SECRETS AND LIES

also by ella monroe

Capital Girls

SECRETS AND LIES

A CAPITAL GIRLS NOVEL

ella monroe

ST. MARTIN'S GRIFFIN ⊯ NEW YORK

This is a work of fiction. All of the characters, organizations, and events portrayed in this novel are either products of the authors' imaginations or are used fictitiously.

www.stmartins.com

Design by Anna Gorovoy

ISBN 978-0-312-62305-0 (trade paperback)
ISBN 978-1-250-02165-6 (e-book)

First Edition: November 2012

10 9 8 7 6 5 4 3 2 1

to my fabulous other half,

charley keyes.

and in loving memory of my parents,

june munro rauber and alan rauber.

to olivia and celia, again,

for your inspiration and support.

ONE

The first week of school was Laura Beth's favorite time of year. It was when the halls of Excelsior Prep buzzed with anticipation, all the girls swapping summer gossip. Who they were dating. Who'd broken up. If the shopping was better in Paris or Rome. But this year was bound to be the best ever, the one Laura Beth had been dreaming about since she was a freshman.

Senior year. Finally.

Not to mention that her summer news should be the talk of the school. After all, who else was dating a gorgeous *college* guy? Unless, of course, you counted Jackie and her boyfriend, Andrew Price, who also just happened to be the president's son.

And that was the problem.

Laura Beth felt her old, familiar jealousy rising at the thought of them. Jackie and Andrew. Andrew and Jackie. *Ankie.* Not that Laura Beth wanted Andrew anymore. She was so over that crush now that she had Sol. It was just that wherever Ankie went, everyone followed, even though their romance was old news at this point. And who knew if they were still even a couple? Jackie certainly wasn't acting like it. Not with the way she'd thrown herself at that sleazy congressional aide, Eric Moran.

But even if they broke up, the press would never let it go. It would be all anyone talked about in the news and in the school halls for months. Laura Beth felt a twinge of guilt—it's not that she wanted Jackie to be unhappy. She just wanted her own turn at center stage.

As Laura Beth strolled down the hallway, students parted to make way. Like royalty. *Well, that's one thing that's good about today,* she thought. Her eyes flicked over the groups of girls pressed against the walls, and she took mental note of who looked thinner and who'd indulged in too many umbrella drinks over the summer.

Halfway down the hall, she stopped next to Lettie's locker and stuck her hand in her brand-new steel-gray Kooba satchel—*the* must-have color of the season. Even though she wore Excelsior's mandatory plaid skirt and collared shirt, Laura Beth knew how to stand out. Her auburn curls had been flattened to a sleek sheen, and one-carat diamond studs dotted each of her ears.

With a tap, the paper she retrieved from her bag disappeared between the vents of the locker. *Lettie needs a new cell phone. She shouldn't be stuck in the stone age. Especially if her family needs her.* Ever since Paz's death, Lettie had been the rock in the Velasquez home. It was obvious the poor girl was stretched thin.

"What's up, LB?"

Laura Beth's heart sank at the sound of Whitney's voice. She turned slowly to face her.

"Planning a party without me?" Whitney smiled maliciously.

And that was the other problem with this school year: She was chained to Whitney.

Laura Beth fought the foul words bubbling inside her and put on a pleasant smile. "Hey, Whitney. Are you finding everything okay?"

Always kill your enemies with kindness. Especially if those enemies know your secrets.

Whitney Remick, the new girl at Excelsior and a constant irritation to Laura Beth and her friends, leaned against the wall of lockers. A hot-pink lacy bra peeked out from beneath her white button-up. Laura Beth envied the way the shirt flattered her caramel-colored skin. Her own complexion was already so pale—especially with everything she'd done trying to get rid of her freckles—that white always washed her out. Even Whitney's yellow feather earrings seemed to dull the sparkle in Laura Beth's studs.

Honestly, how has she not been sent home dressed like that?

"Things are good—if you like sterile, boring, and prison-like." Whitney's smile grew. "But I have a solution. I'm going to ditch and you're going to come with me."

Stalling for time, Laura Beth dug around in her purse and flipped open a compact mirror to check her reflection. At least she didn't look as stressed as she felt.

Over the summer, when she and her friends first met Whitney, Laura Beth loved her carefree attitude and knack for fun. It filled the void left by Taylor's death.

But that was before Laura Beth discovered Whitney's true

motives: spying on them and reporting back to her mother, Gossip Queen Tracey Mills. And before Whitney blackmailed Laura Beth into being friends.

"I can't." Laura Beth snapped the compact shut and began walking down the hallway. Like a yappy dog, Whitney trailed at her heel. "I promised Jackie and Lettie I'd meet them. Right now. Before class."

It was a lie. Kind of. She and Jackie had made plans after first period to meet before third. They wanted to surprise Lettie with a fun lunch off campus—something to cheer her up—and were going to plan it during passing. But Jackie hadn't shown. And that's what had Laura Beth so stressed. Jackie would never forget to meet her. She just seemed to have vanished into thin air.

"Maybe I'll come along." Whitney didn't even bother to hide the threat in her voice. "It'll be a little Capital Girls party."

For a moment, Laura Beth wavered. She'd have to do one or the other—let Whitney come with them or ditch with her. "If you wait until after lunch, I'll come."

Whitney narrowed her eyes. "Fine. But if you back out, I may have to invite Jackie instead. And who knows what might come up then."

Laura Beth curled her fingers tighter around the handle of her bag and prayed they didn't shake too badly as she watched Whitney disappear into the crowded hallway.

There's more than one way to kill a snake, she reminded herself. *But sometimes the best way is to just take off the head.*

Laura Beth wanted, more than anything, to freeze Whitney out completely. But if Jackie ever learned Laura Beth was the reason Uncle Ham—Senator Hampton Griffin, a longtime family friend—caught her in a compromising position with a staffer, their friendship would be over. And as much as Laura Beth sometimes wished Jackie's life were her own, she would never intentionally hurt Jackie.

She glanced back at Lettie's locker and swallowed the lump in her throat. Whitney might own her, but Laura Beth would never be her friend.

Lettie Velasquez wasn't a crier. She couldn't afford to be. Her parents and little sisters relied on her. For the past two weeks, while Mamá wept, Lettie answered the door, accepted condolences and gifts of food from neighbors, and kept the family running.

But as she studied the AP literature reading list, the sobs she kept hidden threatened to escape.

Her older brother, Paz, was dead. Dead. First Taylor and now Paz. Two of the people she most loved in the world. She knew it was illogical and futile, but she kept asking herself the same question over and over: What had she done to deserve this?

Tears sat hot in the corners of her eyes. *Not here, Lettie. Wait till you're alone. Focus.*

With a long sniff, she turned the combination on her locker and flung the door open. A piece of paper covered in hand-drawn hearts fell to the ground.

Lettie recognized it immediately as Laura Beth's handiwork and scooped up the paper. Unlike her two best friends—Laura Beth Ballou and Jackie Whitman—Lettie didn't have a cell phone. At least not anymore. She'd thrown it to take out her anger over Paz's death and couldn't afford a new one. Not that she really needed one or the monthly bill. Well, not all the time, anyway—but it would be nice to not always be the last one to hear about things.

Leaning into her locker to hide her watery eyes, Lettie unfolded the note.

Lets! I haven't seen Jackie since first period and she's not answering her phone. I'm worried. Have you seen her?

xoxo ~ Laura Beth

Lettie frowned. Jackie hadn't been in calculus last period, either, but Lettie had assumed she was meeting with her adviser or something. Of course, without a cell Lettie had no way of checking. And Jackie would have at least texted Laura Beth if she'd had to leave, if only to ask her to pick up her homework.

Something wasn't right. A few weeks ago, Jackie had casually mentioned the threats the White House had been receiving. About her. Jackie and Laura Beth had laughed it off. But President Deborah Price and Jackie's mother, her chief of staff, hadn't found it too funny. They had insisted Jackie tell them every place she went—ahead of time.

"I love my mom and Aunt Deborah," Jackie said, picking at her sandwich. "I know they want to keep me safe. But threats are common if you're in the public eye."

Laura Beth gave one of her typical dramatic sighs. "This year won't be any fun if you have to clear everything first."

Jackie was right about threats being common. But this was different. She wasn't a politician. "I think it's a good idea. Why risk it? If the White House is worried, you should take it seriously."

Jackie rolled her eyes and laughed. "Next thing you'll be suggesting I wear a GPS device."

"If it kept you safe," I told her.

Laura Beth snorted sarcastically. "That would be great! We'd really have fun then."

Jackie pushed her sandwich aside. "Don't worry about it, Lettie. I'm not in any danger."

Lettie's eyes scanned the now near empty hallway. The bell was going to ring any minute, and if she didn't hurry, she'd be late.

With a slam of her locker door, Lettie sprinted toward the stairs at the far end of the hall. She climbed them two at a time and reached the classroom door on the second floor just as the bell trilled.

Hidden just under her desk, Laura Beth's thumbs flew over her iPhone's keypad. Technically, she wasn't supposed to bring it to class, but if the teacher couldn't see it, then what's the harm, right?

J—pls, pls, pls text me. I'm worried about u.

She hit send and doubled-checked the screen to make sure it went through.

Mrs. Stepaniak, the government teacher, shuffled a few papers on her desk as students filed in the door.

Where is she? Laura Beth's stomach roiled. Oh Lord, what if Whitney already told her the truth and Jackie's avoiding me?

Laura Beth stared at the door, willing Jackie to suddenly appear. Despite everything, she was her best friend. And no matter what Whitney thought, Laura Beth had only wanted to protect Jackie.

Stop lying to yourself. You also hoped she and Andrew would break up.

Lettie skidded into the room just as the bell rang. Her eyes, filled with concern, met Laura Beth's as she slipped into the empty desk next to her.

"Have you seen Jackie?" Laura Beth asked even though she knew the answer.

Lettie shook her head. "No."

Mrs. Stepaniak cleared her throat and began calling roll. The desk in front of Laura Beth, the one she had saved for Jackie, sat empty.

"She wasn't in calculus, either," Lettie said softly.

As Laura Beth opened her mouth to ask if maybe they should tell someone, the classroom door burst open.

Startled, she dropped the phone onto the floor.

No one noticed. All eyes were on two uniformed men standing in the doorway, their hands on their sidearms.

"Is Jackie Whitman here?" one of the Secret Service agents asked.

"Jackie?" Mrs. Stepaniak called. Every set of eyes turned toward where Lettie and Laura Beth sat. Without Jackie.

Laura Beth's heart pounded. "I haven't seen her since this morning. What's going on? Why do you want Jackie?"

He stomped down the aisle and stopped at Laura Beth's desk. He kept his gun in its holster, but still, being near it made her skin crawl.

"Are you her friend?" he demanded.

8

"We're her best friends," Lettie said quietly.

The agent pivoted toward Lettie. "Is there anywhere she goes to be alone? Anywhere she may be hiding?"

Bile rose in Laura Beth's throat. Suddenly, the stalkerish calls they'd laughed about didn't seem so funny.

"There's a spot—in the school garden. Sometimes Jackie goes there to clear her mind," Lettie said.

The agent stormed back up the aisle toward the door. "The school is in lockdown. Everyone must remain in this room until further instructed."

The door slammed behind them and the room broke into chaos. Students leapt from their seats and ran to the windows to see the action unfolding out on the grounds. Laura Beth turned in the opposite direction: to Lettie. She folded herself into Lettie's arms and squeezed tightly.

Whitney. The blackmail. Andrew. None of it was important.

Please, Laura Beth prayed. *Please don't let me lose another friend.*

TWO

Late morning sun beat down on Whitney as she slipped through the hedge and into the memorial garden behind the school building. Even though Laura Beth hadn't come with her, Whitney was in a great mood. If everything went according to plan, she'd be out of here before classes ended for the day.

Her iPhone vibrated and she fished it out of her backpack.

"Where are you?" she asked without saying hello.

"Where am *I*? Dude, you're the one who's late," Franklin said, laughing.

Whitney scanned the empty garden. "I'm standing in the garden, Franklin. I'd know if you were here or not."

She had met Franklin Johnson the night of Aamina's party earlier in the summer. If some girl hadn't interrupted their conversation and pulled him and his friend Phillip away,

Whitney probably would have ended up with him in the guesthouse instead of Sol. But it didn't matter. Sol was a good time, and Franklin hadn't forgotten her. It was a win-win. And Sol Molla being Laura Beth's boyfriend made it all the sweeter. LB would be so pissed if she knew about their hookup.

"I'm on the other side. Past the tree," Franklin said in his slow drawl. He wasn't the brightest guy in the world, but Whitney didn't care. He was hot.

"Oh, okay." She turned around and started walking toward the far end of the garden. As she passed a large elm tree, two hands grabbed her from behind.

"What the hell?" Whitney gasped, and dropped her phone.

The rough bark of the tree scratched her legs as Franklin pressed her against it and smashed his lips to hers. His muscular arms braced against the tree, and Whitney—never one for kissing with her eyes closed—admired the outline of his massive muscles. He had to be doing steroids; it was the only way a guy got that ripped.

"You're late," Franklin said, taking a half step back and folding his arms as if he were upset. "It wasn't exactly easy sneaking in here, you know."

Whitney smoothed her hair away from her face and straightened her skirt. "Good things are worth waiting for." She smiled and tapped her finger against his bulging forearm. "Did you bring the chron?"

"What do you think?" Franklin lifted his chin and narrowed his golden-brown eyes. His shaggy blond hair hung over them, so the effect was more comical than gangster. When he brushed his hair back, Whitney admired the contrast of his hair with his olive skin. He had that surfer coloring she loved—sun kissed and golden.

Despite his best efforts to look mysterious, there was nothing complicated about Franklin. Everyone knew he was the only son of one of D.C.'s most influential council members and the star football player at St. Thomas Episcopal—the all-male prep school located conveniently next door to Excelsior.

"Of course I brought it. Can't have a party without the fun stuff." Franklin patted his backpack.

"Good boy."

"I'm not a dog, Whit."

Whitney flashed a smile. "But you *are* good at following orders."

"Whatever." He looked her up and down, lingering on the hint of her pink bra, and gave a lazy smile. "This is better than sitting in class anyway."

Whitney couldn't disagree. So far, all she'd done was recite her name to a bunch of teachers and get loaded down by a ton of books. Not exactly interesting. Unless you counted torturing LB. That was fun.

Franklin began walking to a semi-hidden corner of the garden, but Whitney laced her arm through his and pulled him in the opposite direction.

He pointed up at the second-story windows of Excelsior. "Someone will see us."

Whitney glanced up and shrugged. "I want to sit in the sun—I'm from California, remember? I hate the cold." *If we're hiding, I'll never get caught.* And getting caught was exactly what

Whitney wanted. If Excelsior Prep kicked her out, then her mom would have no choice but to let her move back to L.A.

The sooner the better.

She sat on an old stone bench. It was off to the side, but still in sight of a few of the windows. "Here. Right in the sun."

"If we get caught—"

"Then we get in trouble. What's the big deal?" Whitney challenged. For a second, she felt bad doing this to Franklin. She liked him. At least as much as she'd liked any other guy. Plus, because of Franklin, she was now friends with Angie Meehan and Aamina Al-Kazaz—two girls who knew how to have fun, unlike Jackie and her lackeys.

Whitney's original plan was to get the cush from Franklin, send him on his way, and light up with Laura Beth. *That's* who she wanted to bring down with her. Whitney glanced at Franklin again. *Whatever. I'm sure his dad can buy him out of whatever trouble we get into.*

Franklin flopped down on the manicured lawn, his back against the bench. As if he did this all the time. Which was exactly why Whitney liked him. He didn't give a shit. Just like her.

"You can have this one, I brought my own," he said, offering her a joint.

Whitney straddled the bench and made sure her bare thigh grazed Franklin's arm. His eyes rested appreciatively on the hem of her skirt. *Might as well make it worth his while.*

"Sharing is so much more fun," Whitney said.

Franklin traced a line from Whitney's ankle to the back of her knee. *Damn, that feels good. But first things first. . . .*

She watched him exhale a cloud of smoke and relax against

her leg. "Oh? You want to share one of your hot friends with me?"

"As if." He was all hers. Whitney leaned down to take his lit joint and made sure her loose, curly hair brushed his face.

Franklin's hands darted up and cupped her face.

She held the joint away from them and touched her mouth lightly to Franklin's, her lips parted slightly, and she inhaled deeply. He tasted like weed. Franklin's hand slid up her thigh and under her skirt.

Maybe I should thank LB for not coming.

Halfway through the joint, Whitney's head felt heavy and she leaned against Franklin and ran her fingers over his tight white T-shirt.

Suddenly, Franklin burst out laughing. "Do you hear that? It sounds like a swarm of mosquitoes."

Whitney closed her eyes and tilted her head back, listening to the beat, beat, beat. Franklin's lips pressed against the hollow of her neck before trailing lower to the lacy edge of her bra. "Really big fucking mosquitoes." She giggled.

"Do you know what else is really—"

"Do not move," an icy voice ordered.

Suddenly, Whitney felt herself lifted into the air. As much as she wanted to get caught, this was a bit overboard. "What the hell?"

Something cold and hard locked around her wrists. She looked down, trying to figure out what it was. Handcuffs. "Really?" she asked. "You're cuffing us for smoking a little pot?"

"Whitney, shut up," Franklin said next to her. When she

looked up and focused her eyes, she gasped. This wasn't some school lackey busting them. She and Franklin were surrounded by intense-looking guys dressed in black and carrying guns.

"Oh, shit."

All the sun in the world couldn't make Jackie feel better. Not the birds chirping or the rush of excited students around her. Sure, Laura Beth had rambled on about how the Capital Girls were finally seniors. How the whole school was theirs now.

But honestly, when hadn't it been? After all, Taylor always said—

Stop thinking about Taylor. She's nothing. Just some backstabbing girl who slept with your boyfriend.

But no matter how many times Jackie repeated this to herself, she couldn't make it true. Taylor Cane *had* been her best friend. Which led Jackie back to the thought that kept playing over and over in her mind: Why? Why did Taylor do it? There had to be some explanation.

For the first part of the morning, Jackie had smiled, held her head high, and pretended everything was fine. But after AP English, she heard a throaty laugh that sounded just like Taylor's, and suddenly the walls closed in and her lungs wouldn't fill with air. She had to get out of the building. Away from everyone. Away from the questions about her summer. Away from Laura Beth's nonstop excitement and Lettie's understandable air of despair.

At the end of the science wing, Jackie paused at the side door.

FIRE DOOR. OPEN ONLY IN EMERGENCY.

Freshman year, the first time she'd watched Taylor prop this door open, Jackie's heart had hammered against her chest and she couldn't stop checking over her shoulder.

"Taylor," I whispered. "Wait. Don't. What if it—"

Taylor threw open the door before I could finish. "See? No alarm. Nothing." She gave me the mischievous look I knew too well.

I glanced down the hallway, worried someone would see us.

"I don't want to get caught," I said, arms folded against my chest. I hoped I looked cool, like Taylor, instead of like a girl whose heart was about to explode.

"Jackie, c'mon. Live a little." Taylor stood outside, waiting for me. "Freedom awaits."

With one last look, I slipped through the door and off campus for the first time. Just like Taylor knew I would.

This day, Jackie shoved the door out of her way and stepped into the sunlight without bothering to see if anyone noticed her.

She crossed the small lawn that separated Excelsior from the gym building it shared with St. Thomas Episcopal and circled around to the back. Normally, when Jackie wanted to be alone, she'd tuck herself into a corner of the memorial garden. But today she felt an inexplicable need to be somewhere close to Taylor.

Jackie pressed herself against the gym wall and stared at the stone wall separating the two schools. She used to find Taylor back here, smoking a cigarette—a habit she'd picked up after spending a month in Paris the summer after sophomore year.

Staring at the old cigarette butts littering the dirt, Jackie choked back a sob. Even after what Taylor and Andrew did, Jackie still missed her. And that was what made her angriest of all. Shouldn't this new pain cancel out the old one? Why did she have to feel both?

Taylor always took what she wanted, consequences be damned. We all knew it. But I thought our friendship meant more.

And Andrew. He'd called, texted, and e-mailed nonstop since telling Jackie the truth. But she didn't want to hear his apologies or see his remorse. She just wanted it all to go away.

Jackie snapped her head up at the sound of helicopters hovering near the school.

Curious, she walked to the end of the building to get a better view.

"Jackie Whitman?" a man's voice called from her left.

She froze. *Figures. The one time I sneak out without Taylor, I get caught.*

She turned toward the voice. "I know I shouldn't be out here, but I needed to clear my head and—"

Jackie gasped. A half-dozen Secret Service agents swarmed around her. "What's going on?" she asked, trying to keep her voice level.

"You need to come with us, Miss Whitman." One of the men gently took her elbow and began walking her toward the main entrance of the school.

"What's going on? Where are you taking me?" Jackie demanded. Horrible scenarios swam through her brain: President Price had been shot—or worse, her mother. As the president's top aide, she was almost as vulnerable as the president herself.

"Is my mom okay?" Jackie choked out, and automatically jabbed her hand into her bag. But she'd left her phone in her locker. *Why did I choose today to follow the "no cell phones in class" rule?*

"The chief of staff is secure and safe," one of them said in a monotone voice.

"Then what happened?" When no one answered, Jackie stopped walking. She couldn't take this. "I demand someone tell me what is going on."

Three unmarked black SUVs were parked at the curb, directly in front of the school's entrance. The agent who seemed to be in charge replied, "I'd like you to get in the car, Miss Whitman. If you don't, I'll have these men assist you."

Two impossibly huge men tugged on Jackie's arms. She refused to budge. "James, pick her up. We don't have time for this."

With one quick movement, he lifted Jackie off the ground, carried her to the nearest car, and shoved her inside. The door slammed shut, and before she could right herself, the car was speeding away from Excelsior.

"I told you, I don't know where Jackie is. And I didn't leave any message on the school voice mail. Do I look like an idiot?" Whitney sat in the office of the head of students, her hands held behind her back by handcuffs.

The Secret Service agent, dressed in a gray suit and sitting behind the desk, flipped through a folder. "Why were you out of class, Miss Remick?"

Whitney exhaled loudly. "I snuck out to meet my boyfriend."

As soon as she'd realized what was happening, Whitney had sobered up fast. Getting busted by the school was one thing; being hauled in for questioning was totally another.

Whitney tried to focus on the upside and not the fear coursing through her veins. *There's no way Excelsior won't kick me out now.*

"Are you aware, Miss Remick, that possession of marijuana is punishable by up to six months in jail and a one-thousand-dollar fine?"

Whitney felt the color drain from her face. This was bad. Way worse than she'd imagined. Shit. Shit. Shit.

"But we didn't even have that much. Just half a joint. That's, like, nothing."

The agent slapped the folder down on the table. "All quantities are illegal. How hard is that to understand? You broke the law."

If I don't end up in jail, Mom's going to strangle me and then pack me off to reform school. I'm never going home to Cali.

The door opened and a woman dressed in a suit hurried in and whispered something to the asshole across the table.

He lowered his chin and glared at her with piercing blue eyes. "Well, this is your lucky day. Seems that not only have we located Miss Whitman, but there won't be any charges brought against you."

Whitney stood up and turned around so her back faced the agent. "Then take these things off me. They're killing my wrists."

The agent walked around the desk and lifted Whitney's hands so that she had to lean forward.

The lock clicked open and Whitney massaged her wrists. Angry red lines showed where the cuffs had rubbed her skin raw.

"Can I go now?" she asked.

"You can," he said. "Make sure you give your thanks to Councilman Johnson. He saved your skin."

Whitney rushed toward the door, eager to get out of the room. She'd deal with Franklin and his dad later. First, she had to do damage control.

Do not panic. That's the worst thing you can do. Stay calm.

Jackie stared out the window as the streets of the District blurred into one another. She'd given up begging her driver for information ten minutes ago. It was as if he were deaf. Or, like every other Secret Service agent she knew, very focused.

The SUV turned left, then right, then right again, and Jackie felt they were driving in circles—almost as if evading someone, which didn't help her nerves one bit.

Finally, somewhere near George Washington University, the car stopped in front of an entrance gate. The driver rolled down his window and flashed an ID badge at the security guard. The metal barricade flattened into the ground and the car rolled into an underground garage.

"Miss Whitman? Can you come with me?" Her driver held the door open. Jackie's shaking legs stuck to the leather seat when she tried to climb out.

She glanced around, hoping for some sort of identifying marks on the building, but she didn't recognize anything.

Jackie followed him through an unmarked steel door and down a badly lit hallway. The fluorescent lights flickered and her ballerina flats clicked as she walked over the linoleum floor.

Her heart was still racing. *They said Mom was okay, but they could be lying.*

At the end of the hallway, the driver waved his badge in front of a scanner and the door clicked open. He turned the knob and stood aside.

Before Jackie could register what was happening, her mother rushed over to her and pulled her to her chest. "Jackie! I was so worried. Where were you?"

"Mom?" Jackie choked out. All the anxiety and worry gave way to a flood of tears, and Jackie buried her head in her mom's shoulder. "What's going on? I thought something happened to you."

Carolyn Shaw held her daughter at arm's length and shook her head. "Me? Jackie, we've been worried sick about *you*. The school couldn't find you, and after those messages they received . . . Do you know how worried we were? I thought you'd been kidnapped!"

"Kidnapped? What? No! I just went outside. I needed to clear my mind."

Carolyn shook her head. "You can't just go off, Jackie. I thought you understood that."

Jackie's heart sank. When her mom and Aunt Deborah had explained the situation to her, it hadn't sounded that bad. Nothing more than all the other threats crazy people were always phoning in to the White House. But from the reaction today, she could tell there was more—something they hadn't told her.

"Excelsior received a kidnapping threat," her mother was saying. "When you didn't show up for class, we had to take action."

Someone coughed, and Jackie suddenly realized they weren't alone in the room. About a dozen Secret Service agents, as well as Jackie's father, were there, too. And against the far wall, watching her, was Andrew.

Of course Andrew was there. Technically, as far as everyone knew, he was her boyfriend. The other half of the famous Ankie couple. He shifted under her gaze, moving to cross his arms, and she caught the glint of something on his right hand. The abstinence ring. All it did was remind her of all the fights they'd had, the ones that always ended with Andrew telling her he wasn't ready. And all *that* did was remind her he'd slept with Taylor.

When her eyes met Andrew's Jackie saw the same image that had burned into her mind the night Andrew confessed everything. The image she'd been trying so hard to erase: Andrew and Taylor in her car, having sex. Andrew driving the car and crashing. Andrew lying to her day after day, for months.

"You understand, don't you? This is for your safety, Jackie. Just until we find out who's behind this," her dad said. He kissed the top of her head.

Jackie blinked and turned her attention back to her parents, who stood side by side. A united front. Which meant they were in agreement. "I'm sorry, I wasn't paying attention. My brain is still in overdrive from all the excitement," she lied.

Carolyn squeezed her daughter's hand. "You'll be staying in the White House. I'm gone too much, and neither your dad nor I like the idea of you being alone at home when some madman is targeting you."

"Mom, no." Jackie shook her head, her blond ponytail whipping side to side. "I'll be fine. I don't need to stay at the White House."

"Absolutely not." Her mom had that look—the chief of staff

look that meant her mind was made up and wouldn't be changed. "I was terrified today—we all were. You'll stay at the White House and have a security detail at all times. Is that understood?"

Jackie knew what her role was: dutiful daughter. This wasn't the place to argue with her mom. But that didn't mean she wouldn't bring it up later. "When's your trip?" she asked.

"Tonight. Aunt Deborah and I have to be in South Africa tomorrow."

Jackie sucked on the inside of her bottom lip. There would be no later. She nodded and said what she was supposed to. "If that's what you think is best."

THREE

Jackie had sounded awful on the phone. *Of course, I would too if I'd been whisked off campus because some crazed man threatened my life,* Laura Beth thought as a Secret Service agent led her into the First Family's living quarters.

Even though Laura Beth had been to the White House a dozen times, it never failed to impress—the decor, the formality, the history. She loved all of it.

Though of course she'd love it more if a Republican family lived here.

As Mama says, all in good time. The presidential campaign is not that far off, and Lord only knows what may happen.

Laura Beth caught her reflection in the oversize gilded mirror next to the stairs and smiled. The two hours spent blowing out her curly auburn hair and trying on outfits had paid off. She'd wanted something sexy but not too obvious—just in case she bumped into Andrew. Not that she wanted Andrew anymore. She didn't. *But if he is around, why not show him what he's missing?*

The agent indicated the first door to the left of the landing, which was ajar, before retreating back down the staircase. *You're here for Jackie,* Laura Beth sternly reminded herself. *You need to make up for what you did, even if it was for Jackie's own good.* Still, she felt awful. She hadn't meant to get Jackie in trouble—or send her running to Jennifer Cane.

Laura Beth shivered at the thought of Taylor's terrifying mom and sucked in her breath. *Good Lord, Jackie must have felt desperate if she went to her for help. But if I'm a better friend—one who's a hundred percent there for Jackie—she won't doubt me if Whitney outs me.* At least, that's what she hoped.

She stuck her head into the room. "Knock, knock, anyone home?"

"Laura Beth!" Jackie's blond hair was in a messy bun and she was wearing tacky fuzzy blue slippers and plaid pajama bottoms with a Yale tee.

"Oh, you poor thing! Just look at you!" Laura Beth said.

Jackie grabbed Laura Beth by the hand and led her in. Lettie was already sprawled on the floor next to a tower of magazines and nail polish bottles. She smiled up at Laura Beth, moving one foot in time to the music playing from Jackie's iPod speakers. Laura Beth had offered to schedule mani/pedis and massages at Aveda for the three of them, but Jackie had refused. Probably because Lettie would never let them pay for her and Jackie didn't look fit for public consumption.

Laura Beth darted her eyes back to Jackie and sighed. *So it's the perfect girls' night in—until Whitney shows up.*

She couldn't bring herself to tell her friends she'd invited Whitney. Why ruin the fun early? If Jackie knew ahead of time, she'd sulk all night and then Lettie would try to run interference, and all her plans to be a better friend would be gone in less than a minute. *It's not like I want her here any more than they do. Less, probably. But they'll blame me all the same.*

"Thanks for coming. I can't believe Mom is making me stay here. Total overkill, but you know how she is." Jackie shook her head.

"Don't you think your mama knows best?" Laura Beth asked. "After all, there was a serious threat against your life today."

Jackie shrugged as if it were no big deal, but Laura Beth didn't believe for one moment that she hadn't been rattled—they all had. When Excelsior decided to end classes early and send everyone home, Laura Beth and Lettie had huddled together at Laura Beth's, waiting for Jackie to call or text. Ms. Jenkins, the head of students, had told them Jackie was fine but wouldn't tell them where she was. And that scared Laura Beth even more than the armed agents stomping around campus.

"The president receives threats all the time. And no one acts like this," Jackie said. Laura Beth kind of agreed. Even though she would have loved to be ordered to stay at the White House, it did seem like overkill. But she bit her tongue. Tonight was all about Jackie. And that included making her feel better about having to stay under lock and key, even if it was the most amazing house in the world.

Lettie, who was now painting her toenails a bright shade of blue, looked at Jackie. "The president has the world's top security. And now you do, too."

Jackie fake growled as she flopped back onto the floor and

swirled a bottle of rose-colored nail polish. "You can put your stuff in the study, Laura Beth."

As she moved toward the connecting door, it suddenly hit her. She spun around in wide-eyed awe, taking in the navy walls and masculine decor. "This is Andrew's bedroom—the Queen's Bedroom!" She'd assumed Jackie would be staying across the hall in the Lincoln Bedroom, which was kept free for guests.

Jackie nodded but kept painting her toenails.

"Why did they put you in here?" Excitement crept into Laura Beth's voice.

Jackie sighed like she didn't want to talk about it.

Whatever is going on between Jackie and Andrew is bigger than she's telling us.

"Well, Andrew's back in the Georgetown dorms anyway, and Aunt Deborah says she wants to keep the Lincoln Bedroom for Democratic donors to stay in. And she didn't want me in one of the bedrooms upstairs alone. Which means I get to stay in Andrew's old room." She blinked a little too fast. "But Andrew's here, too. He insisted on staying here tonight. In the Lincoln Bedroom."

Quick, think of somethin' nice to say. "Well, that was kind of him. I'm sure he was worried sick about you."

Jackie wasn't even listening. She stared blankly at the floor. Lettie shook her head slightly, as if to tell Laura Beth to not talk about Andrew.

Add that to the growing list of topics we can't discuss, Laura Beth thought as she carefully placed her bag on a luggage holder in the study. *I would do anything to live in this house. Death threats aside, Jackie doesn't know how good she has it.*

Jackie's hands hadn't stopped shaking all day. She was positive Lettie noticed while they were doing manicures because she suddenly took the brush from Jackie, made some comment about pampering her, and finished the job. That was two hours ago.

Why am I still so upset? Nothing bad happened. Everyone is fine. Her shrink had said to repeat reassuring and realistic phrases when she was catastrophizing things. But that wasn't working tonight, and she was sure she was doing it wrong. As the panic welled up inside her, she couldn't help thinking, *What if I never get control of this feeling?* A lump formed in Jackie's throat. She swallowed it quickly.

"You go first." Laura Beth nudged Lettie into the doorway.

"No, you."

"I'll go first," Jackie said, shoving her hands into the pockets of the hoodie she'd slipped over her T-shirt. Sneaking around the White House at night was a thrilling enough distraction from her worries.

The three girls tiptoed down the long hallway, past the formal Yellow Oval Room to the sitting room. One perk of being the First Son's girlfriend: You knew where the liquor was kept. Trouble was, it was right next to the president's bedroom, and who knew if Bob Price was in there? *Well, if the cat's away . . .*, Jackie thought.

Jackie hadn't heard any noises coming from the Lincoln Bedroom, so she figured Andrew must be asleep. At least she hoped he was. He'd been smart and stayed away while she'd moved her bags into her (his) room. She'd only glimpsed him at dinner—he had decided to eat early.

"Shhh . . . Lettie, stop making so much noise," Laura Beth whispered. She was acting weird. Jumpy.

Maybe the kidnapping threat upset Laura Beth more than I realized.

Jackie paused, turning her head back toward the Lincoln Bedroom. *If Laura Beth were in my place, would she forgive him?*

She heard Laura Beth giggling softly. "Jackie, hurry up."

Something ugly boiled inside of Jackie. She couldn't put a name to it. It wasn't exactly anger or frustration. It wasn't jealousy or guilt, either. But at the same time, it was all those things.

Laura Beth would forgive Andrew in a heartbeat. She'd probably tell him it was all Taylor's fault or some bullshit like that. But Jackie couldn't do that. She couldn't completely blame Taylor or forgive Andrew. Not now. Maybe not ever.

And it pissed her off.

She took a deep breath in an attempt to steady the mess of emotions running through her. Maybe Laura Beth was a bigger person than she was. And that thought pissed her off even more. Laura Beth always seemed to know exactly what Andrew needed—like the time at Libby Ballou's fund-raiser, when he had to make an impromptu speech and she helped him figure out what to say while Jackie's mind just went blank. Or the way she helped him pick out Jackie's birthday and Christmas presents.

She couldn't help but resent it. Even though in her heart she knew Laura Beth had done all those things not so much because she had a crush on Andrew, but because she was a true friend—to both of them.

Jackie must have been walking slowly because Lettie and Laura Beth had moved past her and stood in the middle of the ornate yet comfortable sitting room, waiting.

Laura Beth studied her with a small frown. "Are you okay? You look upset."

An impressive liquor cabinet sat in the corner of the room, and Jackie made a beeline for it. "I'm fine. I just don't want us to get caught," she whispered, although she was pretty sure neither the Secret Service agents nor the household staff would stop them or tell their parents. Their job was security and discretion—not tattling on a bunch of high school girls.

Lettie sidled up to the cabinet. "You sure you're all right?"

Jackie bit the inside of her cheek. No, of course she wasn't. She had some crazy guy threatening her life, a cheating boyfriend, and a dead best friend who'd betrayed her. And what was she thinking? How pissed she was at Laura Beth. Which was ridiculous because Laura Beth had never done anything disloyal to her.

"I'm sure." Jackie picked up a bottle and said in a stuffy British accent, "Here's some bourbon. Do you think we should save this for Miss Libby, Laura Beth? You know how much your mother loves her bourbon."

"Mama only drinks top-shelf liquor. And it has to be made in America," Laura Beth retorted with an equally bad accent. No matter how hard she tried, her accents always came out making her sound like a drunken Southerner. Irish, French, Spanish—it didn't matter, Laura Beth did them all with the same deep, Southern twang.

Lettie giggled. "You two sound ridiculous."

Tucking a black-labeled bottle under her arm, Jackie felt herself relax a little. "What? You don't think I'm a shoo-in for an Academy Award?"

"Not at all." Laura Beth grabbed another bottle, unscrewed the top, poured the amber-brown liquid into three highball glasses, and handed one to each of her friends. "To senior year!"

"Senior year!" they repeated, keeping their voices low.

The liquid burned going down, and Jackie gagged. "What is this?"

Lettie inspected the bottle. "Scotch. It's gross, isn't it?"

"That's an understatement." Jackie set the glass on the cabinet. The maids cleaning up in the morning would probably think the First Husband had had a few drinks. "Who wants to watch a movie?"

"In the movie theater?" Excitement crept into Lettie's voice. "I love it—"

"No. In my room." Jackie motioned for the girls to follow her. "Mom had them bring a TV in for me so I wouldn't be completely bored."

She didn't dare tell them the real reason: She'd have to wake Andrew to ask him to arrange an escort down to the theater, and she couldn't bear to see him. It was bad enough just knowing that she could run into him anytime—she'd overheard Andrew telling her mom that he'd stay at the White House until she and Aunt Deborah returned from South Africa. Like he could stop someone from hurting her.

Like anything could hurt more than his betrayal.

The less time she spent outside her room, the better.

"What DVDs do you have?" Laura Beth asked, her eyes flitting nervously to the door again.

What's she so worried about? It's not like we've never broken into our parents' liquor stash. We do it all the time at Miss Libby's house.

"*Sabrina* or *Chris Moody Gets the Girl*," Jackie said as they walked back to her room.

Lettie opened the door. "I vote for *Sabrina*. I don't really like Chris Moody. He's not very funny."

This room doesn't even smell like Andrew anymore, Jackie thought as the girls entered the Queen's Bedroom. *Which is a good thing, I guess.* Most of his personal stuff had been moved to his dorm, and the sisal mat they'd picked out together had been replaced by a fancy Oriental rug.

"He's so cute!" Laura Beth squealed. For a moment, Jackie thought she meant Andrew. Then she realized she was talking about Chris Moody. "Those lips, that jaw! He could read the dictionary and I'd watch."

Lettie rolled her eyes. "He's handsome, but he doesn't seem very smart."

"Not every boy has to be smart, Lettie," Laura Beth teased.

"But there should be a connection, don't you think?"

The two girls looked at Jackie as if they expected her to weigh in. A connection. She thought she'd had one with Eric—at least a physical one—and that was a disaster. So was her "take it slow" connection with Andrew.

"So you would still date Sol if he were stupid?" Jackie asked.

Laura Beth shook her head. "Well, he is somethin' to look at, isn't he?" She grinned like the Cheshire Cat. "And lucky for me, he's whip smart."

"What if he cheated on you?" Jackie asked before she could stop herself.

Lettie's eyes grew large, and Laura Beth stopped smiling. "*If* Sol cheated on me, I'm sure we'd be able to work it out. After all, sometimes things are just misunderstandin's."

Jackie's heart sank. Not only had she upset Laura Beth, but she also had her answer: Laura Beth would forgive Andrew.

"*Chris Moody* it is," Jackie said, trying to sound chipper. Even though she would rather watch *Sabrina* (she loved Audrey Hepburn), she wanted to appease Laura Beth.

The three girls settled into the bed and passed a bottle of vodka among them. The movie stank. But that didn't stop Jackie from making it fun.

"How about, every time someone just misses finding the person they're looking for, we drink," she said.

"Oh! And we drink every time someone says the name Owen or Katie," Laura Beth offered.

Lettie swigged from the bottle. "That woman just said 'Katie.'"

"Pass it here." Jackie held out her hand and took a swig. All the stress and worry of the day melted away. This was just what she needed: time with her best friends.

"Whitney Mills Remick, are you listening to me? I said put your phone down. *Now.*"

Whitney dropped her phone on the counter and lifted her eyes to her mom's gaze. Even on the computer screen, Tracey Mills looked ready to tear into her.

I wonder if I can accidentally disconnect? Whitney thought. *I mean, who gets bitched out by their mom over Skype?*

"What the hell were you thinking? Cutting class—on the first day—and smoking pot on school grounds. With a boy." Tracey threw her hands in the air. "C'mon, Whitney. I taught you better than that."

They'd been having this discussion for at least twenty minutes now. What was Whitney thinking? Did she want to ruin her parents' careers? If she got kicked out of Excelsior, she'd ruin everything her mother had worked so hard to set up. Blah. Blah. Blah.

But at least her mom was paying attention to her. And she hadn't been hauled off to jail for six months. So there *were* positives.

"So you're not packing me off to reform school?" Whitney sassed.

Her mom gave an exasperated sigh. "Why would I do that?"

Whitney felt all the anger she'd been trying to control for weeks boil over. "You exiled me here. Away from all my friends. During my senior year. Why wouldn't you?"

"I don't hate you, Whitney. And being there isn't a punishment. At least I thought it wasn't." Her mom played with the large silver disk hanging from the chain around her neck. "You know Dad had to go to Washington for his work. You understand, don't you?"

No. She didn't. Her dad took this job to climb the career ladder or some bullshit like that. But Whitney's *life* was in L.A.

The air felt hot in Whitney's lungs. She picked up her phone again, desperate to change the subject. "I have to go. Laura Beth invited me to a sleepover at the *White House*."

The face on the screen changed instantly from concerned mom to ambitious journalist. Whitney had been saving that piece of information until the right moment—either to get out of being grounded or to get off the call. And judging from the look on her mom's face, she'd picked the perfect moment.

"With Jackie?" her mom asked.

Fucking Jackie. I wouldn't be in this mess now if her Secret Service posse hadn't swarmed all over the school.

Whitney nodded. "Yeah. Apparently she's staying there now or something."

Tracey pursed her lips. *As if she's really debating. If she could, she'd body swap with me and be all over that little get-together.*

"Fine. You can go. But you have to get pictures or quotes. Or next time something like this happens—and let's be clear, there better not be a next time—you *will* be sent to reform school."

Whitney knew it was an empty threat. As long as she proved useful, her mom wouldn't send her anywhere. Not even back to L.A. Which was the problem. If she kept being useful, she couldn't go home. And if she wasn't . . . Well, she wouldn't be enjoying the warm L.A. sun, either. She couldn't win. But she could keep her mom happy and out of her hair.

Just outside the White House gates, Whitney idled her new yellow Mini Cooper convertible—a gift from her dad for taking her away from Cali—and waited for her name to be checked off the list. She'd spent her life with the rich and famous of Hollywood, yet she had to admit that hanging at the White House was a pretty big deal.

Maybe tonight wouldn't be so bad after all. She'd hang out with the *Crapital* Girls, listen to them giggle about boys, and get some dirt for her mom. There were worse ways to spend a Friday night—like in a jail cell.

As the Secret Service agent waved her through, Whitney cringed, remembering the way Franklin looked when he'd been led away for his own interrogation. Hopefully he wasn't

too upset with her. He was the only good thing about D.C.
so far.

An incredibly good-looking agent waited for Whitney next to
the assigned parking spot. His close-cut dark hair and square jaw
made him look like a military guy. Whitney's eyes flitted to his
chest. Although there was no sign of the gun she knew he must
have beneath his suit jacket, she couldn't help but shiver. This
guy was dangerous. And danger, to Whitney, was supersexy.

"Miss Remick," he said in a gravelly voice, "I'm Agent Tobbs.
I'll be showing you to the family quarters."

"Fancy," Whitney said playfully as she swung her legs out of
the car. She made sure he got a good look at them. "I get my
own personal escort."

Agent Tobbs smiled politely. "It's protocol. All guests to the
White House are escorted."

Whitney's smile faded when she realized her flirting was
unreturned.

"I believe you'll find your friends in the Queen's Bedroom.
It's right this way."

*Queen's Bedroom, are you kidding me? As if Jackie needs any more proof
she's the It Girl.*

Whitney tried to look blasé as she followed the agent through
the West Entrance of the White House, but her head swiveled
everywhere, trying to take it all in. Agent Tobbs led her upstairs to the family quarters, past the agents stationed at the top
of the stairs, and toward the bedrooms.

Maybe she could force Laura Beth to show her around. After all, LB was at her mercy. Why else would she agree to invite
Whitney to the White House a few hours after the world
thought Jackie had been kidnapped?

"This is Miss Whitman's room." He stopped in front of a regular-looking door. Whitney had expected gold and glitz or something. Not a simple five-paneled door that looked as if it could belong in any of D.C.'s musty old homes.

She pulled her breath in deeply. *Remember, as much as they hate you, you hate them more.*

"Hey, girls! Thanks for inviting me!"

No way. No effing way was Whitney Remick standing in her bedroom smiling at them as if she were their best friend.

Jackie shot a quick glance at Lettie, who looked just as surprised as Jackie felt, and Laura Beth, who was studying her newly polished fingernails, before she turned her glare on Whitney. If looks could kill, Whitney would be the White House's first murder victim.

"What are you doing here? How'd you get in?" Jackie demanded.

The new girl tossed her bag into a corner and flopped onto the couch—between Lettie and Jackie. "LB invited me. I hope you don't mind."

Don't mind? Is she out of her freaking mind?

"Laura Beth," Jackie said evenly, trying not to show her anger, "why didn't you tell us Whitney was coming? We don't have room for her—she'll have to sleep on the floor."

A faint blush tinted Laura Beth's cheeks. Whether it was from the alcohol or from Whitney showing up, Jackie couldn't tell. But she clearly was uncomfortable. Was *this* who she'd been waiting for all night?

"I . . . um, asked Andrew to put her on the guest list." Laura

Beth looked up from her nails and her eyes darted around the room as if a better answer were written on one of the walls. "But I didn't think you'd be able to come, Whitney. Not with your arrest and all."

Lettie's mouth dropped open. "You were arrested? What did you do?"

Whitney grinned, climbed into the bed uninvited, and snuggled into the stack of pillows against the headboard. "Got caught smoking cush and making out with Franklin Johnson in the memorial garden."

Ugh. This girl has no class.

"Did law enforcement press charges?" Lettie asked, concern seeping into her voice. *Leave it to Lettie to actually care.*

"Nah. Just a slap on the wrist. No big. Though my mom was kind of pissed. She totally bitched me out over Skype." Whitney flashed a smile at Laura Beth. "Thanks again for inviting me, LB."

Laura Beth gave a tight smile and gathered up all the nail polish bottles next to her. She disappeared into the bathroom and shut the door.

Jackie stared at the closed door. *I know Laura Beth didn't invite Whitney to cheer me up. So why, exactly, is she here?*

"So what do you say? Should we get this party started?" Whitney held up the half-drunk bottle of vodka. "Oops. Looks like you girls have been at it already. Guess I better catch up." She tilted the bottle back and chugged for an impossibly long time.

Whitney lowered the bottle and smirked at Laura Beth, who had emerged from the bathroom. Red blotches covered Laura Beth's upper chest and neck—a telltale sign she was upset.

"How about a game of truth or dare? LB? You want to play?"

To Jackie's dismay, Laura Beth nodded. "Sure, sounds like fun." But from the tone of her voice, you'd think someone just asked her to sit for the SATs again.

Whatever. Jackie wasn't about to spill her secrets to Whitney Remick. She'd pick dares every time—no matter how bad they were.

Whitney clapped her hands to get their attention. "Great. Jackie—you're first. Truth or dare?"

So much for de-stressing, Jackie thought as she braced herself for what was coming. "Dare."

FOUR

Lettie paced across the Oriental rug in the Queen's Bedroom. The last time she'd been at the White House had been for the sleepover two weeks ago. And that hadn't gone well. No matter how hard Lettie tried to help her, Whitney seemed determined to get on Jackie's bad side. And Jackie wasn't any better. She'd barely given Whitney a chance.

But she couldn't worry about them today. After months of political battle, today was the day Lettie's family had a real shot at becoming U.S. citizens. If they were lucky, they would never have to worry about returning to Paraguay—the country where her older brother, Paz, had died fighting in the escalating civil war.

Lettie slipped a red sheath dress over her head—a loaner from Laura Beth. Paz had been suspicious of Lettie's friends.

He thought that they were spoiled little rich girls who lived in a bubble. That they didn't know the real world and the problems in it. But did running with a gang equal the real world? Lettie didn't think so.

Paz. If you didn't have the wrong friends, Mamá and Papá would never have sent you home! You'd still be here.... She swallowed a sob.

As Lettie studied herself in the mirror, her fingers played with the Capital Girls bracelet on her wrist. Jackie, Laura Beth, Taylor, and she each had one, the clover-shaped charms representing their years together. Four best friends forever. Lettie touched the charms one by one. For her, they also represented a different year of her new life in the United States. The last one, added this past summer after junior year, slipped through her fingers. She'd lost one of her three best friends and her brother, but maybe things were changing—for the better—now.

Jackie's hair dryer hummed in the adjoining bathroom, and Lettie smiled, remembering how her friends had taken her under their wing. How even though Lettie's English wasn't great at first, they'd never made her feel that she wasn't part of the Capital Girls Club, as Taylor jokingly called it.

And she loved them for it. Jackie's loyalty, Laura Beth's kindness, Taylor's sense of fun (even if it did get her in trouble more than a few times)—they were all such a huge part of her life here.

Lettie giggled. She could just imagine if Taylor were still alive. *She'd probably hire some offensive mariachi band or flamenco dancer or something to celebrate.* But Lettie wouldn't care because Taylor would have done it *to be* offensive. And funny.

For the first time in months, thinking about Taylor didn't

open the huge wound in her heart. Maybe it was because of the new scar—Paz's death—or maybe time was starting to heal the pain. It didn't matter. It was nice to remember Taylor and not feel sad.

But the scar with Paz's name on it was still agonizing.

"Paz," Lettie said out loud in Spanish, "Mamá is making her special Christmas tamales tonight. You *know* this must be important if she's doing that." She chuckled under her breath. She and Paz had always joked that only acts of God and Christmas could convince Mamá to make those tamales.

"Who you talking to?" Jackie asked, emerging from the bathroom. She looked perfect, as usual. But lately Lettie worried about Jackie. In the days since the kidnapping threat, Jackie had become more quiet than normal. And she didn't go out as often. In fact, other than school, Lettie barely saw her anymore. It was like she disappeared behind the White House gates after school let out.

"Just myself. I'm nervous."

Jackie laughed weakly, as if it were an effort for her to do it. "For a minute there, I thought Whitney crashed this event, too." It was supposed to be a joke, but the hard set of Jackie's lips said otherwise. Jackie sat on the edge of the bed and buckled her T-strap pumps.

When she stood up, she took a long look at Lettie and whistled. "Whoa, Lettie! I'm not sure you're supposed to look *hot* at these things."

Lettie felt her face heat up. "I, uh . . . maybe I should change?"

Jackie laughed. "No! You look great!" She stood in front of Lettie and fixed a stray piece of hair. "But maybe you should see if Laura Beth will let you wear that for your next date with Daniel."

Lettie's heart fluttered and she shook her head in embarrassment. "I'm not sure he's interested in me anymore."

"Of course he is! How could he not be? Why do you think he's back in D.C.?"

Lettie didn't answer. Taylor's twin brother had decided at the last minute to leave his L.A. boarding school and move back home. She was pretty sure she knew why—and it wasn't because of her.

Jackie applied her rosy red lipstick and smacked her lips together. "You should use some, too," she said, holding out the tube. "The camera washes everything out. This makes your lips look normal."

Lettie took the lipstick. Her hands trembled slightly as she ran the color over her lips. She hadn't seen or spoken to Daniel since the night she'd learned Paz had died. He'd sent messages through Laura Beth, but Lettie had withdrawn into her shell and hadn't returned them. And now? Well, it was probably too late.

"It's been so long," Lettie said.

Jackie rolled her eyes. "If a guy likes you, he doesn't mind waiting." Her expression grew dark. "Besides, you don't want him to get gobbled up by Whitney, do you?"

That was a ridiculous thing for Jackie to say. Although Whitney blatantly flirted with Daniel whenever she saw him, he'd always made it clear he had absolutely no interest in the Cali girl—fending off her advances with a good-natured laugh.

"I don't think Whitney's his type," Lettie said softly.

"That's because *you* are. You don't give yourself enough credit, Lettie. You are a catch and Daniel Cane knows it."

Jackie pulled her hair back into a sleek ponytail before turning toward Lettie.

"What do you think Whitney's up to? She has to know we don't like her, but she keeps coming back for more." Jackie said it carefully and controlled, as though it had just popped into her mind. But Lettie knew better. Jackie had probably wanted to ask her about Whitney since Lettie walked in the door.

To be honest, Lettie had been wondering the same thing since the night of the slumber party. But what she found more confusing was why Laura Beth continued to invite Whitney everywhere. Especially since she didn't seem to like her either.

"She's probably lonely. It's hard moving to a place where you don't know anyone." Lettie remembered the feeling all too well. Being the new girl in seventh grade. Having everyone stare at her as if she didn't belong. Neither Jackie nor Laura Beth knew what that felt like—Jackie had always been the It Girl and Laura Beth the runner-up.

"You always find the best in everyone, don't you?" Jackie smiled.

Not really. I'm not sure I trust your boyfriend. But she kept her doubts about Andrew to herself. "It's easier than always finding the faults."

Jackie nodded and glanced in the full-length mirror. She noticed Lettie was chewing her lip nervously. "Try to relax."

"I can't help it. This could change everything." Lettie slipped her feet into a pair of Laura Beth's navy-blue pumps. She looked like an American flag with her red dress and navy shoes. Which was probably what Laura Beth had in mind when she chose the outfit for her. She could almost hear Laura Beth whispering in her ear, *Stand tall and try not to look too foreign.* In the nicest way, of course.

After one last close look at her face, Jackie turned around. "I don't mean about the new immigration law working out for your family. Are you nervous about being onstage? I know how you get, and there's going to be a lot of photographers and camera crews there."

"Not really." Just this summer President Price had wanted Lettie to help promote immigration reform. Thankfully, Jackie had intervened, knowing that Lettie hated the idea of being used as a token minority—even if it was for an issue she cared passionately about. But this day was major. It was historic. Her entire future depended on this White House ceremony where President Price would finally sign the immigration reforms into law.

Senator Hampton Griffin hadn't even seen it coming. That was the beauty of it. After all his underhanded, blackmailing ways, he was brought down by jobs—the very thing he said the country would lose if Congress passed the immigration reforms. In a backroom deal, President Price had negotiated a major jobs program in the high-unemployment states of two wavering Republican senators—and they had jumped. All the way across the aisle and into the president's pocket.

Jackie couldn't help smiling over the irony.

As soon as her mother and President Price returned from South Africa, they'd holed up in the Oval Office, strategizing how to win back the two Republican votes they needed to pass the bill. In a way, staying at the White House was a gift because it meant Jackie actually got to see more of her mom. In fact, one night Carolyn Shaw, too tired to go home, collapsed on Jackie's bed. She said it was more comfortable than sleeping on the couch in her office—which she seemed to do more and more.

I'm so proud of her, Jackie thought as she watched her mom stand just behind President Price. A small desk with the presidential seal had been brought out to the lawn, and a group of lawmakers, students, and immigrants—including Lettie—surrounded President Price.

Next to her, Andrew shifted his weight from one leg to the other. *Someday, he'll learn not to fidget like a ten-year-old.* When his arm brushed hers, Jackie didn't flinch. She kept her smile firmly in place even as her stomach knotted. She and Andrew used to play a game at these things, to see how much touching they could get away with. Now she wanted nothing more than to get away from him. The sooner the better.

Tension rolled off Andrew, and Jackie hoped it wasn't obvious to everyone watching. With all the cameras trained on them, Jackie knew one dirty look would result in headlines screaming, "Ankie: Is It Over?"

She wasn't ready for that. Yet.

But she wasn't sure *what* exactly she wanted. Andrew had apologized. Shouldn't that be enough?

Still, when he'd texted this morning, Jackie had deleted it without even reading it—just like she had every day since he'd told her about him and Taylor. She didn't want to hear more of his apologies. After all, if he loved her—like he claimed—he wouldn't have given in to Taylor. And he would have told her the truth, about everything, as soon as it happened.

Jackie's eyes wandered over the crowd. There were so many smiling faces and even some tears. *This new law will change millions of lives.* A warmth spread over Jackie's chest, neck, and arms as she thought of it. But it quickly dissipated when she caught the eye of someone in the crowd. He wore a baseball cap and sunglasses, but she could tell by the set of his jaw that he was scowling. *Is he looking at me?* It was difficult to tell. Then the man did something strange. He shook his head from side to side once. Jackie gasped.

"What is it?" Andrew whispered so low that Jackie almost didn't hear it. And even though she didn't want to be near him, she felt herself move a few inches closer.

Jackie looked to her mother and President Price. Then at the security detail behind them. She knew this was the worst possible time to create a scene, but if it was a matter of life and death . . .

She raked her eyes over the crowd again, but the man in the baseball cap was gone. *How could that be? He was just here! Or was he?* Jackie chewed on the inside of her cheek to stifle the panic welling up inside of her. *Everything is fine. See? No stalker in the crowd. I mean, a baseball cap and sunglasses? That's so cliché.*

"Hey," Andrew hissed. "What's wrong?"

Jackie shook her head and pretended it was nothing, because it *was* nothing. She forced another smile for the crowd to see her give her boyfriend. Andrew smiled back, and it seemed genuine.

Everything is fine.

She found Lettie, just to the left of her mom. Her face was glowing.

Focus on how happy you are for Lettie. And how Senator Griffin's plan totally backfired, Jackie thought as President Price prominently signed her name across the bottom of the bill with a swish, swish, dab.

48

It was done. No one could take it away—not Senator Griffin and not the PAPPies—the populist conservative group he was always trying to suck up to. Relief washed over Jackie. *Because of me, this day almost didn't happen. I would have been the reason Lettie's family couldn't become citizens. I would have killed Lettie's dreams.*

A polite round of applause brought Jackie back to the moment. As cameras flashed, a few reporters rushed toward the velvet ropes, eager to get pictures of Ankie.

"Hey, Andrew. When are you going to pop the question?"

"Jackie—are you staying in town for college? To stay close to Andrew?"

She swallowed hard and forced her breath to stay steady. But she couldn't fight the knot in her stomach or the beads of sweat breaking out along her hairline. Desperately, she stared at her mom, hoping to be rescued from the media vultures, but she was too busy shaking hands to notice. Despite the anxiety tearing through her, Jackie kept smiling as if nothing bothered her. Just as everyone expected her to do.

"Let's get out of here," Andrew said, folding her hand into his.

As much as Jackie dreaded being alone with him, she wanted to stay here even less. And she still couldn't shake her unease about the baseball cap guy. *You're being ridiculous.*

Jackie glanced over at Lettie, whose smile stretched ear to ear. *She's ecstatic. And I'm falling apart.*

With a slight nod to Lettie, Jackie replied, "Let's go."

She walked side by side with Andrew into the White House, fully intending to ignore him once they were out of camera range. Or at least busy herself talking to other people.

But there was no one else inside. Only Andrew. And her. Alone. She dropped his hand and took a couple of paces back.

"Jackie." She froze. Andrew had a way of saying her name that sent shivers down her spine. "Please talk to me."

Blood pumped hard through her body, and she wanted to run away. Barricade herself in her room and wait for Lettie. *We're going to have to do this sometime. But why today? Why ruin the celebration?*

She lifted her eyes to tell him no, she wasn't doing this. But when she looked at him, really looked at him, she gasped. Andrew's normally carefully disheveled hair looked dirty—almost uncombed. And the makeup caked on his face barely covered the bruiselike circles around his eyes.

God, he looks awful.

Andrew took two strides across the wide hallway and closed the distance between them. Jackie's heart sped up and she chewed her bottom lip. Something about Andrew looked raw and vulnerable in a way she had never seen before.

"I miss you, Jackie. Please—"

"There you are!" Lettie ran through the entrance doors, taking small, quick steps to avoid falling in her heels. "Isn't it amazing!"

Andrew backed away, giving the two girls room to hug.

When Lettie finally released her, Andrew was gone.

As soon as Lettie saw Jackie and Andrew disappear into the White House, she knew she had to intervene.

I don't know what's going on with Andrew, but if Daniel's right and Andrew somehow caused Taylor's death, I don't want him near Jackie.

"C'mon, I want to see the interviews, don't you?" Lettie asked.

Jackie smiled and nodded. "Of course. That's usually the best part. It's where Aunt Deborah gets to say all the good stuff."

"Like eff you, Senator Griffin?" Lettie asked before covering her mouth. "I shouldn't say that, should I?"

Jackie giggled. "Probably not. At least not where you may be overheard." They were back outside, and Jackie jabbed her chin in the direction of the press. "They'll print anything they hear and make it sound worse."

"Like someone is secretly engaged?" Lettie skipped ahead, trying to lighten the heavy mood hanging over Jackie.

"More like I'm a slut who does slutty things because I talked to a boy." Thankfully, the whole Princeton mess had died down and the press had forgotten about it. Or forgotten about it enough to not mention it every time they saw her.

"In a bar, drunk. *And* doing a provocative dance for the patrons. Don't forget that part," Lettie teased.

Jackie groaned. Each version of the story had been worse than the one before. One version even had her running off and eloping with the guy.

Jackie's iPhone buzzed in her hand.

"Are you going to check it?" Lettie asked quietly.

But Jackie's eyes were already staring at the screen. Her mouth hung open slightly, as if what she was reading caught her completely by surprise.

Curious, Lettie asked, "What is it?"

Jackie blinked and shook her head slightly, as though she were confused. "Scott."

"Scott Price?"

Jackie nodded yes.

"What does he want?"

Scott had hardly been in touch with her since he got caught with pot and the Prices packed him off to some sort of reform school in an effort to keep it all out of the press. But before that had happened, he'd been one of her closest friends.

"He asked if everything's okay. He was watching the signing on TV and says I looked upset." Jackie's voice trembled.

Jackie still looked a little shaken. "*Are* you okay?" Lettie asked.

"I think so," Jackie said with less of a waver in her voice.

President Price stood behind a podium, fielding reporters' questions. Lettie led Jackie to a spot out of sight of the press.

"If we stand here, we can still see, but we're not in the spotlight," Lettie said.

"Yeah, I've had enough of that today," Jackie replied, her eyes trained on the president. "This is perfect. Thanks, Lettie."

Lettie patted Jackie's forearm. "That's what friends are for, right?"

Before Jackie could respond, someone shouted, "Liar!"

All heads swiveled to the source of the accusation.

"You want immigrants to take over this country! You should be impeached!" screamed a tall man with salt-and-pepper-colored hair from the back of the press pool.

President Price leaned into the podium. Her face showed absolutely no emotion. "Our new bill will create hundreds of thousands of new taxpayers. And, if you've forgotten, sir, immigrants founded this country."

Lettie's heartbeat thundered in her ears and she curled her fingers around Jackie's arm. "Why is he saying that? Why does he think the president should be impeached?"

Jackie clasped her hand over Lettie's. "He's with the Patriotic Americans Populist Party. Look."

The man's suit jacket fell open, exposing a PAPPies T-shirt. Four Secret Service agents surrounded him and forcibly removed him from the news conference.

"We won't go down without a fight, you liar. PAPPies for real Americans!"

Senator Griffin flipped off the television. "Moran, that's how we do it. How we destroy that woman."

Eric Moran, the senator's aide, ran his hand through his hair. "Senator, I don't see how one person acting like a lunatic at a news conference destroys the president's credibility."

"Not him. Did you see her son and that Whitman girl? Something's going on there and I don't think it has anything to do with your little fling."

Eric felt heat spread across his cheeks. Jackie Whitman kissed like no other girl he'd had before. And that body. *Goddamn if she isn't hot. And smart, too.*

"What do you mean?" Eric asked.

The senator slammed his fist onto his mahogany desk. "I want you to dig up dirt on those two while you're looking into the rest of the Price family."

Eric flinched. Politics was politics, but getting dirt on a couple of teenagers? That seemed overboard. "But—"

"Do I need to remind you your career is in jeopardy? After the hack job you did on the immigration bill, I should fire your ass."

You're the dumb-ass who couldn't close the deal. I got you what you needed. You blew it. And you ruined whatever chance I had with Jackie in the process.

"I'll get started on it right away." Eric strode toward the door.

"Oh, and Moran?" the senator called after him. "Let's keep this between us for now."

"Of course, Senator."

FIVE

Steam rose off the streets of downtown D.C. as Lettie navigated her way through the crowds. The District was always busy, even after all the summer tourists had gone home. Lettie never did get why tourists flocked to the nation's capital during the worst of the heat. Every summer she wanted to stop a group of them, apologize for the horrible humidity, and invite them back in the late fall.

Sweat dripped down her back as she descended into the mouth of the Metro Center train station.

She clutched the bakery box of cupcakes to her stomach—an American dessert to celebrate the signing of the immigration bill with her family. Technically, they were still in mourning for Paz, but if Mamá had made tamales, surely her parents wouldn't disapprove of Lettie spending some of her money from her embassy job on a treat.

Even with the crowds and the heat, Lettie didn't regret refusing Jackie's offer to pay for a taxi home. The other girls couldn't understand why she preferred riding crowded metro trains and buses, but Lettie liked the egalitarian nature of them. Plus, they were fast and efficient. And affordable.

A group of high school students blocked the entrance to the fare gates, unsure how to get through. She'd seen this a million times—tourists unfamiliar with how the mass transit system worked.

"Do you need help?" she asked, moving to the front of the line.

A boy around her age with close-cut brown hair and the biggest brown eyes she'd ever seen turned to face her. He was cute in an almost pretty way, but not really her type. Lettie preferred blonds . . . like Daniel. Her heart fluttered at the memory of him, which was all he was at the moment. Maybe Jackie was right, maybe she shouldn't assume it was over yet.

"It's not working. Is there a trick or something?" The boy with the metro card held it up and waved it around. A PAPPies button was pinned to the strap of his backpack, front and center, with the words ILLEGALS GO HOME for everyone to see.

Wonderful, he's one of them. What does Laura Beth say? Kill them with kindness?

"Let me try," Lettie said, holding out her hand with a smile on her face.

The boy narrowed his eyes, looked her up and down, and gave her a dirty look. "I don't need your help."

Lettie felt herself turn crimson. Why did he give her that nasty look? Was it because she had olive skin and black hair? Did he assume she was Hispanic and therefore illegal?

Around her, people moved quickly through the gate, but she felt frozen.

"Are you waiting for us to let you through? Do you need to sneak in?" the boy snapped. Another student snickered, and Lettie was sure the entire station was listening to their exchange.

"C'mon. Either go through or don't," someone shouted from the back of the line.

That was enough to snap the power the boy had over her, and she inched away from him. She tapped her SmarTrip card against the fare reader. When the gate swung open, she hurried through.

Lettie's heart pumped hard as she rode another escalator down to the platform. When she stepped off, people swarmed around her, eager to get where they needed to be. None of them seemed to even notice her. Which was exactly what she wanted.

I thought when President Price signed the bill this morning, things would be better. She kept her eyes down and leaned against a tiled wall. She wished she could fold into herself and disappear. Or at the very least, never see those PAPPie kids again.

Oh, who am I kidding? The PAPPies won't change. And they're even madder now that the bill is law.

A train sped into the station and came to a smooth stop. Lettie waited for the passengers to exit before entering and finding a seat. It was a short ride, but her whole body shook from the confrontation with the boy.

For the first time, Lettie wondered if she was deluding herself. Princeton and Harvard Law wouldn't change how people saw her—at least not at first. She'd always be a poor Latina girl who was granted citizenship out of charity. Just as she'd always be the scholarship student to Mrs. Ballou.

Lettie, balancing the cupcakes on her lap, stared at the blackness outside her window. It was unfair, but it was also reality. People didn't change overnight. And prejudice didn't just evaporate with the swish of a pen.

She changed trains, then got off at Columbia Heights station and waited for the 43 bus. Most of the people with her were immigrants like her or yuppies who had gentrified her Mount Pleasant neighborhood. Out here, she was anonymous—no one gave her a second glance.

In some ways, Paz was right. But it wasn't about her friends. It was the whole place. D.C. is a bubble, she thought as the bus bumped along before stopping at Lamont Street. *Out there, in the real world, some people don't think I'm worth the air I breathe.* The realization sent chills down her spine.

She climbed the steps of her apartment with a heavy heart. As much as she wished differently, nothing had changed.

Music and laughter floated down the stairwell. Lettie stopped and tilted her head. A slight smile crossed her lips. *At least someone is happy. I wonder if the Díazes' daughter finally got engaged?*

But the closer she came to the top floor, the more it seemed like the sounds came from her apartment. Lettie paused. Her family was still in mourning for Paz, and even though Mamá and Papá were excited about the bill signing, it seemed unlikely they'd throw a party. Mamá making tamales was as far as their celebrating went. Even the box of cupcakes was pushing it.

Yet the instant she opened the front door, music poured into the hall and Mamá ran to greet her. "Lettie! Isn't it wonderful! Your brother! He's home!"

Lettie stared at Mamá, her brain trying to process the impossible news. "Mamá, you know Paz is dead. Come now, I'll make you—"

"It's true, little sister." Paz stood in the doorway to the kitchen. His dark hair was disheveled, and he looked a little thin. But it was Paz. Despite the dark circles under his eyes, he was grinning. "I have returned from the dead."

Lettie's legs turned to a wobbling mess of Jell-O. As sure as she breathed, Paz stood before her, crooked smile and all. Their two little sisters were squealing with delight, hanging on to his legs. And he seemed *whole*.

"Paz?" she squeaked weakly.

"In the flesh."

Her knees buckled and Paz's arms immediately encircled her.

"You . . . you idiot!" she shouted, suddenly finding her strength. "You're supposed to be dead. We mourned for you! Cried for you! Mamá lit candles every day at church for your soul."

Paz gently pried off nine-year-old Maribel and seven-year-old Christa and led Lettie to the couch. "I can die again if it makes you feel better."

She shook her head. "No!" She buried her face in her brother's chest and sobbed tears of joy.

Carolyn Shaw poured a glass of bourbon and handed it to her best friend, Deborah Price. The two women had been pals since college. Over the years, they'd weathered divorce, infidelity, and the brutal firestorm of national politics. But today they'd scored their largest victory when Deborah signed the landmark immigration bill.

They'd campaigned hard on the idea, even when all the pundits said Deborah's reelection chances would be ruined if she didn't get it through Congress. Many thought they had no hope of succeeding—especially that old Republican windbag Hampton Griffin. He underestimated them—they all had.

"To success," Carolyn said, raising her glass and glancing at her daughter and Andrew, who stood on opposite sides of the room not making eye contact with each other. Normally, Andrew's arm would be snaked around Jackie's waist and they'd be acting like a unit. But not tonight. Despite the excitement in the room, both looked as if they didn't want to be there.

Something's not right. I haven't seen the two of them look happy together in a few weeks.

She watched as Deborah's husband hoisted his glass a little too enthusiastically and amber liquid sloshed over the edge and onto his shoes.

And to think I used to envy Deborah for keeping her marriage intact. You couldn't pay me enough to put up with that.

Deborah's new communications director and a few other select staffers rounded out their small group. Other than the obvious tension between Jackie and Andrew, the celebratory atmosphere reminded Carolyn of the night they won the Iowa caucuses.

Across the room, Jackie slipped out the door with her iPhone pressed to her ear. She hadn't been the same since Taylor died—she often grew quiet and spent more time alone. It was as if Taylor took a piece of Jackie with her. And Carolyn didn't know how to fix it. She thought time would help, but lately Jackie seemed even more withdrawn. Maybe it was time for Jackie to see the psychiatrist again.

Lettie rolled over on the couch, her hands pressed against her overfull stomach. For the first time in weeks, food didn't taste bitter and she'd stuffed herself.

She'd offered to help Mamá with the dishes, but her mother insisted Lettie spend time with Paz. "I've had him all afternoon. It's your turn," she told her daughter. "Come on, little ones, you can help your mama and papa clean up." The two little girls protested loudly but wriggled off the sofa and did as they were told.

Paz's head rested against the couch. "I'm sorry I couldn't call. I wanted to, but . . ."

The excitement of Paz's arrival overshadowed the question of how exactly he'd returned. Mamá and Papá claimed it was a miracle. That the Lord had heard their prayers and kept Paz safe. But Lettie knew it was more than divine intervention.

"What happened?" she asked, not fully convinced she wanted to hear the truth.

Paz sighed, ran his hand through his hair, and didn't speak. This didn't look good. Not at all.

"What did you do, *mi hermano?*" Lettie rolled onto her side so that she could see her brother's profile. He still looked like Paz, but something darker lived inside him now. And it frightened her.

"There was so much fighting. And killing." He kept his eyes straight ahead. "I won't lie, it was the scariest thing I've ever done. But I was a soldier fighting on the wrong side. Taking orders from a corrupt government that was ordering the army to kill the people. Our own people. So I left."

"Did you think about staying and fighting on the other side?" Lettie asked gently.

"Of course I did!" Paz turned and glared at her, then shook his head sorrowfully. "But I couldn't. You can't imagine what it was like, Lettie. So much bloodshed. So many bodies." His shoulders seemed to sag under the weight of the memories. "You probably think I'm a coward—"

"No!" Lettie interrupted quickly. She took his hand. "You are not a coward. You are brave for refusing to keep fighting for the wrong side."

Lettie could see the fear lurking behind his eyes. Her own memories of Paraguay, though faint, were of happy family times. But to be honest, in many ways she thought of the United States as her *real* home now. That was why Congress passing President Price's immigration reforms meant so much to her. It would allow her to stay here for as long as she wanted, go to law school, and then go back to Paraguay—maybe temporarily or maybe forever—to help lift the country out of poverty and corruption. To return it to the people.

She turned her attention back to Paz, who sat slumped and silent.

"How did you get out?" she asked, although she dreaded his answer.

"I told you. I ran away," he whispered in English—the language their parents didn't understand.

The blood in her veins turned icy as she absorbed the information. Absent without leave from the army. An offense punishable by firing squad. She shuddered. "But if you went AWOL, how did you get back in the U.S.?"

"I did someone a favor. I snuck a package in." He held up his hand when she began to protest. "Don't judge me, Lettie. You'd be a drug mule, too, if it meant getting out of that shit hole."

Lettie's mouth fell open. Not again. The whole reason Paz had been sent away to the military was that Papá had caught him running with a local gang of drug dealers. What was the expression? "He'd fallen in with the wrong crowd." But he *hadn't* been a dealer. And he was actually trying to break free of the gang when Papá found out. Instead of his plan to get a U.S. work permit, go to college part-time, and make something of himself, he found himself on an embassy plane headed for Asunción.

"Paz, Lettie, come to the kitchen," Papá called.

The two siblings exchanged worried glances. Papá had sounded stern. The only time he sounded like that was to admonish them or break bad news. Did he know about Paz?

Lettie slipped her arm through her older brother's. "Don't make Mamá cry, Paz. Please," she whispered before they entered the small but cozy kitchen. It still smelled like dinner, and Lettie's mouth watered.

"Sit," Papá ordered. It was just the four of them, their younger sisters already tucked into bed in the room they shared with Lettie.

They sat in silence, waiting for Papá. Next to her, Paz tapped his foot.

"I am so happy that we are all a family again. But I have some news." Her father rested his hand on Mamá's shoulder. She wasn't crying, but she looked worried.

"The ambassador has been recalled to Paraguay."

All the air seemed to get sucked out of Lettie's lungs and the blood pounded in her head. "And our family has to go home with him."

"Lettie, slow down. I can't understand you." Jackie paced the hallway outside the First Family's living room. Even though her mother was back in D.C., she and Aunt Deborah had insisted Jackie stay on at the White House. It made Jackie wonder if the threats against her were continuing. But she didn't ask. She didn't want to know.

"We have to go back! To Paraguay." Lettie sniffed. "I won't be going to Princeton, Jackie. Or Harvard. I'll never be a lawyer."

Jackie leaned against the wall. She couldn't save Taylor, but she sure as hell wasn't going to lose Lettie. "Back up and tell me everything."

"I guess I should start with Paz. He isn't dead."

"What?" Jackie's mouth dropped open.

"He went AWOL and snuck back into the States. If he goes back, they'll arrest him. But my parents think he was discharged as a war hero."

"That sounds easy enough to fix. Just tell your parents the truth. They'll understand why he had to leave, won't they?"

"No! They think the president can do no wrong—" Lettie's voice cracked. Jackie listened in stunned silence as Lettie poured out the rest of the story: how the country was on the verge of civil war and the Paraguayan president had declared a state of emergency and ordered his top ambassadors home.

"Why don't your parents just stay? They could easily get jobs, there's so many people needing reliable drivers and maids," Jackie said.

"Mamá and Papá's visas only allow them to work at the embassay and nowhere else," Lettie said miserably. "Even if they had a choice, which they don't, they would never disobey the ambassador. They are loyal employees who do whatever their government tells them, without questioning anything the government says or does." Jackie could hear the bitterness in Lettie's voice.

"What's Paz going to do?"

"Paz told me he's not going with us. He's going to stay, Jackie. And what will he do for money? He can't get a job without an immigration card, so he'll go back to his gang and start dealing drugs in order to survive. I know it."

Jackie closed her eyes as if to block out the sound of Lettie's sobs. She tilted her head back so that it touched the wall. "I'm not going to lose you without a fight, Lettie. Let me talk to Mom and Aunt Deborah."

There was a long pause. *At least she's stopped crying.*

"Lettie?"

"I'm sorry. I'm . . ." Lettie trailed off. "I'm so lucky to have a friend like you."

"You, me, and Laura Beth—no matter how bad things are, we stick together."

Lettie sniffed. "Always."

After they said their good-byes, Jackie studied her phone.

Would Lettie still think she was a great friend if she found out Jackie had been keeping secrets from her? Would she judge her for stealing information for Senator Griffin, the way Jackie judged Taylor? Or did friendship mean looking past those things, forgiving, and moving on? Jackie didn't know anymore.

Suddenly, Jackie flipped her iPhone over and pushed a button. She had to talk to someone. Someone who would never judge her.

"Scott? Hey, it's Jackie."

"Jackie! What's up?" He sounded excited, as though she'd just made his night with one phone call.

"I just felt like talking to someone outside the Beltway," she said, studying the raised pattern on the wallpaper.

"I'm all yours." He laughed. "So long as it's not inside-the-Beltway bullshit you want to talk about."

"My life's so boring that's *exactly* what I was going to talk about."

"You need cheering up." He laughed again. "And a hug. I'd give you one if I was there."

Right now, that sounds like the best thing in the world.

SIX

Laura Beth adjusted the collar on the front of her Lanvin ruffled blouse one last time before opening her laptop. Every night at nine thirty, she and Sol Skyped. It wasn't the same as actually *being* with him, but at least she could see his face. And that was better than just hearing his voice.

As she waited for his image to appear, she ran through her e-mails in a separate window. Whitney, Whitney, and more Whitney. When she wasn't texting or calling Laura Beth, she flooded her in-box. Laura Beth had hoped once Whitney started hanging out with Angie Meehan and her group, she'd back off. But no luck.

She clicked through the list, deleting as she went. Most of Whitney's e-mails were asking about Laura Beth's weekend plans.

As if I'd tell her!

Since Jackie's sleepover, Laura Beth had successfully pushed Whitney off by saying she was busy with her mom or Sol. Which was true—mostly.

After clearing out her in-box, Laura Beth clicked over to the *Washington Tattler* Web site. The very first picture showed President Price signing the immigration bill. And right behind her was Lettie, dressed perfectly for the occasion.

I did such a good job on that outfit! It photographed beautifully. Laura Beth studied Lettie a little closer and smiled. *Jackie must have convinced her to wear a little makeup. She looks great.*

She scrolled through the article, not really caring what it said. She just wanted to see the photos. On the second page was a picture of Andrew and Jackie standing side by side, smiling but keeping a polite distance from each other.

That's new. Usually they're all over each other, playing that silly game of theirs.

"Hey, Laura Beth . . ." Sol's voice came through her computer speakers loud and clear.

She panicked, worried that she'd been squinting or making a funny face when he logged on. Laura Beth hated Sol to see her looking anything but her best.

"Hi! How was your day?" She couldn't take her eyes off his tousled hair. It looked as if he'd just taken a shower. And his arms! *Oh. My. Lord. How much does he work out?*

He smiled sleepily. "Long. But I wouldn't miss this for anything."

She inhaled deeply and grinned at her boyfriend. Whatever was going on with Jackie and Andrew could wait. She had better things to think about right now.

Still clutching her iPhone, Jackie slipped back into the First Family's living room. Aunt Deborah, her press secretary, Brian Gillespie, and Jackie's mom sat around the low coffee table, nursing drinks. Everyone else had left for the night.

"Madam President, if you don't mind, I'd like to leave for the evening," Brian said. He was a large man—six feet five—and had the deep, rumbling voice of a newscaster. Her mom said they'd hired him because no one else could stare down a reporter quite like Brian.

Aunt Deborah finished her drink and set it on the table. "Of course, Brian. Your wife probably would like to see you sometime this year." She flashed the famous Price smile at him—the one that was both kind and a little mischievous.

Brian hurried toward the door. Long hours were the norm at the White House, but some people—like Brian and her mom—worked all day, every day. Jackie couldn't remember when she and her mom last took a vacation together. Or when her mom had taken a real vacation at all—completely unplugged and tuned out from D.C. life.

"Is that what you really want, Jackie? To live for work? How boring is that?" Taylor shook her head at me.

We'd had this conversation before. Taylor thought I was too focused on breaking into politics, and I thought she was too laid-back about the future.

"My mom gets to travel the world. The things she sees—"

"Yeah, from behind ten inches of bulletproof glass and only on a carefully

scheduled itinerary." Taylor played with the end of her white-blond hair and raised her eyebrows. *"After we graduate, come with me to Spain."*

"I thought you wanted to caravan across the U.S.?" Taylor's plans changed so regularly, I couldn't keep up with the trip du jour.

She waved her hand. *"It doesn't matter where we go. Let's just do something."*

I am doing something. I'm going to keep Lettie and her family here, Jackie thought as she sank into the deep cushions of the couch. Unlike the rest of the White House, this space was decorated to Aunt Deborah's taste and had a slightly more modern feel. Like maybe mid-1900s instead of being stuck in the 1800s.

Her conversation with Scott had cheered her up a little, even if it was short. His school operated on a restricted schedule, and he had to go before Jackie had been able to really get into what was bothering her. Still, just hearing his voice and listening to him discuss his total hatred of Frisbee golf cracked Jackie up.

"What's up?" Carolyn Shaw asked. "You seem upset."

Jackie swallowed the lump in her throat. Now was as good a time as any. Who knew when she'd get some time alone again with two of the most powerful women in the world?

"The Paraguayan ambassador has been recalled and Lettie's family has to go home." The words tumbled out of her, faster than she wanted. But she didn't cry. That's not how powerful women behaved.

The door to the room opened and in walked Andrew. *Wonderful. Just what I need, another awkward interaction to cap off this day.*

Andrew came around the back of Aunt Deborah's chair and

picked up her empty glass from the table. "Want another?" he asked.

Jackie narrowed her eyes. Classic Andrew trick—offer to refill the adults' drinks and skim a little off the top. They'd spent many nights during the campaign sneaking sips of alcohol.

Aunt Deborah leaned back into her chair and rolled her head from side to side as she moved from "president" mode to "mom" mode. "I'm fine, and no, you cannot have a drink. You're still underage, in case you've forgotten."

With a sigh, Andrew slumped into the empty chair across from Jackie. He didn't speak to her or even look at her. *So much for keeping up appearances.*

"What were you saying about Lettie and her family?" her mom asked gently.

Andrew leaned forward in his seat, concern clouding his eyes. Jackie knew that of all her friends, Lettie was the one Andrew liked best. Sure, he and Laura Beth went back years, but Andrew admired Lettie.

The cool metal of her iPhone comforted her. Taylor used to joke that it was Jackie's third arm—especially when Jackie would misplace it and go into a panicked search. And she needed to be calm now. Especially with Andrew sitting across from her, simultaneously ignoring her and paying attention to everything she said. His presence felt a lot like the Secret Service—always there, but pretending not to be.

"Lettie's family has to return to Paraguay with the ambassador. But Lettie can't go—she has to graduate with our class." She heard the strain in her voice. The one thing she'd learned from her mom and Aunt Deborah was to never, ever let the other side see how badly you want something. But here she could drop her guard. "She wants to go to Princeton. Sending her back will destroy her dreams."

President Price rubbed the bridge of her nose and closed her eyes. She was so still that for a moment, Jackie thought she'd fallen asleep. "That poor girl. First her brother is killed and now she has to abandon her life here."

"Oh!" Jackie had completely forgotten to tell them. "Paz isn't dead. He went AWOL and turned up at their apartment. Lettie said he couldn't fight for a government he didn't believe in and that this was his home, not Paraguay."

She realized too late she'd just told the president that Paz had snuck into the United States. But she kept talking. "And now, if he goes back, he'll be arrested and shot for deserting. Isn't there something we can do?" Jackie was always careful to say "we" and not "you." She never wanted Aunt Deborah to feel taken advantage of.

More silence. *Please, somebody say something. Lettie's counting on me.*

To her surprise, Andrew said, "Paz graduated from high school, didn't he?"

"Yes," Jackie said hesitantly.

"And the bill allows students studying at the college level, with a job or internship, to remain in the country, right, Mom?"

The president opened her eyes, a smile forming on her lips. "It does."

Next to Jackie, her mom shifted forward in her seat. "Deborah, if this isn't the time to use the new law, I don't know what is. Paz is exactly the type of person we're trying to help."

Aunt Deborah turned her thoughtful eyes toward Jackie. "There may be a way to keep Paz here."

If advocating for Lettie's brother gets Jackie to speak to me, I'll do it.

Andrew watched his girlfriend—still his girlfriend because they hadn't officially broken up—volley ideas with his mom and Carolyn Shaw. She crossed her bare, tanned legs, and Andrew's eyes traveled up, up, up to the hem of her skirt.

Instead of the usual excitement, all he felt now was an *Access Revoked* punch to the gut.

It didn't help that he'd overheard Jackie on the phone to Scott. Jackie and Scott had had something more than friendship freshman year. And now, if she was turning to Scott instead of him for help . . . Well, that wasn't good. It meant she wanted out. And in with Scott?

So why hadn't she done it yet? Why were they still in this limbo of being a couple but not really being together?

Jackie's mom leaned back in her chair, her legs crossed at the ankles. "Since he has a diploma, I'm sure I could pull a few strings and get Paz into Montgomery College. But Lettie? She has a year left of high school."

Andrew seized the moment. If he could help fix this for Jackie, maybe it would show her how much she meant to him. "What if we have Lettie declared an exchange student? It would buy her another year, and then with college, she'd be a foreign student and eligible for citizenship."

Jackie's eyes grew large and she nearly leapt out of her seat. It was just the reaction Andrew wanted. "Can we do that? Can you get Excelsior to change her status?"

His mom nodded. "I don't see why not. Especially since it

might mean she'd no longer be a scholarship student and would have to pay full tuition."

Jackie deflated into the couch. "Oh."

And there goes my moment, Andrew thought.

Carolyn and his mom exchanged some wordless communication that Andrew had given up trying to understand years ago. They were so in sync, always knowing what the other one needed—it was eerie sometimes. Kind of like Jackie and Taylor.

Shit. Don't think of Taylor now, you dumb-ass. That's how you ended up in this mess.

Carolyn reached over and squeezed her daughter's hand. "We'll make sure Lettie's tuition is paid for. Don't worry about it."

"Really?" Jackie's glossy pink lips broke into a smile. "You'd do that?"

"Just let me work out a few details before you tell Lettie, okay? And I'll have to speak to her parents, of course."

Jackie jumped up from her seat and hugged Carolyn. "Thank you! Thank you!"

She stumbled around the table and leaned down to hug his mom. "Thank you! Thank you! Thank you!"

Jackie's deep blue eyes rested on Andrew. He began to look away, but before he could, her hand darted out and grabbed his. "And thank you, Andrew."

She hadn't meant to grab Andrew's hand. Hell, she was still eight shades of pissed at him. But when she touched him, the look of surprise on his face melted away some of those hard feelings. He'd spoken up for Paz—and kept the info about his gang past secret. Jackie didn't really care about the *why*, just that he did.

After Aunt Deborah and her mom left, Jackie found herself alone with Andrew again. Neither of them spoke, just stared at different corners of the room.

When that became too awkward—and really, how can anything be more awkward than sitting in a room, alone, with the boy who cheated on you with your best friend—Jackie started toward the door.

She felt Andrew move next to her before she saw him. "Jackie, wait." His voice shook slightly. "We need to talk."

"Do we?" She spun around to face him. "I think I've said everything I need to."

Andrew took a step back, as though he were afraid she might hurt him. His shoulders rolled forward a little. "Yeah. We do. And this avoiding thing, it's not going to work forever. People are starting to notice."

Figures. He cares more about his reputation than my feelings.

But he had a point. She'd overheard Brian Gillespie telling her mom that he was getting press calls about Ankie's relationship status. Not that the White House commented on such things, but still, reporters were obviously nosing around. And the way her mom and Aunt Deborah looked at them tonight, they knew something was wrong, too.

For weeks, she'd been avoiding this moment. She'd imagined it a million times: She'd be firm, pissed, and to the point. Andrew would repent and then... It was the *then* that she had no idea about.

"Did you even like me, or was it all a big joke? A political ploy to look good?" Jackie asked. She wanted to sound hard, even cold, but her words came out in a whisper. Not at all how she'd imagined.

"You know I love you." His bright green eyes locked on to Jackie's. "Shit, when we thought you'd been kidnapped, I felt like my life was over. Like someone cut out my heart."

It was dramatic, but something about the anguish in his eyes made Jackie feel better.

"But I wasn't. And I'm fine." *Everything is fine,* she repeated in her mind. "So you can go back to your normal program of being a cheating asshole." She knew it was too harsh, but those were the words she'd wanted to say for weeks.

Andrew raked his hand through his sandy brown hair. His remorseful eyes focused on her. "Please, Jackie. I want to make this up to you. I need you to forgive me."

A tremor shook Jackie's body. This was what she'd wanted: for him to beg. To show remorse and regret. But she wasn't going to let him off so easy.

"This is a good first step, but you've got a lot of work to do." Without waiting for a response, Jackie slipped into the hallway and walked, as fast as she could, back to her room.

SEVEN

No one told her. *Why would they? Half the time, they don't even remember I exist.*

Whitney slammed her bag down on the kitchen counter and threw open the fridge door. All the food had been replaced with her mom's organic smoothies, tofu, and vegetables for making cleanses.

"Whitney? You home?" her mom called from her home office.

As if you care. Supposedly, Tracey Mills had moved to D.C. earlier than planned to keep an eye on Whitney. Her parents claimed that her near arrest made it clear she needed more supervision than her dad could give her on his own. But something about their explanation sounded fake to Whitney. First, they'd never batted an eye when she'd gotten into trouble in L.A. Second, her dad had seemed just as shocked as Whitney to see his wife on the doorstep of their Watergate apartment. And third, her mom wouldn't be paying attention to her. She'd be too busy working her way into D.C. society.

"Yeah, I'm here." Whitney shut the door. *I should call Angie and see if she wants to grab dinner.*

Since crashing Jackie's little slumber party, Whitney hadn't seen much of her or Laura Beth or Lettie. Other than annoying LB, she hadn't really tried to weasel her way into any more *Crapital* Girl get-togethers. Why should she have to hang out with the most boring people in D.C. when she could hang with girls like Angie Meehan? Besides, things with Franklin had heated way up despite their little memorial garden fiasco. In fact, he'd told Whitney that getting busted just made him want to finish what they'd started even more. Horny boy.

Tracey Mills marched into the room.

"How was school?" *Translation: Did you get anything good on the* Crapital *Girls?*

"Fine."

Her mom rolled her eyes. "Just because I'm here, Whitney, doesn't mean you can't go back to L.A.—if you play your cards right."

When her mom turned up yesterday with no advance warning, Whitney's stomach had dropped into her shoes as fast as the bile rose in her throat. With her mom in D.C., Whitney would never get back to L.A. That was obvious. Or so she thought.

Whitney raised one carefully sculpted eyebrow. "Oh?"

"You know what I need. Just give me some good, usable info on Jackie and Andrew or Laura Beth or their families, and I'll buy you a one-way first-class ticket."

Same old, same old. Her mom had been dangling that carrot in front of her all summer. But no matter how hard she tried, nothing Whitney delivered was good enough. Or it proved to be a full-on lie. Like the fake engagement.

"I've been hanging out with this girl Angie Meehan. Her father's a rich Republican fundraiser and she's Jackie's frenemy."

That got her mom's attention. "Good girl. Befriend the friends *and* the enemies. Smart thinking for once."

"Oh, yeah, and Angie just introduced me to a new junior, Dina Ives. Her dad's some senator or something."

Her mother clapped her hands. "Yes! Brilliant!" Then she frowned. "For your information, Whitney, her father is one of *our* senators from California. I can't believe you don't know that."

"Well . . . ," Whitney started to say. She wanted to ask if she could stop forcing herself on Laura Beth, Lettie, and Jackie. After all, she hated them just as much as they hated her. (Well, not Lettie. Lettie was actually nice to her.) But something about the spark in her mom's eye told her this wasn't the time. "You know, I learned from the best."

Her mom swatted her on the ass as she walked past. "That you did. That you did."

Laura Beth pushed the steamed vegetables and brown rice around her plate and sighed. Sol was coming down from New York tonight and they had a romantic dinner planned. Which was perfect, but after-school dance practice always left her ravenous and she didn't want to look like a pig, inhaling her dinner or eating more than Sol.

Another bite of dry rice, chased by a swig of iced water. *The things I do to look good.*

"Laura Beth, what are you doing sittin' here eatin' that plate of rabbit food?" her mother asked, flipping on the dining room light. Libby Ballou insisted all meals—even breakfast—be eaten properly, in the dining room. As far as she was concerned, only the staff ate in the kitchen.

"Sol's taking me to dinner tonight." Another mouthful of bland food.

Her mother winked. "I see. When do I get to meet this boy's family? Seems only fittin' as he's here so often."

Laura Beth blushed. Things were moving fast with Sol—just last night, he'd told her he'd never met a girl like her, and her heart still hadn't settled down.

He was so perfect. Except they mostly got together via computer.

Modern romance wasn't very romantic.

Laura Beth hesitated. She hadn't told her mother the truth about Sol—that not only was Sol not Spanish, but he was Iranian *and* Muslim. And when she did screw up the courage to tell her, oh Lord.

Mama's not racist. She has all different kinds of friends. She'll be fine with it. . . . Or not. Laura Beth wrinkled her nose slightly. *Better just get it over with.*

She hadn't intended to introduce the families yet, but if Mama was asking, or rather demanding . . .

"Maybe we can arrange something for next week? Mr. and Mrs. Molla will be in town," she said.

Her mother nodded. "Why don't we invite them to join us at Vidalia?" Vidalia was one of her mother's favorite restaurants—Southern food with an upscale French influence.

Laura Beth picked up her now half-empty plate and started

toward the kitchen. "Thursday?" she asked as her stomach flip-flopped. *No going back now.*

"Sounds lovely. I'll make the reservation for the six of us," Mama called from behind her.

"Six?" Laura Beth stopped midstride and spun around.

This time, her mother blushed. "I'll bring Jeffrey, of course." When Laura Beth stared blankly, her mother added, "Senator Ives, darlin'. He and I have been seeing quite a lot of each other. Haven't you noticed?"

Laura Beth felt awful. Of course she'd noticed. It was impossible not to when her mama was always talking about him. "I just thought, with Congress in session, he would be busy." She hoped that covered her gaffe.

"Darlin', a man still has to eat. Don't ever forget that." Libby smiled widely. "And like any well-bred man, Jeffrey appreciates a proper meal with good company."

There was something about the way her mom said Senator Ives's name: *Jeffrey.* Like honey and molasses. *She must really like him.*

Love was in the air at the Ballou house, and it filled Laura Beth with a warm, cozy feeling. Her mother had been a widow too long. "Mama, Senator Ives is quite a catch!"

Libby Ballou placed one hand on her hip and patted her dyed ash-blond hair with the other. "And so is your dear old mama. Don't you forget that!"

Laura Beth pecked her on the cheek. *If she's so wrapped up in Senator Ives, maybe she won't pay attention to where Sol's parents are from.*

A short sigh escaped Laura Beth's lips as she climbed the stairs. *Fat chance. Libby Ballou pays attention to everything.*

Once safely in her room, she threw herself down on the

oversize four-poster bed that dominated the space and stared at the tray ceiling. She loved her room and its feminine touches— the canopy, the ruffled bed skirt; the pale pink textured wallpaper; the vanity covered in cosmetics and perfume.

Mama always said a lady's room was her sanctuary. Men should never be allowed to see a woman without makeup, and they should never, ever be invited into her dressing room. No need to show off the arsenal. Still, it didn't stop her from wishing Sol were right there, lying next to her.

But soon enough. He'd be here any minute and she wouldn't have to just imagine the feel of his lips. And Laura Beth planned on doing as much kissing as possible.

Her phone dinged and Laura Beth automatically scooped it off her nightstand. She regretted it immediately. It was Whitney:

This weekend you're going shopping with Angie and me. Saturday. I'll email you the time and place later.

Laura Beth sighed again. When did things get so complicated? Blackmail, boyfriends, college. When did life change from playing with Barbies to *this*?

Oh, stop your bellyachin'. Your problems are nothing compared to Lettie's.

No one knew what would happen to Lettie. Jackie had reassured the girls that her mom and the president were taking care of it, and though the ambassador's departure had been delayed for another month, Lettie's future was still unclear.

Laura Beth swung her legs over the side of the bed and hopped down. When she was little, she'd told her daddy she wanted to sleep way up high, like "The Princess and the Pea." He'd found the tallest bed he could and surprised her with it on her eighth birthday. She'd had to use a step stool to climb up and down.

If Excelsior can change Lettie's status, she'll need a place to live. . . .

Laura Beth's eyes darted around her room as she considered what it would be like to share. As an only child, she'd never shared anything—not her toys, her room, or her parents. *If Lettie stayed with us, it would be like having a sister. But she'll have to use one of the guest rooms. Mine is too small for two people.*

From her color-organized walk-in closet, Laura Beth selected a short Pucci shift in swirls of green. Sol had admired the way her dark red hair looked against green. And she was dying to wear this number.

With a pair of scissors she retrieved from a drawer, Laura Beth snipped off the tags and let them fall to the ground. She draped the dress over the back of her vanity chair and removed her yoga pants and wrap sweater. She'd showered at the dance studio, and of course, she wore full makeup already.

Once she had slipped the dress over her head and admired the fit, she quickly rolled her hair up—she'd just had it straightened again at Aveda—into a loose chignon. Sleek and sophisticated.

As she applied one last coat of gloss, the doorbell rang. Laura Beth placed her hand over her heart to calm herself.

Showtime.

"So, tell me again. Your mom just showed up, and you didn't know she was coming?" Angie Meehan swirled the straw in her toasted marshmallow milkshake.

"Pretty much. She and all her crap moved in, and now I have no shot of getting back to L.A." No need to tell Angie about their deal.

The noise of the dinner crowd at Good Stuff Eatery roared

around them. Franklin had brought her here one night for dinner and Whitney'd loved it. It reminded her of the kitschy burger joints in L.A., but with better food. At first, when Whitney had suggested meeting here, Angie had laughed. *Apparently, if you're from California, you can only ever eat tofu and bean sprouts. You're also a hippie and spend all your free time hugging trees.*

Obnoxious congressional staffers from the Hill crowded around the girls and pressed into their small table near the stairs. *What a bunch of lame-asses. Who even wears khakis besides old people?* Whitney adjusted her tank top to show off more of her cleavage. *Might as well give them some excitement that doesn't involve pages of hard-on killing legalese.*

"D.C. isn't *that* awful, Whit."

Whitney scowled. "Not if you like boring and old."

Angie leaned across the table and pushed the corners of Whitney's mouth up. "C'mon. You have me and Aamina ... and Franklin. I bet there's no one in L.A. as fabulous as us."

Actually, just about everyone is more fabulous. But Angie and Franklin were vast improvements on the *Crapital* Girls. At least her new friends knew how to party.

Whitney snorted. "And no one is as big of a priss as Jackie Whitman. What's her deal, anyway? Has anyone even tried to get the stick out of her ass?"

Angie practically choked on her milkshake. "Shhh ... Whit, most of these people know who she is."

"So?" Whitney tore off a piece of her burger bun and shredded it with her fingers. Now that she was here, staring at her burger, she seemed to have lost her appetite. "Aren't you tired of kissing her ass all the time?"

Angie swung her head left and right, as if someone cared

what two high school girls were talking about. But then again, Whitney's mom cared. So maybe other people did, too.

"I've been watching people grovel at the feet of Jackie Whitman since third grade. Well, Jackie and Taylor." She made the obligatory sad face when she said Taylor's name. "I thought, for a few months, Jackie was totally losing it. After the accident. But now, I don't know. It's like nothing happened. She prances around school like a prima donna. And Laura Beth isn't any better. Don't even get me started on their charity case. Sure, she's cute and all, but ugh."

Whitney bit her tongue at the swipe at Lettie. Lettie had more balls than the other two put together. Too bad no one else seemed to notice.

"Then maybe we should do something about it."

Angie raised her eyebrows. "Like what?"

"I'm not sure yet. But I think it's time D.C. got a new It Girl, don't you?"

A smile spread across Angie's face. "Definitely."

The booth's dark wood paneling created a cozy atmosphere, and the candlelight cast a warm glow across Sol's olive skin. Ever since they'd sat down, the woman across from them had been staring at him. At first, Laura Beth thought it was because he looked so handsome in his suit jacket and tie, with his black hair carefully messed up. After the third time she'd caught the woman staring, Laura Beth had asked Sol about it.

He'd smiled and told her it was nothing. That the woman probably wondered how someone like him ended up with such a beautiful girlfriend.

Of course, Laura Beth just about died. Especially when she caught sight of his cute dimple.

"Tell me again why you want to go to Juilliard?" Sol asked, pulling her back down to earth.

Laura Beth let out a sigh. "I want to be a Broadway star, and they have the best training program in the world." She'd admitted that to only a few people—him, Jackie and Lettie, of course, and her dance instructor. Sol was so interested. He was so easy to talk to. And a great listener.

"What's stopping you?"

Laura Beth placed her hands in her lap and frowned. "Mama wants me to go to Sewanee, her alma mater in Tennessee."

Sol reached under the table and squeezed Laura Beth's hand. "You have to tell her about your dreams. It's your life. You need to do what's right for you."

As usual, Sol cut right to the heart of things.

"You don't know Mama like I do. She gets an idea in her head and she doesn't let go. Why, just this evening, she decided she must meet your parents when they're in town next week."

"Oh?"

Heat flared across her cheeks. That wasn't how she'd wanted to tell him, but it had just tumbled out. "She's old-fashioned, and believes in courtin'." Laura Beth lowered her head and peeked up at Sol through her lashes, just as she'd seen Jackie do to Andrew a thousand times. "If I'm your girlfriend, then it's only proper."

"Laura Beth." Sol placed his finger under her chin and raised her head until their eyes met. "I'd love for you—and your mama—to meet my parents, but I'm afraid they had to change their plans. Business, you know."

Actually, I don't. I have no idea what your parents do other than oversee a foundation. "Maybe another time, then?" Laura Beth kept her voice perky to hide her disappointment.

"There's plenty of time, Laura Beth. I'm not going anywhere."

With that, she melted into her seat.

EIGHT

Laura Beth shut the front door and leaned against it breathlessly. Her lips tingled and she ran her tongue over them, remembering Sol's mouth against hers. The taste of wine he'd drunk lingered.

Such a perfect evening. Perfect. Perfect. Perfect.

Once she was sure her legs wouldn't buckle beneath her, Laura Beth climbed the main staircase to the second floor.

"Is that singing?" Laura Beth said aloud to herself as she passed her mother's room. She paused outside the door, listening. Sure enough, Libby Ballou's rich voice belted out a jazz number.

"Mama?" Laura Beth stuck her head in the door.

"In here, sugar."

Libby Ballou, in a silk nightgown, sat before her impressive vanity, removing her makeup.

"You sound happy," Laura Beth said as she sat on the velvet

chaise near the vanity. "Did you have a nice evening with the senator?"

"Did I!" Her mama ran a silver brush through her hair. "I don't want to jinx myself, but I think he may be the one!" She turned toward Laura Beth, a smile stretched wide across her face. "What do you think, darlin'? Do you want a good-looking *senator* for a stepdaddy?" Her mother added softly, "Of course, no one will ever replace your daddy, God rest his soul. You know that, darlin'."

Even though her father, a powerful Republican consultant who'd had the ear of senators and presidents alike, died years ago, Laura Beth had a hard time imagining her mama married to anyone else. *But look at her—she's positively glowing. I haven't seen Mama this happy since that little fling with my voice coach.* At the time, Laura Beth had been so totally traumatized by her mother's behavior that she'd quit singing. *Thank God I'm over it now.*

Laura Beth returned her mother's smile. "I think I like the sound of that."

Libby Ballou threw back her head and a deep, rich laugh tumbled out of her. "Me too, darlin'. Me too." Her eyes fixed on Laura Beth's face. "It looks like we both had lovely evenings?"

Had she ever. Sol had been a perfect gentleman: opening doors, ordering for her—all the small things most guys thought were corny.

But before she launched into details, Laura Beth knew she had to press her advantage. She was on cloud nine, and what better time to bring up something difficult? And if she never tried, then she'd never know.

"Mama," she began hesitantly, "would you be mad if I didn't go to Sewanee?" How many times had her mother drummed into her that Sewanee: The University of the South was where all the best Southern families sent their children?

Laura Beth's heart hammered hard in her chest. She'd imagined this conversation a million times, and every time it ended with Mama sobbing and carrying on about how Laura Beth was turnin' her back on her heritage.

A sigh.

Here it comes.

"You know I've had dreams of you going there since you were a tiny thing. That's all we ever talked about."

That's all you ever talked about. Because you want me to be you.

Laura Beth picked up one of the soft velvet pillows and hugged it tightly to her chest. She'd rehearsed this moment in her mind many times, but actually having the conversation . . . She pressed her nose into the pillow and stared at the floor.

"And that's where your dear old daddy wanted you to go, sugar. It's tradition. And being a Ballou is all about tradition."

All her life, Laura Beth had been told she'd go to Excelsior, graduate, attend Sewanee in Tennessee, meet a nice *Republican* boy, and get married. But that's not what she wanted. Maybe when she was little and didn't know better, but now she wanted to dance. And be on Broadway. Marriage was definitely in her dreams, but that could come later.

"Mama," she said, sitting up a little straighter, "if I went to Sewanee, it wouldn't be for the right reasons. I'd be miserable."

Libby Ballou finished smoothing moisturizer over her face and turned to her daughter. "Is there somethin' you need to tell me?"

This was it. No going back. "I want to go to Juilliard. I want to dance." Laura Beth held her breath and waited for the new info to sink in.

"Oh, my Lord, Laura Beth, dancing is somethin' you do with a gentleman in a ballroom. It's not a career." She wiped the grease off her hands and stood up, looking agitated. "And it's not even in the South."

"But I could be onstage, Mama. Isn't that why you've spent so much time on my lessons? So I could have a shot at being famous?"

Libby stood up and tied a robe over her nightgown. "As a hobby, Laura Beth. Even if you go to Juilliard, you realize how hard it is to break into Broadway? Why, New York City is just littered with thousands of broken hearts, young people just as talented as you are, darlin'."

"I know, Mama, but if I don't try, I'll never know. And I couldn't bear not trying to chase my dream."

Her mother closed her eyes, silent. *Please, please, please, please,* Laura Beth prayed.

Finally, Mama looked down at her and took a deep breath. "I was so looking forward to Family Weekend at Sewanee and showing you all my old haunts." She gave Laura Beth a small smile, then squared her shoulders. "Are you sure you want to do this?"

Relief exploded in Laura Beth's stomach. "Yes."

"Then we have some work to do, don't we? Auditions to schedule and tapes to put together?"

Laura Beth's mouth dropped open. Surely the unwavering Libby Ballou didn't just give her permission?

"Now, don't you look like a child given the whole cookie jar! Say something."

Laura Beth flew out of her seat and wrapped her arms around her mother's tiny frame. *Sol was right. Telling Mama was the right thing to do.*

"I love you! I love you! I love you!"

Laura Beth was ecstatic, the excitement tingling up her spine. First a perfect evening with Sol and now this. Today was the best day ever.

Jackie held her iPhone away from her ear as Laura Beth rambled on and on and on. First it was about Sol and their perfect date. Next about Juilliard and finally being allowed to apply. No questions about how she was *or Lettie*. Just a one-sided conversation with Laura Beth as the star.

Really, Jackie should be sleeping. But that still didn't come easily. Not when every time she closed her eyes, she saw some creepy guy with sunglasses and a baseball cap. No matter how many times she tried to shake his scowling image, she just couldn't. It had been almost a month since the kidnapping threat. Everything was back to normal now. So why wasn't she? Jackie squeezed her eyes shut. *Stop it.*

"But I completely forgot to tell Mama Sol's parents aren't coming to town!" Laura Beth wailed.

The cell fell on the bed and Jackie scrambled to pick it up. "I'm sure she'll get over it."

"Maybe. You know how she is about protocol and manners."

I'm so not in the mood for this. She makes everything into a life-or-death situation. Her problems are nothing compared to Lettie's . . . or mine.

"We should do something special for Lettie," Jackie said abruptly. "To take her mind off everything. Maybe throw a little party or something and invite Daniel. I know she wants to see him again, but she just doesn't know how to do it."

Dead silence.

"Laura Beth?"

"I guess. But Lettie would probably hate being the center of attention. You know how she is." The giddiness had evaporated from Laura Beth's voice. "Now, did I tell you about what Sol was wearing? He looked amazin'. Like he stepped right out of GQ or somethin'."

Jackie rolled her eyes. She loved Laura Beth and was truly happy for her, but she couldn't take one more detailed description of what they ate or what Sol said to the waiter. "I have to go. It's late and I don't want to be a zombie tomorrow."

"Wait! Are you mad? Don't be mad. We can have a party here, at my house."

Jackie frowned. "No, you're right. Lettie wouldn't like that. See you tomorrow?" She pressed the end key before Laura Beth had a chance to protest and tossed the phone on the bed.

Eleven o'clock at night and she still had on her school uniform. She hadn't bothered to change. What was the point? She wasn't allowed to go out—at least not without an escort. Which meant she didn't go anywhere. Just to school and back to the White House. With an ever-present Secret Service agent following discreetly behind, of course. At least they respected her space at school and didn't actually sit in her classes.

Jackie pulled a pair of pajamas out of her drawer and marched into her private bathroom to wash her face.

Oh, my God. I look like hell.

Taylor's voice echoed in her head. *I slept with your boyfriend, Jackie. And there's nothing you can do to change that.*

Dark circles surrounded Jackie's eyes, and her skin had lost its glow. *If I don't pull myself together, the press will definitely know Andrew and I are having problems.*

"When you're at the top, the fall's a lot harder," Whitney had whispered in her ear the other day as she'd shoved books into her locker. When Jackie had spun around to confront her, Whitney was already halfway down the hall, arm in arm with Angie Meehan. And to her surprise, Dina Ives and Aamina Al-Kazaz had been with them. Whitney had picked up an entourage and Jackie hadn't even noticed.

I'm not falling. I'm still on top. I'm Jackie fucking Whitman, and I don't give up.

But no matter how many times she repeated the phrase, Jackie couldn't make it true.

She splashed cold water on her face, slipped on her pajamas, and walked slowly into her bedroom.

Her eyes burned with exhaustion, but her mind whirled.

Maybe I should be more like Whitney and not care. She lives by the "No publicity is bad publicity" policy and look where it's gotten her—on the popularity express track.

In the short time she'd been in D.C., Whitney somehow had moved seamlessly from new girl status to the girl everyone wanted to hang out with. Even Laura Beth kept inviting her places, despite the fact that Whitney drove her crazy. It made no sense. Why did everyone like her?

Jackie sighed and slipped on her headphones, hoping to drown out the thoughts pummeling her brain.

With music blaring, she started to drift off to sleep.

You think I'm bad? What till you see what my mom will do to you, Taylor whispered.

Jackie's eyes flew open. Her heart raced.

That was why she hadn't been sleeping. Nothing was as heart-stoppingly frightening as this. Not her problems with Andrew or worry about Lettie. Not the stalker no one had been able to find. Not even losing her social standing.

Her worst fear, her biggest problem, was Jennifer Cane. The Fixer. The woman who knew everyone's secrets and who now knew Jackie's. *I didn't have any choice. She was the only one I could turn to for help, who could stop Senator Griffin's blackmail.* But in Washington, more than anywhere else, favors were never free. Jackie knew it was only a matter of time before Taylor's mother named her price for getting Jackie off the hook.

Still floating on a cloud, Laura Beth hummed to herself as she waited for the maid to bring her breakfast. She ate the same thing every day: a soft-boiled egg and a side of fruit. Washed down with water, naturally.

"Good morning, Mama," Laura Beth said as her mother entered the room wearing a long silk robe. Of course, her hair and makeup looked perfect. Laura Beth had never seen her mother outside of her bedroom looking anything less than pulled together.

Her mother dropped a folded newspaper onto the mahogany table and tapped her finger angrily on it. Laura Beth caught her gaze and knew. *It has to be about Sol. Mama has found out he's a Muslim.* But before Laura Beth could explain, Libby said, "I will not have my daughter running around town with a suspected terrorist. I won't."

Laura Beth's mouth dropped open. Her mother was completely overreacting. "Terrorist? Mama, what are you talking about? Sol's not a terrorist. He's Iranian and Muslim, but that doesn't make him a terrorist any more than being Southern makes us Klansmen."

Libby shook her finger at her daughter. "There will be no meetin' of the families, Laura Beth. You cancel those plans immediately, do you understand?"

Laura Beth furrowed her brow, trying to understand what had happened. She expected her mama to be a little upset over Sol's heritage and religion, but this was ridiculous.

The *Washington Tattler* lay faceup on the table, and Laura Beth read the top-of-the-fold headline, upside down.

Prominent Iranian American Couple Suspected of Terrorist Front

By Tracey Mills

Her stomach lurched as she reached across the table and picked up the paper.

Iranian Americans Javad and Tehernah Molla have it all: a lavish lifestyle spanning three continents, a son attending Columbia, and a charitable foundation that builds hospitals in impoverished areas of the Middle East.

But where does the money come from and where does it really go? How do unknowns like the Mollas manage to climb the international social ladder in a matter of a few years?

There are growing rumors about the Mollas—specifically that they have ties to terrorist organizations and that their charity is merely a front for a terrorist money-laundering scheme. The *Tattler* has learned exclusively that investigators in Congress are looking into the allegations. Mr. and Mrs. Molla did not return our calls.

Laura Beth stared at the paper in disbelief. "Mama, this isn't true. I swear it. You've met Sol—you've seen how good he is. Mama!"

"I'm sorry, Laura Beth, but I can't let this romance of yours continue. I want you to call that boy and break it off. Now. Before school."

That boy. How fast she's forgotten his name.

"Mama, no! There has to be an explanation. Let me talk to Sol. Give him a chance to explain."

"I have to think of your safety, darlin', not to mention our reputations. I can't get muddied up in this! Especially if there's the slightest chance it could touch my Jeffrey—"

"You're worried my love life will ruin yours?" Laura Beth glared at her mother. Her heart pounded in anger.

"*I'm* a grown woman, with a real chance at marrying a decent, ambitious man. *You* are still young and there will be other boys, even though that might seem impossible to you right now. I'm sorry, but you have to break this off, Laura Beth. You need to forget Sol Molla. It's for your own good."

Tears stung Laura Beth's eyes. Unable to speak without sobbing, she nodded. Satisfied, Libby Ballou scooped up the paper and stormed out of the room.

As she sat there crying, Laura Beth resolved to do two things. First, there was no way in hell she was breaking up with Sol until he had a chance to explain. And second, Whitney and her mother were going to pay for ruining her life.

NINE

"Shhh. Don't let her see us." Jackie grabbed Laura Beth's arm and tugged her back into the doorway of the school's massive entrance. They'd already interfered enough, and if Lettie found out, she'd be embarrassed.

Down on the lawn, in the common area shared by Excelsior and St. Thomas, Daniel was doing grinds on his skateboard while Lettie watched.

"If he doesn't hurry up and ask her, we're going to be late for class," Laura Beth said as she crept out of the doorway and along the portico. For someone who just spent the past twenty minutes bawling in the girls bathroom over Sol, Laura Beth was acting surprisingly composed.

I don't know how she does it—just pushes all the bad out of her brain and acts like things are normal.

Before Jackie could stop her, Laura Beth darted along the hedge.

"Where are you going?" Jackie asked.

"To make sure he doesn't mess this up."

"He's not going to mess it up. Daniel isn't exactly the shy type."

Two days earlier, Laura Beth had decided she had to do something about Lettie and Daniel—the something being a phone call to Daniel, where she proceeded to dominate the conversation until he finally could get a word in. He told her he fully intended to ask Lettie to Homecoming and really didn't need her help.

Jackie crouched down and hopped over to where Laura Beth peeked through a hole in the shrubs. Her lips twitched into a smile. "He's doing it! Lettie better say yes. If she doesn't, I'm going to—"

"Shhh!" Jackie pressed her finger over Laura Beth's lips. "Listen."

"I wanted to ask you about Homecoming," Daniel said. Jackie almost giggled out loud. He actually sounded nervous. Unusual for Daniel, who always seemed so confident.

"It's fun. We go every year, you should come with us," Lettie said.

Laura Beth's eyes grew wide. "What is she doing? Inviting him on a group date?"

Jackie rolled her eyes. Leave it to Lettie to misunderstand when a boy was asking her out.

"I'd rather just go with you. You know, on a date?" Daniel interrupted, grinning.

Silence.

"C'mon, Lettie. Say yes. I won't bite," Daniel joked. "Not unless you want me to."

Poor Lettie, she's totally frozen up. Come on, before he changes his mind.

"I'd love to," she finally said, flashing Daniel what looked like a flirtatious smile. Daniel dropped his skateboard, picked Lettie up, and swung her in the air. She let out a shriek of surprise and laughed.

Laura Beth grabbed Jackie's arm, pulling her back to the building. For a few minutes, it was nice to see everyone happy—even if it wouldn't last.

"We make a sorry group," Lettie said, squeezing between Laura Beth with her tear-streaked face and Jackie, whose dark circles looked even worse today. Most students ate indoors on cold days like today. But Laura Beth had asked them to meet here, on the lawn. "People are going to start calling us the *Crapital* Girls if we keep moping around like this."

"Whitney already does," Laura Beth said, then gave a little sniff.

Jackie pulled a dark pair of designer glasses from her handbag and slid them over her eyes. "Figures."

A Secret Service agent was hanging around the school entrance, glancing their way every few seconds. It had been a few weeks since the big kidnapping scare at school, but Jackie still had an escort. And even though Jackie pretended it was no big deal, Lettie felt bad for her. Lack of privacy was something Lettie knew all too well, living in a tiny apartment and sharing a room with two younger sisters.

On the end of the bench, Laura Beth sat wringing her

hands. "How do you tell your boyfriend you can't see him any-more because his parents might be terrorists?" She leaned for-ward and stared at her stacked-heel Mary Janes.

"You don't," Jackie said.

Lettie's eyebrows shot up. That was a very Taylor thing to say, and she wasn't sure she liked where it was going. "Oh?"

Jackie pivoted on the bench so that she and Laura Beth now faced each other. "You don't have to listen to your mom. You are almost eighteen, after all. You can date whoever you want."

Right. Because you clearly follow this advice, Jackie.

"But Mama said it could ruin Senator Ives' career aspirations if he were dating a woman whose daughter was datin' the son of accused terrorists." She giggled. "Oh, my Lord, that sounds like a bad plotline from a soap opera."

Lettie perked up. Listening to her friends' problems made her forget her own for a few minutes. For one thing, Paz had made it clear that if the White House couldn't help him after all, he'd have to get an illegal job on his own and risk being de-ported. "I don't want to, Lettie, but what choice do I have?" he'd said when she'd called him on it.

"You should call Sol, Laura Beth. He probably thinks you don't want anything to do with him." Jackie checked her iPhone for the hundredth time. Sometimes the habit crossed over from annoying to downright rude.

Laura Beth grinned. "I'll do one better than that. What if I, you know . . ."

"Sleep with him?" Jackie stole the words from Lettie's mouth.

That was the worst idea she'd heard today. *I have to tell her about Sol and Whitney. Or at least what I suspect.*

"Maybe," Laura Beth replied coyly. "I mean, I do like him. A lot. And how better to show him that I don't care what the press says?"

"Shouldn't you talk to him first—you know, to find out his side of the story—before you decide to have sex with him?" Jackie asked.

Laura Beth huffed. "I think I know my boyfriend. That story is ridiculous. Sol's no more a terrorist than you're a PAPPie."

"But having sex with him, Laura Beth? You've only been dating since the summer." Jackie didn't hide her concern, and Lettie was happy she spoke up. If she'd tried to say something, Laura Beth probably would have laughed at her. Jackie had wanted to sleep with Andrew so much, that was practically all she used to talk about.

"You wouldn't say that to Tay," Laura Beth accused her. It was true. They never questioned Taylor about her choices. They simply accepted them. Even when they thought she was making bad decisions. Because Taylor was tough.

But Laura Beth? She tried so hard to be a steel magnolia, but her feelings got easily hurt.

"Why is it different for me? Why can you sleep with Andrew, but I can't sleep with Sol?"

Lettie watched the color drain from Jackie's face. Laura Beth knew things between her and Andrew were tough, and she had thrown it back in Jackie's face.

"But I didn't sleep with him. And I'm happy I didn't." Jackie shoved away the rest of her lunch.

Lettie hated it when they disagreed, but this was different. Laura Beth was making a mistake. And bringing up Andrew was the worst thing she could have done to upset Jackie.

Best to change the subject. "I have some nondepressing news."

Jackie and Laura Beth exchanged knowing looks. As though they knew exactly what was coming.

"Daniel asked me to the Homecoming dance," Lettie said. "I know it's not as major as what you two are going through, but . . ."

"It beats possible deportation?" Laura Beth suggested.

Jackie leaned over Lettie. "Laura Beth!" She tapped her on the shoulder. "Have some tact." She turned her attention back to Lettie. "That's awesome, Lets."

"What are you going to wear?" Laura Beth asked.

Lettie blushed. Even though she'd never ask, she hoped one of the girls would offer to loan her something. Laura Beth, who had a closet full of clothes she'd worn only once and would never wear again, always came through for her.

"I don't know. I haven't given it much thought." That was a lie, of course. Since Daniel had invited her, it was all she could think about. What to wear. What songs they'd dance to. How he'd smile at her. Whether they'd kiss.

"It's weird seeing Daniel around town again," Laura Beth said. "Every time I catch a glimpse of his white-blond hair, I can't help but think of Tay."

Daniel had been telling everyone that his parents needed him close by now that Taylor was gone. But Lettie thought he had other reasons. Like keeping an eye on Andrew Price.

"It's kind of nice to have him around again. Right, Lets?" Jackie grinned at her.

Lettie laughed. "Taylor would freak if she knew I was going to a dance with her brother."

The lunch bell rang and she stood up, offering a hand to each of her best friends. "We better get inside before someone sends a SWAT team after Jackie."

"Hey now!" Jackie protested as the three girls linked arms and headed back into the school, giggling.

"Oh. Hell. No. We have to ride around in those?" Whitney asked, staring at the three plain white vans parked near Excelsior's main entrance.

"Were you expecting limo service?" Jackie asked with a sugary sweet smile.

I'd love to knock that smile off her face.

"Whatever." Whitney searched the small group of girls until her eyes landed on Laura Beth. "Hey, LB. Kiss any terrorists lately?"

Whitney admired the way Laura Beth's face went from serene to rage-filled within seconds. She balled her fists and clenched her jaw. "I haven't and I don't ever plan to."

"Your loss. Sol's hot."

Next to Whitney, Angie giggled. "You're so mean."

Whitney shrugged. "I only speak the truth."

Their teacher, Mr. Martin, shouted above the din of the girls, "Ladies, before we get in the vans, I want you to remember why we require each of you to volunteer your time."

"Boring," Whitney whispered. Who cared why they had to go? It was just one more thing to make her life in D.C. hell—spending one day a week working at a hospital for wounded veterans. *Probably changing adult diapers and wiping drool off senile old men's faces.*

It had been Lettie's idea—after Paz went MIA from the army—to make veterans their volunteer project, and Mr. Martin had loved the idea. Jackie, Lettie, and Laura Beth moved toward the first bus. Whitney grabbed Angie's hand. She wasn't about to pass up an opportunity to hang out with her *best friend,* LB, and torture her a little.

"Let's ride with them."

The two girls pushed ahead of the rest and onto the ten-person van. It smelled stale, like old people. So gross.

"Hey, girls! This is just like old times. Remember when we all took the train up to New York? Wasn't that the best?" Whitney spoke high and fast, making sure to ooze fake excitement.

All three of the girls looked everywhere but at her. "Yeah," they mumbled one by one.

Angie plopped down into the seat next to Whitney and turned around to the three girls behind her. "I don't see any of you nearly enough."

You could practically see the tension rippling off the two groups of girls, but that didn't stop Whitney. No—she had a job to do.

"So, Jackie. What's up with Andrew?" Next to her, Angie giggled. "Things better now?"

Jackie leaned back in her seat, her blazing eyes meeting Whitney's. *If Jackie could burn a hole through me, she would.*

"I don't know what you're talking about."

Whitney hopped up on her knees and leaned over the back of her seat. "I heard you were fighting. Is he still mad about the whole Princeton, 'kissing a random guy' thing?" It was brief, but Whitney saw Jackie wince. That was all she needed to keep going. "I bet he wasn't too happy about that. Did he try to get back at you by kissing someone else? That's what most guys would do." Jackie pressed her lips together and stared out the window as if she weren't listening, but Whitney knew better. Jackie sat rigid in her seat. Too tense not to be pissed. "Oh..." Whitney twisted her hands together in faux worry. "Is that it? Did he cheat on you?"

The van hit a pothole and Whitney slipped forward into her seat, but not before catching the death glare Jackie shot at her.

Bingo.

But who did he do it with?

Jackie scanned the list of possible jobs. SAT tutoring, food service, activity center, dance, advocacy.

"I bet I know which job you don't want," she said to Lettie.

"And you would be correct. I have no plans to wash dishes in my off time." She ran her hand down the list. "Maybe tutoring? How about you two?"

Laura Beth shimmied. "Dance, of course."

"Advocacy sounds interesting. I wonder what it involves?"

"Sounds like politics and more politics to me," Laura Beth said. How could a girl with the Ballous for parents not love politics more than anything else?

Jackie shrugged. "I'm going to go learn more about it. I guess I'm on my own?"

Her eyes flitted over to Whitney and Angie, who stood ridiculously close to a young vet. He clenched and unclenched his prosthetic arm for the girls with a huge grin on his face. *Figures. Whitney flashes her legs and all the boys come running.*

As much as she didn't want to, Jackie felt herself wondering if Andrew found Whitney attractive. She was gorgeous and had the same made-for-trouble attitude Taylor had.

Would he have cheated with her instead of Taylor if Whitney had been around? Or was it a perfect storm: Had he always wanted Taylor but needed an excuse to act?

Stop it. You're going to drive yourself crazy, she thought as she walked past Whitney and Angie.

The meeting room was at the end of the hall, and when Jackie slipped through the doorway, only one other student sat in the rows of seats. Vanessa Crawford.

"Is it just us?" Jackie asked her.

Vanessa nodded. "I guess no one else cares about really making a difference."

Jackie sighed. Her classmates were either apathetic or simply burned-out from being fed politics 24/7. Either way, two students out of twenty-seven wasn't exactly a strong turnout. The door opened again, and for a moment Jackie thought it would be three students instead of two . . . but it was only her Secret Service agent.

At the front of the room, a tall man with salt-and-pepper hair stood with a young, slightly built soldier. He quickly glanced at the near empty room and smiled. "Believe it or not, this is the best turnout I've had all week."

Jackie squirmed in her seat, feeling bad for him. *No one likes to put on a party and not have guests, as Laura Beth would say.*

"Let me introduce myself. I'm Dr. Paul Rosen and I run the Veterans Rights Activist Group—VRAG, for short.

"This young man," he added, gesturing to the soldier, "is Private Vic Hazelton, who is a patient at the hospital and also my invaluable assistant."

Vanessa raised her hand. "You're a medical doctor? In the military?"

"I am a doctor, but I'm a civilian. What's your name?"

"Vanessa."

"Well, Vanessa, the military has thousands of enlisted doctors, lawyers, engineers—almost every job you can also find in the private sector. But my organization is a group that volunteers with veterans and fights to improve their lives."

Vanessa's eyes grew wide in amazement. Jackie had always thought Vanessa was nice, but in a totally nonmemorable way. Jackie noticed the soldier, who hadn't spoken a word, was staring at her. As soon as she gave him a friendly smile, he dropped his gaze. *He must be shy,* she thought. He looked young, maybe twenty. He didn't seem to be injured, and she wondered why he was still in the hospital.

Dr. Rosen flipped a chair around and straddled it backward. "That's why my job—and yours, if you choose to work in advocacy—is important. Many of our veterans receive injuries that make going back into their careers, either in the military or out, impossible. That's where we come in."

Jackie raised her hand. "Do you train them for new jobs?"

"We do." He held out his hand. "I didn't get your name."

"Jackie." She shook his hand but purposefully left off her last name. She'd learned long ago that people tended to change their attitude toward her once they knew *who* she was, though Dr. Rosen didn't look like the type to read gossip magazines.

"Imagine this," he said, rising from his chair. "You're a field doctor with the marines and your hand gets blown off. Or maybe you're a young mechanic, used to spending all day under tanks. But mortar fire leaves you paralyzed. What do you do then?"

"Doesn't the government pay them a salary for life? And medical care?" Jackie asked.

Dr. Rosen shook his head. "It isn't enough, Jackie. Some of our guys have to wait months for reconstructive surgeries and years for job training. The pension sometimes barely covers living expenses. And we haven't even touched on depression and other mental illnesses that plague our vets."

Vanessa played with her simple gold necklace. "What can we do?"

"You can help us speak out. Raise awareness about the problems vets face and help us get more help, sooner."

Jackie's heart sped up. This sounded like the perfect volunteer job—getting her feet wet in advocacy and redeeming herself for almost destroying the immigration bill. It also meant getting out of the White House on a regular basis.

"Where do we sign up?" she asked.

Dr. Rosen smiled and walked to the door. "Just meet me back here same time next week."

TEN

"What does it feel like? When the panic starts to set in?" Dr. Rachel Edmonds sat across from me in her usual hippie-era long flowery skirt and Birkenstocks. So not D.C. I liked her the first time I met her.

"Like a football player just tackled me and won't get off my chest, no matter how hard I try to push him away." I could feel that weight right now, just a little. Dr. Edmonds scribbled something down on her notepad. "I also get this lump in my throat. Like if I let it grow, I'll never be able to speak again."

"And when do these feelings come about?"

I hardly needed to think about it: Andrew and Taylor, her long hair falling around his shoulders as she straddled him, Angie Meehan and Whitney linked arm in arm down the hall, my mother working late into the night yet betrayed by her only daughter, Jennifer Cane and what price I'll have to pay. Then I thought of the man in the baseball cap and the kidnapping threats and *the prickly feeling I got on the back of my neck when I was in a crowded room—like I was being watched.*

"They happen all the time now," I admitted.

"Jackie," Laura Beth whispered next to her, nudging Jackie with a finger. It took her a second to realize she was still in class.

"Do you want to hit Georgetown or Neiman's first?" Laura Beth asked.

"Whatever you want." She'd promised Laura Beth days ago that they could go dress shopping today for Homecoming. Lettie, as usual, was working in the embassy kitchen.

Laura Beth rested her chin on her hand. "I'd rather look at the boutiques, find something no one else has. I want Sol to think I'm the most beautiful girl in the world."

Ever since Laura Beth had decided to sleep with Sol, every conversation circled back to what Sol thought. *I love Laura Beth, but sometimes she lives too much in her fantasy world. Her whole life is singing and dancing and boys and clothes.* It seemed trivial compared with everything else going on. Even more so since they'd been working with the wounded vets over the past few weeks.

Jackie rubbed her temples and tore her eyes away from the clock. At least she was doing something useful, even if it was just once a week. Not that the other girls weren't, too. Lettie tutored soldiers for the SATs, and Laura Beth taught a dance and movement class to vets learning to use their new prosthetic limbs. Hell, even Whitney, in her own slutty way, seemed to enjoy her volunteer time, even if it was just flirting with the soldiers.

But Jackie's job made a *difference.* Last week, Dr. Rosen asked if she'd like to accompany him to speak before a congressional committee—just to see how it all worked, of course. She didn't have the heart to tell him she'd been on Capitol Hill a hundred times when Aunt Deborah was a senator, and probably into some areas he couldn't go. Like the secret hideaway offices given to Senate committee chairmen that were inaccessible to anyone without an invitation. Everyone assumed the rooms were where the senators cut their under-the-table deals with lobbyists and had afternoon trysts with their mistresses.

"You should wear something green..." Laura Beth was still rambling on about what to wear at Homecoming. *You can have an entire conversation with her without saying a word.* "It will look gorgeous with your blond hair. And it will match Andrew's eyes."

Jackie frowned. She wasn't sure if Andrew was her date. They hadn't discussed it, but Aunt Deborah had mentioned in passing how she wanted pictures. So...

"Then again, I saw this gorgeous McQueen at Barneys. It has gold appliqué over pale gold chiffon. It looks a little like a long flapper dress. Very 1920s." Laura Beth came up for air. "Maybe we should hit the big stores first?... Jackie, are you even paying attention to me? This is important! It's Homecoming!"

Mr. McCaffery rapped his desk twice. "Girls, I'd appreciate it if you'd hold the chitchat for between classes."

Jackie nodded, hoping the warning would shut Laura Beth up.

No such luck.

"Are you still obsessing over that article today?" Laura Beth whispered. She didn't bother to hide her annoyance.

The front page of the *Washington Post* had a picture of Jackie, flanked by Dr. Rosen and Private Hazelton, walking up the steps of Congress to appear at yesterday's hearing. During the doctor's testimony, Jackie sat behind him, kept her head down, and took notes. But as soon as they left the committee room, they were mobbed by reporters bombarding her with questions.

And then it became *The Jackie Whitman Show.*

"Hey, Jackie, what does the president think about you siding with Dr. Rosen against her administration?"

"This isn't an issue of choosing sides," I said carefully. "Every one of us—Dr. Rosen's organization, the Price administration, and the entire American public—we all support and respect our brave veterans, and we all want to do whatever we can to improve their quality of life."

The crowd of reporters was buzzing like a swarm of yellow jackets ready to sting, and I could feel a trickle of sweat run down the back of my neck. Thank God there weren't any cameras behind me.

An older woman with a bad face lift shoved a microphone in my face. "Dr. Rosen has criticized President Price for deserting veterans once they leave the battlefield. Do you agree?"

"You are mischaracterizing Dr. Rosen's position," I said, trying not to let my irritation show. "His job, our job, is to make public officials and the American people aware of the issues facing our military men and women returning from war. Government cannot solve all the problems. It's a shared responsibility."

After a couple more minutes—it seemed like hours—Dr. Rosen cut off the questions and a congressional aide ushered us into the elevator. As soon as the doors slid shut, Dr. Rosen grabbed me in a bear hug.

"Congratulations! You were great!" He grinned. "I knew you'd be a pro in front of the cameras."

I noticed Private Hazelton, his face flushed and his back pressed against the rear wall, scowling.

"You all right?" I asked, concerned.

"Those vultures," he muttered. "How dare they question you like that? They have no respect."

I shrugged. "I didn't mind, really."

It was true. Now that it was over and I was no longer stressed, I realized I'd almost, kind of, enjoyed it. For once, no one had hounded me about Ankie. Or Taylor's accident. Sure, the reporters had tried to drag me into a fight with Aunt Deborah. But I'd handled that pretty well. And it was the first time they'd asked me anything substantive, about things that mattered, serious issues that affected real people.

Jackie just wished her mom felt the same way.

She sighed. This morning, her mother had woken her up before the alarm clock sounded. For a blissful second, Jackie thought she was back home in her own bed. Then she remembered—her mother had worked so late with Aunt Deborah last night, she'd slept in one of the third-floor guest bedrooms.

"Hey! I wanted to see you before you left for school." She was on the edge of the bed with the Washington Post *in one hand and a mug of freshly brewed coffee in the other. She handed me the coffee and waited as I took a sip.*

"Why didn't you tell me you were involved in this veterans rights advocacy group?"

"It's my volunteer project through school. You know how we're working at the hospital."

Mom held up the newspaper, showing the front page. "First Girlfriend Speaks Out!" jumped out at me. "You know I want you to be involved, but Jackie, you've got to clear this with me first. You're associated with the

White House—everything you do or support can be seen as White House support."

"I only answered one or two questions. I hardly said anything, and they've made an entire article out of it?"

She folded the paper in half and kissed my forehead. "It's a good article. You handled yourself well. And your points are spot on. But next time, give us a heads-up, okay?"

I set the mug down on my nightstand. "I'm sorry. When Dr. Rosen asked me to come, I said yes without thinking. I'll take more of a behind-the-scenes role, if you want."

Mom shook her head. "Aunt Deborah and I think this is fine, but we want you to get briefed on our official position. Can you come by after school? I'll have Brian prep you."

"Maybe tonight? I told Laura Beth I'd go dress shopping with her."

"That's fine. He'll be there until at least ten, anyway."

Laura Beth nudged her again, and Jackie leaned in closer. "My mom wants me to come by later today for an official briefing by Brian Gillespie." When Laura Beth's face fell, Jackie added, "Don't worry, we have plenty of time for Barneys and Neiman's and all the little boutiques you want to visit."

"And dinner?"

"Sounds like a plan."

The dress looked horrible on. It clung in all the wrong places and barely covered her nipples. Which was too bad; it had such promise on the hanger.

"Would you like to see anything else, Miss Ballou?" asked Stuart, the sales manager.

Laura Beth sighed and nibbled on a strawberry, wishing they came with a little champagne like they did for her mama. "I don't think so."

As soon as he left, Laura Beth surveyed herself one last time in the mirror. "Too bad." She ran her hand over the dress. "Look at the fabric! It's so pretty!"

Jackie stood next to her, wearing a one-shouldered Marchesa dress in plum. *Of course she looks stunning. Everything looks good on Jackie.*

"I think the color washes you out. Maybe something richer? To play off the color of your hair?"

Laura Beth stripped off the dress and laid it over the velvet chair for the staff to hang. "Are you getting that?"

Jackie tossed her long blond hair over her shoulder. "I'm not sold on it. Let's keep looking."

Laura Beth soaked up the late afternoon sunshine as she and Jackie strolled down M Street. "Do you want to have dinner or just stop by Georgetown Cupcake?"

"Is that really a question?" Jackie joked. "Today's Friday, which means . . ."

"Lemon blossom," they said in unison. When Tay was alive, the girls made treks over to the cupcake shop three times a week: Tuesdays for salted caramel, Thursdays as a treat for Lettie, and Fridays for lemon blossom.

The streets around Georgetown were unusually quiet as the girls strolled. "Did I tell you Sol's parents are issuing a formal statement to the press?" Laura Beth had wanted to talk about this with Jackie all day, but she didn't want anyone—well, mostly

Whitney—to overhear. And Whitney was always around, hovering just behind them or popping up out of nowhere. Laura Beth sometimes wondered if she'd hidden a GPS on her or something.

Jackie turned her head and raised her eyebrows. "What are they going to say?"

Laura Beth sighed. The whole thing was awful. Tracey Mills's article had blindsided Sol's family, and donations to their foundation had dried up overnight. Several benefactors were even insisting on having their money returned. "There's no evidence. None," Laura Beth said forcefully. "It's like Ms. Mills wrote it just to get herself famous."

Jackie stopped abruptly and turned to her. "Didn't your mom say something about this hurting Senator Ives?"

"Yes," Laura Beth said hesitantly. She realized where this was going.

"Don't you think she was on to something? That this was a ploy to link the senator to something shady? When is he up for reelection?"

"Same as the presidential election."

"Maybe Tracey Mills doesn't want him reelected. Or somebody else doesn't want him reelected. Though I don't know why they wouldn't have leaked it closer to the elections." Jackie sped up a little. "C'mon, I'm hungry."

Laura Beth's mind spun. If what Jackie and Mama said was true, then Sol's family was being ruined because of her. She suddenly felt ill and grabbed on to Jackie's arm to steady herself.

"Hey, are you okay?" Jackie asked. They had stopped just outside the shop.

"I'm—"

"Hi, girls. I haven't seen either of you in ages."

This time Laura Beth's stomach really did do a somersault, and she felt Jackie tense up next to her. Jennifer Cane—Taylor's mom—stood before them holding a Georgetown Cupcake box in one hand and a coffee in the other.

"Mrs. Cane!" Always one for manners no matter how bad the situation, Laura Beth composed herself and air-kissed the older woman's cheeks. "How are you? Is Daniel with you?"

Jackie followed Laura Beth's lead and greeted Taylor's mom in the same manner, only much less enthusiastically, and her hands were clenched.

Poor Jackie. She's probably worried that Jennifer's going to call in that favor. And who knows what she'll want.

"I'm fine, and I believe Daniel is meeting Lettie after she gets off work."

Laura Beth fought the surprised look threatening to break her calm façade. *Really? Lettie's been holding out on us.*

Mrs. Cane smiled at Jackie. "I saw the article in this morning's paper. You handled yourself well. Carolyn and Deborah must be proud."

"Thank you. Mom said I did a nice job."

With a flick of her wrist, Jennifer checked her diamond-encrusted watch. "I've gotta run, girls. So nice bumping into you."

"Bye, Mrs. Cane," they said as she rushed away.

All color had drained from Jackie's face, and her hands shook. She looked worse than Laura Beth felt.

"Jackie! Darlin'! You okay?" Laura Beth asked, wrapping her arm around her friend.

"I'm fine."

"You are not. Look at you—shakin' like a leaf." Laura Beth wouldn't say it out here, not in public, but she'd be trembling too if she owed Jennifer Cane a favor.

Jackie grabbed the door handle. "Let's get our cupcakes. Maybe the sugar will help."

Laura Beth let her friend go in first. From the circles under her eyes and the color of her skin, she had a feeling nothing short of a good night's sleep and being rid of Jennifer Cane would make Jackie feel better.

Lettie balled up her apron and shoved it into her cubby before locking herself in the bathroom and scrubbing her hands. She didn't want to smell like a kitchen for her date.

Not that it mattered. Daniel claimed to admire the fact that she worked hard. That he liked how Lettie wasn't pampered and privileged, like the other Excelsior girls.

One last glance in the tiny, scratched mirror after pulling on a pair of jeans and a sweater. *Laura Beth would die if she saw what I'm wearing on a date. But then again, maybe that's why Daniel likes me.*

She hummed as she stepped out the back door and into the dimly lit parking lot.

"You should totally wear that to Homecoming."

Lettie jumped at the sound of Daniel's voice. "What are you doing here?" she gasped. They were supposed to meet at the diner—just as they had a few other times this week.

Daniel stepped out from the shadows, and Lettie's heart fluttered. He looked amazing in jeans, a fitted tee, and an un- zipped hoodie. "Change of plans."

"Oh?" Just like Taylor, Daniel liked spontaneity.

He leaned against the wall, his blue eyes sparkling in the dim light. "I picked up two burritos from the taqueria on my way here. They're probably cold, but they'll still taste good."

"Yum. Cold burritos. Just what every girl wants," Lettie joked. Somehow, being around Daniel loosened her up. Things didn't seem so awful or serious.

Daniel threw his hand over his heart. "I'm hurt. You don't know how hard I had to search for real burritos—like the ones they make in L.A."

"You could have asked me, you know. I happen to know a place or two."

He shook his head. "And spoil the surprise? No way!"

Lettie liked the way Daniel's eyes lit up when he was excited. She also liked the curve of his lips when he smiled. . . . "Does our night involve *that*?" she said, pointing to the board at his feet.

Daniel kicked up the board and draped his arm over Lettie's shoulders. "Burritos, a board, and a beautiful girl. The only thing that would make it better is beer."

Yup, Laura Beth would be hyperventilating right now, she thought as she walked to Daniel's truck with a huge smile on her face.

"Oh, my Lord!" Laura Beth jerked the steering wheel of her gray BMW to the right and careened around the corner. "Is that Daniel Cane driving a *pickup truck* with Lettie in the passenger seat?"

Jackie squinted, trying to make out the occupants of the dilapidated vehicle two ahead of theirs. "Maybe?"

"It is! I know it." Laura Beth hit the gas harder and blew through a yellow light. Jackie dug her fingernails into her seat and tried to relax. To let go of the ball of anxiety that had been sitting in her stomach since running into Jennifer Cane an hour earlier. She tried to tell herself that Laura Beth's driving had her on edge. But the truth was, seeing Jennifer Cane had rattled her. *It went fine. Nothing bad happened.*

"Why would he be driving that horrendous thing?" Laura Beth shrieked.

Jackie swallowed hard and inhaled sharply as the car made another high-speed turn. Every time she got in a vehicle, she thought of Taylor and Andrew and how dangerous cars were. And Laura Beth's crazy driving didn't help any.

"Not everyone needs a sixty-thousand-dollar car to be happy," Jackie said through gritted teeth.

Her friend eased off the gas and let another car slip between them. "You're following them?" Jackie asked, her eyes instinctively moving to the side mirror, where she could see her own Secret Service tail. "Seriously, Laura Beth, leave them alone."

Laura Beth pursed her lips. "No way. Lettie hid this from us and there's a reason. I'm going to find out."

"Probably because she doesn't want us meddling."

"If it weren't for us, Daniel might have waited too late to ask her to Homecoming, remember?"

"There's a fine line between helpful and interfering, Laura Beth."

Laura Beth drummed her fingers impatiently on the steering wheel. "I'm a concerned friend."

Jackie sighed. She didn't want to stalk her friend, she didn't want to meet Brian Gillespie this evening to discuss the official White House position on veterans affairs, and she definitely didn't want to see Jennifer Cane ever again.

Actually, all she wanted to do was be a normal teenager. And stalking Lettie on her date was about as normal a teenage thing as she had at the moment. Even with the agents following them a few cars back. Part of Jackie wanted to tell Laura Beth to gun it and see if they could outrun them.

"Look, they're slowing down." Laura Beth scrunched up her face in disgust. "What in the world? Why would he take her here?" She pulled the BMW to a stop down the block from Daniel's truck. The agents' car stopped behind them.

Warehouses lined both sides of the street, and a few broken streetlamps cast weird shadows everywhere. Suddenly, Jackie felt less safe parked than she did speeding along in the car. Even with her security detail.

Daniel jumped from the driver's side and ran around to open Lettie's door.

"At least he's a gentleman," Laura Beth said. "But he has weird taste in dates. If Sol ever tried to bring me to a place like this, well, I don't think I'd get out of the car."

Jackie chuckled. The image of Laura Beth, in designer clothes, driving around in a pickup was pretty funny.

From the bed of the truck, Daniel lifted a bag and two skateboards. Lettie held a white plastic bag in her hands and followed him toward a metal door.

When Daniel turned his head toward them, Laura Beth slouched in her seat. "If I hadn't known Daniel almost all my life, I'd swear he's about to murder her."

Jackie rolled her eyes. Leave it to Laura Beth to be dramatic. "So what's the plan now, Miss Detective? Do we wait here and get carjacked or do we *leave them alone*?" she asked.

"Just a quick peek?" Laura Beth said, pouting.

Jackie couldn't help it; she laughed. "Fine."

They hopped out of the car and clicked their doors lightly closed so as not to make any sound. Though Jackie winced when the agents let their car doors slam as usual.

"Which way did they go?" Jackie asked. Despite the stealthy faux pas, she was feeling more confident having security.

Laura Beth pointed. They started off toward Daniel's truck when there was a commotion behind them. Agent #2 was speaking into his phone. "I'll bring them in," was all that Jackie heard before Agent #1 was grabbing her arm and dragging her back to the car. The security car. *No. No, no, no.*

"What in God's name . . . ?" Laura Beth started, but she was being led away from her car, too. "What about my car?"

"I'm sorry, Miss Ballou, but you'll have to leave it until it's been searched," said #2.

"Searched?" both girls asked in unison.

"What's happening?" Jackie asked, pushing down the panic. "Is it the stalker? What about Lettie and Daniel?"

They were quickly ushered into the car, and #1 sat in the back with them. "The White House received another threat, Miss Whitman."

"But Lettie—"

Agent #2 interrupted. "He seems to know your movements."

Agent #1 held up his hand, cutting off all conversation. "We were told to bring you back to the White House at once."

Lettie eased down onto the curb. Her butt hurt from falling, but at least she hadn't broken her wrist, thanks to the gear Daniel insisted she wear.

"I think I'm getting the hang of it," she said, sliding her borrowed board back and forth with her feet.

Daniel popped his board and flew through the air. An ollie, he called it. He made it look easy, but Lettie barely managed to stand upright without falling.

A cool, late September breeze blew over her, and Lettie shivered.

"Hey, are you cold?" Daniel shrugged out of his hoodie and handed it to her.

"I'm fine. I'm working up a sweat."

But he insisted, helping her on with the soft jacket around her, zipping it up for her, and kissing her forehead. He stepped back, a quizzical expression on his face—as if expecting her to step away—and stared at her. Lettie looked up at him, smiled, and inhaled the scent of his hoodie. It smelled like Daniel—sweat and cologne.

"Thank you," Lettie said shyly, but she didn't move away.

"It looks good on you," he whispered. "Everything looks good on you." Then he closed the space between them and touched his lips to hers.

Lettie felt the softness of his lips all the way down to her toes. She leaned into him, nervous but tingling with excitement and . . . something more. Then Daniel slipped his arms around her and slowly dragged his right hand up her back to cup her neck. She could feel every move his body made as he kissed her and kissed her and kissed her. Lettie didn't want it to end.

But then it did. Daniel slowly pulled away with a final peck on the nose. It was sweet, but for some reason Lettie felt she had done something wrong.

Daniel sat on the curb and pulled Lettie down with him.

He threw an arm over her shoulder. "That was nice," he said, grinning.

"Yeah, it was," she said. *Do boys usually categorize kissing as just "nice"?* Lettie was too shy to ask, and thankfully Daniel suddenly changed the subject.

"So, any news yet?"

He didn't have to elaborate. "Other than Paz being accepted to Montgomery College, we haven't heard a thing. He's still looking for an internship or job." She massaged her aching left hand. "The ambassador leaves the day after Thanksgiving." The date had changed a few times, but her parents told her this one was final. "It gives us some time."

Daniel unwrapped his half-eaten burrito and tore off a piece of tortilla. "Any idea on when they'll know about you?"

Lettie shrugged. "Jackie said to be patient. That President Price would take care of it."

"Riiight. Just like the Prices take care of everything."

She didn't have to see the hard look in his eyes to know he meant Taylor's death. As many times as they'd discussed it, she still wasn't convinced that Andrew was to blame. But she wasn't unconvinced, either.

"Daniel, unless you have evidence—"

The specialness of the evening evaporated. Daniel folded his arms and a dark shadow fell across his face. Inside the hoodie, Lettie felt more chilled than before.

"I know he did something, Lets." He tapped his chest with his fist. "I feel it here. It's like Tay wants me to know what happened. Every night, when I close my eyes, I see her face. Do you know what that's like?"

Lettie stared off into the dark. Losing Taylor affected them all differently, but revenge seemed to be driving Daniel. He wanted someone to pay. And Andrew Price was the logical target since he was the last person with Taylor.

She moved her hand over his balled fist and gently pried open his fingers. "I know that I miss her every day. And I understand how you hurt. When I thought Paz had died, it was like a piece of my soul had been cut away. And we're not even as close as you and Taylor."

Daniel's face softened and he laid his head on her shoulder. "Thanks, Lets."

"You're my friend. I care about you."

Daniel lifted his head and stared into her eyes. "How about *girl*friend?" he asked sweetly.

A wide smile stretched across her face and she laughed. "Do you think Taylor would like us . . . being together?"

Daniel looked puzzled. "Of course she would." Then he grinned. "Now, if you were dating Sam, she'd be ballistic."

Lettie blushed at the mention of his older brother's name. She'd never told Daniel that she'd once had a little crush on Sam, who was now in college in L.A. The only person she'd told was Taylor, who'd promptly told her to forget him.

"I thought he was . . ."

"A total womanizing creep?" Daniel helped her out. "Yeah, he is."

"A creep? No! Taylor told me a long time ago that he was gay."

Daniel laughed. "I guess she wasn't taking any chances. Because one time, when Sam let slip that he thought you were cute, Tay told him not to waste his time. That *you* were gay."

"What?" Lettie's mouth dropped open.

Daniel laughed. "Don't worry, I knew she was lying." He pulled her in closer and kissed her until she thought she'd melt.

Jackie rubbed the sleep from her eyes and stared at the list of e-mails the press secretary had forwarded to her. Twenty-seven speaking engagement requests. All because of her impromptu press conference on the Capitol steps.

OMG.

Too bad she wouldn't be able to go to any of them, at least not until her mother calmed down. The threat last night had been a hoax. Not only did the phone operator get the message wrong (it was "I see where she's parked," not "I see she's at the park"), but it turned out the call was traced back to Franklin Johnson and his stupid friends. And they would have gotten away with it, too, if Franklin hadn't accidentally butt-dialed the White House operator again, long enough for them to trace his phone. *Idiot.* Let's see his father bail him out of this one.

The only one thrilled about last night's fiasco was Laura Beth. Once all real danger was taken out of the equation, she played quite the damsel in distress with her "Oh, my word!" and her "I'm feeling faint from all this excitement!" It was as if this were the best thing that ever happened to her.

For Jackie, it was just another sleepless night and another reminder that she was never going to get back to her own home. She was stuck here, trapped, under constant surveillance. And she had to admit, she had been terrified when she'd thought it was the stalker. There was still just the slightest pressure in her chest from her nightmares.

Now she stared at the computer screen. She scrolled through

the list, marking the obvious passes (umm . . . hello, club that sounds like an S&M bondage group) and starring a few others for follow-up. Maybe. Brian Gillespie made it clear she didn't have to accept any. But she had an obligation . . . or did she?

Yesterday, hanging out with Laura Beth, she'd felt like a normal teen for the first time in ages. Well, until they got dragged away by the Secret Service. But she really had, before that. Not part of Ankie, not a political activist or a pawn. Just a girl hanging out with a friend.

Laura Beth would tell me to worry about finding my Homecoming dress, not anything else, especially not public speaking. But it's just that this is my life.

Jackie had grown up wanting to be just like her mom or Aunt Deborah. Powerful, in control, and a force to be reckoned with. The impromptu press conference at the Capitol had shown she could pull it off. But now, lying on her bed in pajama bottoms and a tank top, Jackie wondered whether a normal life wouldn't be so bad. One where best friends didn't die and boyfriends didn't lie. Oh yeah, and the whole drama didn't play out in front of the American public like a bad reality TV show.

Always worried about saying the wrong thing, or wearing the wrong dress, or associating with the wrong people. I can't sneeze without someone commenting on it. I'm so over it.

Since moving into the White House, she'd felt even more suffocated. Her movements in and out of 1600 Pennsylvania Avenue were recorded. And even when she wanted to be alone, she wasn't. An agent was always somewhere nearby.

It hadn't seemed so bad when she was with Andrew, who never went anywhere without a Secret Service agent. But he liked his main protector, Mark Davenport.

Jackie shivered and pulled the comforter higher. Since learning about Mark's role in the accident, Jackie had a hard time being around him. If he was willing to cover up Andrew's involvement in Taylor's death, what else had he done?

From its spot on the bed, Jackie's phone dinged. On autopilot, she picked it up and checked her message.

from: **Friedrick VonDrak**<FVD@FVDdesigns>
subject: **Fashion Show**

Jackie paused and studied the preview in her in-box. *Friedrick VonDrak?* The designer?
She opened the e-mail and read quickly.

Jackie—I do hope you don't mind me calling you
that—I'd love, love, love to discuss you modeling my
signature piece at my spring preview for my patrons.
It's gorgeous and you would look *stunning*. And of
course, you can bring that too handsome boyfriend of
yours, too, if you'd like.

Call me as soon as possible, love. My cell is always on—
212.555.FVDD.

xoxo Friedrick

What the hell? Is this a joke? An image of Whitney sitting at her desk laughing maniacally floated through her mind. *It's weird it came directly to me and not through Brian.*

Jackie squinted at her phone. It was ten thirty. Even a late sleeper like Laura Beth had to be awake by now.

As she waited for her friend to answer her phone, Jackie hit speaker and opened her Mac Book so she could search Friedrick.

"Hello?" mumbled a groggy Laura Beth.

Jackie picked up the iPhone. "You sound like hell."

"I didn't get home until late and I still don't have my car. Oh, and I was Skypin' with Sol until two."

"Video sex?" Jackie teased. "Giving him a little preview of what's to come?"

Laura Beth gasped. "Jackie!" She could practically *hear* Laura Beth blushing through the phone as she sputtered, "I'm saving that for the big night."

"Hey, what do you know about Friedrick VonDrak?" Jackie asked, getting back to the reason she called.

"The designer?"

"Yeah, I got an e-mail—supposedly from him—asking me to model his signature look at some preview thing." *It sounds even more ridiculous when I say it out loud.*

Total silence on the other end of the phone.

"Laura Beth?"

"Oh. My. Lord. Are you serious? Jackie, you're not teasing me, are you? Really? Friedrick VonDrak? Oh. My. Lord."

Laura Beth's breathless shock made Jackie laugh. "Whoa. Slow down. I'm not even sure it's from him. It was sent directly to my private account. Not through Brian Gillespie."

"And?" Laura Beth was still hyperventilating.

"And, what if it's a joke? Like maybe from Whitney or Angie? Aamina has my private e-mail address, remember?"

More silence. Jackie studied her fingernails. *If I'm going to be a model, I really need to have my nails done.*

"Well . . . it does seem a little strange. But why would Aamina do that? She's always liked you."

"Not so much after Whitney showed up. Now she hangs out more with her than with us."

Laura Beth huffed. "Well, don't worry about that right now. Did Friedrick give any contact info?"

"His e-mail and a phone number. Do you think I should call him?"

Laura Beth tsked. "No. Give me the number and I'll do it. I'll pretend I'm your assistant. And I'll call from my house phone. Whitney won't recognize that number."

Jackie gave her the info while suppressing a laugh. Of course Laura Beth wanted to call. She was a fashion show fanatic who would do anything to talk to one of the few designers she hadn't yet met—even if it meant pretending to be a mere assistant.

"And if it's really him? What will my assistant say?" Jackie asked, knowing the answer.

In a very businesslike voice, Laura Beth said, "Why, Miss Whitman would be honored to walk in your show. Of course, she'll need seating for her entourage."

"Entourage?" Jackie asked, cocking an eyebrow.

Laura Beth giggled. "Lettie and me, darlin'. You can't forget your friends. Now, do you want to hold the line while I call or have me call you back?"

"I'll wait." Jackie heard the hard clatter of Laura Beth dropping her phone.

"It's ringin'," she shouted. "Hello. My name is Regina Walford, I'm the assistant to Miss Jackie Whitman." A pause. "Why, yes, I'll hold. . . .

"They're putting me on— Oh, hello, Mr. VonDrak." Laura Beth sounded a little breathless. She cleared her throat. "I'm calling on behalf of Miss Whitman."

There was a long, long pause. Presumably Mr. VonDrak was describing the gig in agonizing detail. Finally, Laura Beth said something.

"Hmm. Well, we'll need to see it in writing. Miss Whitman is extremely busy, as you can appreciate, and she will have to check her schedule. Of course, provisions would have to be made for her assistants and her security detail." Laura Beth was really laying it on thick.

"Why don't you send the details right over and we'll get back to you?"

There was another pause, then: "Of course. A pleasure speaking to you, too."

Jackie heard the phone drop back into the receiver, followed by a decidedly un-assistant-like scream.

"Oh. My. Lord. It was really him! Jackie! You're going to model for the hottest designer!"

Jackie jumped up and down, her scream matching Laura Beth's.

It's crazy, but this may be just what I need.

ELEVEN

"Lettie, stand up a little straighter, darlin'. You don't want to look like the Hunchback of Notre Dame, do you? And Laura Beth, stop fussin' with your hair. You're goin' to turn it into a frizzy mess."

Libby Ballou held a glass of bourbon in one hand and a camera in the other.

"At least four drinks," Jackie whispered as she and her two best friends stood together on the stairs, posing for the mandatory Homecoming pictures. Over the years, photos of the girls on the Ballous' grand staircase before any event had become a tradition. Jackie had a scrapbook full of them: as scrawny third graders (without Lettie), as eighth graders with braces, and finally as young women. These were the first without Taylor. No one had felt like going to junior prom after the accident.

Laura Beth giggled. "Five. She pre-gamed before y'all got here."

The camera flashed without warning.

"We're going to look back at this and think we were all headless," Jackie whispered.

"Shhh, she might hear you." Lettie gave them each a stern look before cracking a smile.

All three of the girls wore Friedrick VonDrak dresses—Laura Beth, acting again as Jackie's assistant, had asked for samples. "We need to make sure the product is something Miss Whitman can endorse," she'd said in her faux adult voice.

Two days later, three dresses—more gorgeous than anything Jackie or Laura Beth had seen in the stores—arrived at the White House. Laura Beth's was deep green and one-shouldered, with a short crinoline skirt. Lettie's was a rich orange strapless number with a skirt of ombré-dyed feathers (Lettie at first balked out loud at the idea of killing birds for the sake of a dress—until she tried it on and admitted, to Jackie's amazement, that it made her look sexy). Jackie's dress was a simple midthigh backless sheath covered in ice-blue sequins. All outrageously expensive and totally fabulous.

The girls posed and waited for Laura Beth's mom to steady the camera and finally get a usable shot. Against Miss Libby's wishes, they'd arranged for their dates to meet them at the school—far away from her and her camera and with no way for her to find out that Laura Beth was taking Sol.

"Libby, why don't you let me help you?" Silver-haired Senator Ives walked into the Ballous' oversize foyer with a highball glass in his hand. He wore D.C. weekend casual: khaki trousers, a Brooks Brothers oxford with the top two buttons undone, and loafers. Everything fit him perfectly and showed off the time he spent in the congressional gym. He was good-looking—in that entitled, old-money Republican way that Miss Libby liked.

"Okay now, girls. Squeeze together and give me a big smile. . . . That's good. One, two, three."

Flash.

The senator checked the image and showed it to Libby. "That's the winner," she proclaimed. "Jeffrey, I do believe you have a knack for photography."

Jackie rolled her eyes and elbowed Laura Beth, who fake gagged.

"I've taken a million of these pictures for Frances and Dina and their friends. After a while, you get the hang of it."

Jackie ignored the fact that the adults were acting as if pointing an automatic-focus digital camera and snapping a shot were a herculean feat. She looked over to Laura Beth, who was scowling at the mention of his daughters. Dina was a new junior at Excelsior Prep, and her older sister, Frances, worked for a congressional panel on education. She'd been ecstatic when she'd learned that Dina was getting ready at Angie's house, not hers.

Oops. Better leave that topic alone. For now.

When the girls' limo pulled to the curb in front of St. Thomas Episcopal, Daniel and Sol, both dressed in suits, were waiting near the front door, talking.

Andrew, however, was MIA.

He knows better than to stand me up. Jackie felt the panic starting to bubble up.

"Maybe he's running late? Or there was traffic?" Lettie, seeming to read her mind, squeezed her hand.

Jackie forced a smile. "You're probably right. Do you know how long it takes for him to look so perfect?" Her lip trembled slightly as she spoke, and her heart raced. If Andrew didn't show, then everyone would know something was wrong between them. Andrew missing her Homecoming would be all over the tabloids tomorrow—despite Excelsior's "no press" policy. Not even the threat of suspension stopped the girls from talking when something juicy happened. And how long would it take for the press to get to the bottom of "why"?

"I'll wait with you," Lettie said, climbing out of the car.

Laura Beth had already launched herself from the vehicle and into Sol's arms. "You look amazin'! I could just eat you up!"

If her enthusiasm embarrassed him, Sol didn't show it. *Gotta give the guy credit, he knows how to handle her.*

"We'll catch you girls inside, okay?" Laura Beth practically dragged Sol through the double doors of the school like a prize. Jackie wondered how she was going to keep their date a secret from her mother. Laura Beth's fib—that she was sharing Andrew with Jackie—was too lame to believe. Besides, Miss Libby had eyes and ears everywhere. But whatever, Jackie had bigger problems to worry about. Like Andrew being AWOL.

Standing on the curb, she checked her iPhone, pretending her hour-old messages were interesting. Out of the corner of her eye, she saw Lettie take Daniel's hand and felt a sharp stab of jealousy.

Fan-freaking-tastic. Now it's just me, Lettie, and her Andrew-hating boyfriend. Way to be the third wheel, Jackie.

"You solo tonight, Jackie?" Daniel asked. "That's probably more fun."

She and Daniel had always gotten along, but lately he seemed bent on bringing down Andrew. When Lettie confided a few things he said—his accusations that Andrew was somehow responsible for Taylor's death—Jackie had to bite her tongue to keep from blurting out the truth: that Andrew was driving. That he was more responsible than anyone knew.

But Andrew's reputation and her mom's and Aunt Deborah's careers were more important than unloading a burden—especially one that explosive.

And what difference did it make now who was driving? Taylor was dead. She wasn't coming back. Why ruin more lives?

"Guess not. Speak of the devil," Daniel said as Mark Davenport exited the front seat of a town car that had just pulled to the curb.

Jackie swallowed the lump in her throat, both relieved and annoyed he'd shown up. She hadn't wanted Andrew to come, but she knew he had to. Just like he knew he had to. They hadn't really discussed it. And honestly, she was relieved that they were meeting their dates at school. Not because of Libby or Laura Beth's secret romance, but because she wanted to be around Andrew as little as possible.

Mark pulled open the rear door and Andrew stumbled out. *Oh, my God, he's drunk.* She turned a sharp eye on Mark. *He's not really going to let Andrew go inside like this, is he?*

Apparently he was.

Instinct took over and Jackie darted forward to take Andrew's arm. "Hey, Jackie. You look pretty tonight," he slurred.

His breath reeked of hard alcohol—whiskey, most likely. *Well, at least he isn't driving. We'll go in, do a quick loop to be seen, and leave.*

Thankfully, there was no one else outside to see Andrew stumble. "Andrew, let's go in. We won't stay long, okay?" She tugged gently at his arm.

He gave a goofy smile, one that used to crack her up but now just seemed . . . pathetic. Suddenly, his eyes turned cold and his body stiffened.

"Son of a bitch. It's all your fault." Before Jackie could stop him, Andrew flew across the sidewalk and punched Daniel in the jaw. "It's your fault! Taylor told me—she was screaming at me when we crashed. Yelling at me. About you. About all the lying. About having to cover up for everyone." His fist made contact with Daniel's jaw again.

Lettie jumped back. "Jackie! Stop them!"

Jackie tried to throw herself between the boys but was pushed to the ground.

Where the fuck is Mark? she thought as she hit the concrete. "Andrew! Stop!" she shouted.

Andrew ignored her and used his extra thirty pounds and three inches on Daniel to his advantage, pinning him against the sidewalk.

"Mark!" Jackie screamed. "Do something." She looked around for her Secret Service agent, who was making no move to intervene either.

The Secret Service agents gave her a blank look, as if they had no clue how to handle this. Fury built in Jackie, but she wasn't sure whom she should direct it at. Andrew for punching Daniel? Daniel for everything he'd been saying about Andrew? Or the agents for just standing there? Any minute someone would come outside. All it would take would be one photograph. The weight in her chest grew into a hard fist in her rib cage.

Beneath Andrew, Daniel tried to cover his face with his hands. "You're crazy! Out of your fucking mind."

"I'm not! I know what she said. I know!" Andrew sobbed as his body went limp and he collapsed on Daniel.

Jackie reached over and grabbed at the back of Andrew's jacket, but he slipped through her hands and rolled onto the ground.

At the same time, Lettie yanked on Daniel, pulling him away from Andrew.

"What the fuck, Jackie? What the fuck?" Daniel yelled as he sat up. His eyes flashed with rage. As if it were Jackie's fault. Like she could control him any more than Lettie could control Daniel.

"Don't blame Jackie!" Lettie cried. "She's not the one who attacked you."

Jackie brushed herself off and stepped back, stunned. Instinctively, she searched the street to see if there were any witnesses. From behind her, Mark—finally—brushed past her and hauled Andrew to his feet. "You two go inside, wash up, and enjoy the dance," he said to Lettie and Daniel.

Mark propped up Andrew with his arm, and the two agents conferred in low whispers. "Jackie, come with me," Mark said.

She nodded but didn't move. She felt as if she'd been cast in cement. There was no way she could go inside now. "Lettie..."

Lettie turned slowly. She, too, seemed to be in shock. Blood from Daniel's cut face stained the bodice of her dress and her hair had fallen loose. "Go take care of Andrew. We can talk later, okay?"

Jackie wanted to follow after her. She wanted to distance herself from Andrew, forget about this whole mess, and enjoy herself at the dance with a new gorgeous guy she could fall in love with. But she knew showing up without Andrew would be the worst thing she could do.

"Okay," she whispered as she watched her friend disappear inside the school.

Whitney pressed her face against the dark tinted window of the limo. "Oh, my God, do you guys see what I see?"

Franklin leaned over her, the scent of his aftershave overwhelming. "Is that Daniel Cane and . . . *Andrew Price?*"

"I sure as hell hope so. Stay here."

Angie strained her neck to get a better view. "Oh shit! Andrew just clocked him!"

Franklin slumped back into his seat as Whitney climbed out of the far side of the limo and snuck down to the end of the car. From here, she could hear everything without being seen.

"It's your fault!" Andrew was shouting. "Taylor told me—she was screaming at me when we crashed. Yelling at me. About you. About all the lying. About having to cover up for everyone."

This is it, my ticket home. She flattened herself to the sidewalk, peeking out from underneath the car. *Who cares about the dress when I can get pictures?* From her bag, she slid out her cell phone and snapped a few shots before a guy—Andrew's Secret Service agent, probably—pulled Andrew away.

As soon as Lettie and Daniel disappeared inside, and Jackie and Andrew were hustled into the back of their town car, Whitney slipped back into the limo.

"Dude, Price nailed him," Franklin crowed. "Punk totally

deserves it. I hate that Cane kid. The way he thinks he's better than us cuz he's some skateboarding champ. Who the fuck cares how high you can jump on a board? Right, bro?"

Angie's boyfriend, Carter, held out his fist and Franklin bumped it. "True that."

I don't have time for their bromance; I need to find out what's going on.

As Andrew's town car pulled away, Whitney weighed her options: Go follow the car, which was probably headed for the White House, or go to the dance and see what she could pry out of Lettie. *Lettie's probably the safer bet.*

"You're totally sending that to your mom, aren't you?" Angie asked, pointing to Whitney's phone.

She shrugged. "Maybe. Depends what else I can find out."

Franklin shoved open the door. "Then let's get inside. I didn't shell out a hundred bucks to hang out in a limo all night. Unless, you know . . ." He grinned at Whitney.

She smiled at him prettily. "You help me get what I need, and I'll give you what you want."

"Deal."

Lettie dabbed the dampened napkin against Daniel's face. "Stop wiggling, you're going to make a mess."

Daniel rolled his eyes. "I've had worse, Lets. I'm a skateboarder, remember? I'm constantly bruised and broken."

Maybe that was true, but she didn't like the look of the cut under his eye.

As soon as they'd entered the dance, one of the teacher chaperones demanded to know what had happened. Daniel lied, saying he'd been goofing around and fell off his board.

Surprisingly, the teacher didn't ask any more questions. Probably didn't really want to know.

All around them, music thumped and Excelsior and St. Thomas students danced. Other than prom, this was *the* big joint dance of the year. But Lettie didn't want to be here. Not anymore.

Something about the hysteria in Andrew's voice troubled her. Sure, he was drunk—make that completely plastered—but it was clear he was hurting inside.

"Why did Andrew say Taylor was tired of everybody lying? Lying about what?" she blurted out.

Daniel pulled his face away from her hand. "Hell if I know. He's drunk and crazy."

"Oh, my Lord! Daniel, what happened to you?" Laura Beth, with Sol in tow, pranced toward them.

"I had on the same jacket as Andrew and he got a little upset about it," Daniel joked.

Laura Beth's mouth dropped open. "Andrew *Price* did this?" She spun around and her head moved back and forth as she scanned the dance floor. "Where's Jackie?"

"I think they went home. Andrew's really drunk," Lettie said.

Before Lettie could stop her, Laura Beth had her phone pressed to her ear. "She's not answering! What in the world is going on? Daniel, *what* did *you* do to Andrew?"

As he stood up angrily, Daniel's chair tipped over. "Do to *him*? Seriously? I was minding my business, talking to my girl-friend, when that asshole decked me for no reason. If you want to be mad at someone, be mad at your fantasy boyfriend." His voice turned icy, and Laura Beth blushed.

"Daniel, stop it!" Lettie, pale as a ghost, grabbed his arm.

"Right now!" When he saw Lettie's frightened look, his face softened.

"You're right," he said, giving both girls a rueful smile. "I'm sorry, Laura Beth. It's been one helluva Homecoming." He bent over and kissed Laura Beth softly on the cheek. Then he did the same to Lettie. A typical Daniel gesture. Lettie couldn't help wondering if maybe it wasn't Daniel she should be worried about after all.

"Hey, LB, mind if we join you?"

Of course she'd pick this minute to show up.

With her hand linked through Sol's arm, Laura Beth smiled sweetly at Whitney. "Actually, we're headed to the dance floor. Y'all can have the table if you'd like."

Whitney tossed her wild curls and smiled. "What do you say, Franklin? Wanna dance?"

Franklin ran his hand over Whitney's hip. *I bet she's not wearing panties,* Laura Beth thought, noticing Whitney's lack of panty lines. *So trashy.* "How did you manage to get out of your latest arrest, Franklin? Does your father have an attorney on call for you 24/7?"

Even Lettie laughed at Franklin's slack-jawed look. Whitney ignored it.

"Lets, come dance with me." Whitney pulled at Lettie's hand and dragged her along. "C'mon. Didn't anyone teach you not to run after boys? Make them come to you."

It was such a Taylor thing to say. Laura Beth's heart sank. *Last Homecoming, it was the four of us, hanging out, dancing, sneaking sips of vodka from Tay's flask. Now look at us. I'm the only one who's even remotely happy.*

On the dance floor, she quickly forgot everything as Sol swung his hips to the music.

"Why didn't you tell me you could dance?" she shouted over the din.

Sol laughed. "And destroy my mysterious aura?"

She shimmied to the music, thankful Friedrick had sent her a one-shoulder, and not a strapless, dress.

If he can move like that on the floor, just imagine what he'd be like in bed, Taylor would say. *If he has rhythm, he has rhythm.*

Laura Beth smiled and let the music flow through her body. *I miss you, Tay.*

Sol touched her arm and gestured to the side of the room. "Can we talk for a minute? I haven't been alone with you all night."

Laura Beth smiled. She'd been hoping for some alone time with him.

Once they'd found a spot in the corner, away from everyone else, Sol leaned into her.

"Hey," she said softly. The smell of the soap he used filled the narrow space between them. She inhaled deeply, wanting to remember everything about this moment forever.

Sol ran his finger along her bare shoulder, and Laura Beth closed her eyes as heat worked through her body. *If he doesn't kiss me right now, I may actually die.*

"I wanted to thank you again, for standing by me and not believing that garbage in the paper."

Laura Beth's eyes flew open. A conversation about Sol's parents and the terrorist allegations wasn't what she'd been expecting. "Oh," she said, trying to hide her disappointment. "Well, Tracey Mills is nothing but a gossipmonger. There's not a lie she won't print to get attention. And besides, if your parents are anything like you, they're good people."

Sol touched his lips to Laura Beth's neck and the room spun. What was it about this guy that made him so sexy? "Thank you, that means a lot to me. Not everyone was as understanding." He pulled away from her. "Andrew hasn't returned my phone calls. I was hoping we could talk tonight."

"I wouldn't worry about Andrew, he'll come around once this blows over." Actually, even though Andrew and Sol were good friends, she wasn't so sure. As the president's son, he couldn't afford to be associated with any hint of scandal, true or otherwise. But there was no reason to upset Sol with that kind of talk. Laura Beth stroked the back of her hand across his cheek. The stubble of his five o'clock shadow scratched her hand, but she didn't care. Impulsively, she stood on her tiptoes and brushed her lips across his. "Let's not worry about all that. We're here to have fun."

Sol leaned against the white cinder-block gym wall. A relaxed smile formed on his mouth. "You always know what I need. It's like you can read my mind."

Laura Beth sashayed back toward the dance floor, her fingers wrapped through Sol's. She knew all the girls along the walls—the ones without dates—were watching them. Jealous, of course. Just like she'd been so many times before, watching Taylor with her guy of the week, or Jackie with Andrew. So many times she'd stood with Lettie on the sidelines, waiting for just the right guy to ask her to dance. But not tonight. Tonight, she—Laura Beth Ballou—was going to be the star of the show. She had a hot guy by her side, and she planned on dancing up a storm.

And if she was chosen as Homecoming Queen—and the odds had just narrowed without Jackie here—even better.

They'd just reached the center of the dance floor, near Daniel and Lettie, when her handbag brushed her thigh. Through the thin fabric, she felt her phone vibrate. For a split second, she considered not answering it. But it could be Jackie. Needing help. She stopped dancing to check.

It *was* a text from Jackie.

"Is everything okay?" Sol asked.

"It's Jackie," Laura Beth said, her eyes fixed on the phone. "I want to make sure she's okay after what happened." *And I want to know what made Andrew attack Daniel.*

The text, though, was brief. Jackie was asking her and Lettie to meet her at the Lincoln Memorial. Now. Without the guys.

"Is that Jackie?" Whitney asked, sliding up to her.

Laura Beth flipped her phone over. "No. My mama. She wants to make sure I'm home at a decent hour."

Whitney smirked. "LB, you'll never get laid like that."

Sol squirmed uncomfortably, and heat burned Laura Beth's cheeks. "Maybe some of us have more than one thing on our minds," she said.

Whitney snorted. "Sure. Right, Sol?"

Laura Beth shoved the phone in her bag and looked around to grab Lettie. "I need to use the restroom."

Thank the Lord for the time-honored tradition of the bathroom break.

"I'll come too. I had too much to drink before we got here." Whitney fake staggered. Laura Beth didn't believe for one moment she'd been drinking. She didn't smell like alcohol, and she'd been fine minutes earlier. But she couldn't tell her not to come. That would look suspicious.

In the bathroom, Laura Beth barricaded herself in a stall, and Lettie took the one next to her.

How about in an hour? I need to get rid of Whit, she texted Jackie.

Laura Beth passed her iPhone under the stall for Lettie.

As worried as she was about the Andrew and Daniel fight, Laura Beth didn't want it to ruin her night. She'd come to have a good time—*with her boyfriend*—at her last high school Homecoming ever, not leave after an hour because two immature guys couldn't get along. Besides, she and Sol had plans after the dance, which Laura Beth hoped included a stop at his parents' D.C. pied-à-terre. She could already imagine it, the two of them, alone, in the glass-and-steel condo overlooking the Capital. Sol would build a fire and the two of them would drink champagne and—

"Laura Beth? I'm not feeling well," Lettie moaned from her stall. "I think I need to go home."

Leave it to efficient Lettie to figure a way to ditch Whitney. "Can you hold out for a little while? I want to have at least one slow dance with Sol."

The two girls met at the sink. Whitney leaned against the wall near the paper towels.

"You look fine to me," Whitney said.

Lettie sighed heavily and parted her lips. "My head hurts. I think I'm getting a migraine. If I don't get to a dark room soon, I'm going to puke."

Laura Beth swallowed her giggle. Taylor often used migraines as an excuse to get out of class, even though she'd never had one. They'd both seen her performance so many times that reenacting it was a breeze.

"I'll get Sol to call our car around. You just sit at the table and wait, okay?" Laura Beth said, guiding Lettie out of the bathroom and back into the pounding music and lights of the dance.

Lettie moaned. "I can't go in there. I need somewhere quiet. Maybe outside—on the steps?"

I guess I'm not getting that slow song after all.

Across the room, Sol stood near the punch line with Daniel. His face lit up when he saw Laura Beth, only to fall when he noticed she was holding on to Lettie. He nudged Daniel and they both rushed across the dance floor.

"Are you okay?" Daniel asked, his hand on Lettie's shoulder.

"Apparently, she's going to puke everywhere if she doesn't leave ASAP," Whitney said.

Laura Beth sighed. She hated lying, but with Whitney standing here, what choice did she have? "Lettie has a migraine, Sol. I need to take her home. Can I take a rain check?"

Sol had come down from New York City especially for this dance. Now that Columbia was back in session, Laura Beth didn't get to see him much anymore—only their daily late night Skype sessions kept her from going crazy from missing him.

My one night with my boyfriend and Jackie makes me ditch him. She so owes me.

"I'll come with you," Sol offered. "We'll take her home and then grab something to eat. Or we can just go back to my parents' place."

Daniel looked up at them.

"I'll take Lets home," he said firmly. "We can call a cab."

Lettie shook her head. "I need someone to stay with me until my parents get home—from Carolina Baustita's *fiesta de quince*. They wouldn't like me being alone with a boy."

She lied for me so I wouldn't have to.

Laura Beth pressed her lips together, not even bothering to hide how upset she was by the whole turn of events. She turned to Sol, who looked almost as dismayed as she was. "Lettie's parents are very traditional. I'm afraid you can't join us, either."

Sol's dark eyes searched Laura Beth's face as if he knew she was lying—which technically she wasn't. "I understand. Can we still meet for breakfast tomorrow?"

She squeezed his hand and pecked his cheek. "I wouldn't miss it."

TWELVE

"Where are you going?" Mark Davenport asked as Jackie stepped off the bottom step of the Grand Staircase.

Startled, she whipped around and looked up at him. Mark's close-cropped dark hair had a hint of gray around the temples, and his dark suit hugged his muscular frame.

"Out."

"Don't you think you should be with Andrew right now?"

Who the hell does he think he is? My babysitter?

Jackie flipped her long blond hair over her shoulder and buttoned up her coat. "I think I've done all I can for Andrew. He's on his own now."

The car ride back to the White House had been painful. Andrew had whimpered like a baby over his bloodied hand until he'd passed out. Mark had decided to bring Andrew back to the White House instead of his dorm, and once there, he and

Jackie's agent had helped him upstairs to the Lincoln Bedroom.

Not only did Andrew ruin my evening, he messed up Laura Beth's and Lettie's. Poor Lettie, what if this is one of the last dances she gets to go to?

Jackie stepped into the entrance hall and walked to the North Portico.

"I can't let you go out alone, Jackie. You need to have an agent with you, the president's—and your mother's—orders. You know that."

She sighed and waited near the exit. He was right. For once, though, the stalker was the last thing on her mind.

"Miss Whitman?" A young female agent approached Jackie. "I'm Agent Ellen Fellows. I'll be with you for the rest of this evening. Have you called a car yet?"

Jackie nodded. At least Mark wasn't coming with her. Something about him bugged her—the way he watched her. Not like a normal agent, but something more.

"Would you like to wait here or outside?" Agent Fellows asked.

"Outside."

A sleek black car pulled to the curb and the driver hopped out to open Jackie's door.

"The Lincoln Memorial, is that correct, Miss Whitman?" the driver asked.

"Please."

Agent Fellows sat up front, leaving Jackie alone with her thoughts. She slumped into the corner of the car with one shaking hand over her face and pressed her eyes tightly together.

I'm so tired of being strong for everyone. Of holding everything in. It's too much.

She'd come close to calling Scott tonight and telling him everything. About Taylor and Andrew, the accident, and how she felt like she was breaking apart. But just as she'd started to dial him, she'd realized it would be a mistake. A big one.

So she'd texted Laura Beth instead.

The car slowed and came to a stop in front of the mammoth granite-and-marble memorial. No matter how many times she saw it, or from what distance, its sheer size awed her. Now, late at night, it glowed in the darkness and was almost deserted.

"Is this okay, Miss Whitman?" the driver asked over his shoulder.

"Yes. Thank you." She didn't wait for him to open her door. Sometimes the formality of the White House was ridiculous with all the door opening and Miss Whitman–ing. She didn't bother to tell him to wait. He would, regardless of what she wanted. Agent Fellows would see to that.

A chilly wind whipped up the steps from the direction of the Reflection Pool. Jackie shivered and pulled her scarf up a little higher.

"Jackie! Over here!" Laura Beth called from one side of the colonnade.

In seventh grade, their teacher had made the girls learn the proper architectural terms for the monuments and memorials. Jackie had taken great pleasure in annoying Andrew and Scott with her newfound knowledge. These columns weren't just columns. They were *Doric*. And there were porticoes, friezes, and bas-reliefs.

When did I stop studying architecture? Jackie stopped and studied the building. The answer was obvious. *When I started loving politics.*

She jogged up the steps, her hands shaking inside her coat

pockets. Her friends still wore their Homecoming dresses, and neither one had a coat warm enough for outside. "Thanks for coming, guys."

Lettie's teeth chattered. "Yes, please." They staked out a corner of the vast open-air room, moving away from a couple of late night tourists lingering by the giant statue of the slain president.

Not two seconds later, Laura Beth started complaining. "You know, Jackie, I had plans, *with my boyfriend,* who came all the way down from *New York,* to be here."

Tears stung Jackie's eyes, and she blinked rapidly. *Don't cry. Be strong.*

But she couldn't do it. Not anymore. The tears rolled down her cheeks.

"What's wrong?" Lettie asked. She immediately threw her arms around Jackie as if she wanted to both protect and comfort her.

Jackie shook her head and sniffed.

"I need to tell you something—about Andrew." She paused and swallowed hard. "And Taylor."

Neither of her friends said anything, as if they knew bad news was coming.

"The night of the crash, they slept together."

Laura Beth's hand flew over her mouth. "No."

Not Andrew. He wouldn't do something like that to Jackie. Neither would Taylor. She loved Jackie. She loved the three of us. This has to be a mistake.

She watched Jackie wipe her tears with the back of her hand and try to compose herself. Next to her, Lettie stood still, as if stunned.

"He told me. That's why we've been having problems. After the accident, I thought he didn't want me anymore, but then, he admitted everything. How guilty he felt. And . . . well, how am I supposed to be his girlfriend now?"

Laura Beth knew the answer: A good Washington wife—or girlfriend—was supposed to smile and get over it.

"That's not all. They crashed because Taylor was hysterical. Screaming about people lying to her and cover-ups. Andrew said she was out of control, hitting him and stuff. She kept threatening to jump out of the car."

Laura Beth narrowed her eyes. Something didn't add up. Why would Taylor threaten to jump out of the car? Why wouldn't she just pull over? Or make Andrew get out?

Oh. My. Lord. The ground swayed beneath her and she grabbed Lettie's shoulder to steady herself. *Andrew must have been driving.*

Her breath came in short spurts and dizziness engulfed her.

"Laura Beth? Are you okay?" Lettie finally broke her silence, worry creeping into her voice.

"I'm . . ." Her voice hitched. "Fine. I'm just in shock. I can't believe they'd do something like that to Jackie."

Her eyes met Jackie's panicked blue ones. *She knows Andrew was driving, but she doesn't want us to know. I don't blame her; if this gets out, it could ruin everything.*

"How long have you known?" Lettie asked, trying to keep her voice steady.

Jackie tucked a strand of blond hair behind her ear. "Since early summer."

Lettie squeezed her eyes shut, not to force back tears, but to hide her anger. But who was she angry at? Jackie for keeping this a secret from her two best friends? Or Taylor for doing it?

At least Jackie had a good reason. Taylor and Andrew had no excuse for what they did.

But Taylor was dead.

Andrew, however, wasn't.

Laura Beth sat hyperventilating next to her, and Jackie stared off across the memorial, her face now composed—just like always.

"You should break up with him."

"Lettie, no! Don't say that. Andrew made a mistake, that's all." Laura Beth's fingers curled around Lettie's arm.

Jackie swung her gaze back toward Lettie. "I can't."

The way she said it, slowly, as if she were being careful about her words, troubled Lettie. *There's something she's not telling us.*

Daniel was right. There was more to the crash than Andrew had admitted.

Whitney hadn't bought Lettie's story about having a migraine, not for one minute. Still, they almost threw her off when they left without their dates.

But Whitney wasn't a gossip columnist's daughter for nothing. And her instincts proved correct: Lettie wasn't sick, and the girls didn't go home. She'd ordered Franklin to call their limo back, and the two of them had followed Lettie and Laura Beth to the Lincoln Memorial.

And she had gotten exactly what she needed.

As Whitney walked away from the tourists and headed down

the memorial steps, her heart pounded with excitement. Andrew Price had cheated on Jackie. With her best friend! On the night of the accident. And she had it all recorded on her phone.

If this doesn't get me home, nothing will.

She flung open the door of her waiting limo and the smell of pot wafted out. Franklin lay stretched out across the back, one arm under his head, one foot on the floor, and his dress shirt slightly unbuttoned. In his other hand, he held a half-smoked joint.

She grinned at him. "It's your lucky day. Remember how I said I'd give you what you want if you helped me out?"

His lips moved into a lazy smile and his eyes lit up. "Yeah."

Whitney pressed the intercom button. "We'd like to drive around town for"—she hiked up her skirt and straddled Franklin the best she could—"the next two hours."

She released the button and the car sped off.

Franklin grabbed Whitney's hips and slid her forward a little. "What about Angie and Carter?" he asked.

Whiney leaned forward slightly and ran her hands under his shirt. "They're big kids. They can find their own way home."

"You're in a good mood. What did you get?" he asked.

Whitney placed her finger against his lips. "I could tell you, but then I wouldn't be able to do this." She bent her head down and pressed her lips against his. Franklin tasted like spiked punch and cush.

His empty hand traveled under her skirt and he inhaled sharply. "Whit, did you forget to put panties on?"

She giggled and plucked the joint from his hand. "That's not the only thing I forgot to put on."

A thick puff of smoke billowed around Whitney's head as she tugged down the top of her dress. "See?"

Franklin smiled. "The next time you need help, let me know."

With one last puff on the joint, Whitney leaned over him and nibbled his lip. "Hopefully, there won't be a next time."

THIRTEEN

Whitney had been waiting in the restaurant for twenty minutes. She looked at her phone for the hundredth time. Her mom had said to meet her at Potenza at one thirty and not to be late.

So, where the hell is she?

The hickey on Whitney's neck still stung, and she touched it absentmindedly. Her parents gave up caring what she did years ago, as long as she didn't get pregnant or contract some awful disease. And really, a hickey was nothing. Not that her mom would notice in the dim light of the restaurant.

"More Diet Coke, miss?" the waiter asked.

"Yes."

Her stomach rumbled. After she and Franklin had their fun in the limo, the driver took them to a late night dive in Maryland. It was seedy and run-down, but Franklin said it had the best fries ever. He must have meant it because he polished off two baskets, three burgers, and several sodas.

God, he eats like a pig when he's stoned. It was so gross, she hadn't touched her food.

Out of the corner of her eye, she saw her mom walk into the restaurant and hand the maître d' her jacket. Underneath it, she wore a beige suit, nude-colored pumps, and a large beaded necklace.

She's beginning to dress like every other woman in Washington. Boring.

"Hi, Mom!" Whitney said as her mother slid into the leather booth. Her heart beat hard. She'd sent her mom the audio file of Jackie talking to her friends as soon as she had woken up that morning.

The waiter hovered next to the table.

"I'll start with a Pinot Noir. Whichever you recommend," her mom said, using her snappy, I'm-in-a-hurry voice.

When he walked away, Whitney leaned forward and said, "So?"

Her mother stared at her blankly. "So, what?"

Whitney sat back abruptly, as if slapped. "The file I sent you."

"Oh, that? Was it something special?" The waiter came back with the glass of red wine.

What the hell? I send her a recording of Jackie admitting Andrew slept with Taylor the night of the accident, and she asks if it's special?

Her mouth opened and then shut, like a fish gasping for air.

"How do I know Jackie didn't set you up the way she did last time, letting you 'overhear' that fake story about getting engaged to Andrew?"

Whitney glared at her. Was she ever gonna drop that?

"Oh, don't look at me like that, Whitney. That caused me a major embarrassment. Almost destroyed my credibility. It's a wonder the *Tattler* didn't fire me."

"But it's *Ankie*!" Whitney protested. "America's sweethearts! The fairy tale is a lie. They're not even really going out anymore, it's just a front." She racked her brain, trying to come up with more angles, something that would convince her mom that *this* was the story.

The annoying waiter appeared again. "Ladies, are you ready to order?"

Her mom handed him her menu. "A caprese salad."

"Excellent choice. And for you, miss?"

Whitney's appetite vanished. She shook her head. "Nothing."

"You can't eat nothing, Whitney," her mom scolded. "She'll have the same."

"Very well."

Whitney's mom fake-smiled at the man and then turned her head back to Whitney as soon as he walked away. "Ankie isn't a story anymore. The election campaign is around the corner and I need real dirt, Whitney. *On the adults.*"

"But how am I supposed to do that?" Her voice sounded whiny, like a three-year-old's.

Her mother took a large swallow of her wine as the waiter carried two tomato-and-mozzarella salads to their table.

"If I knew the answer to that, I'd do it myself, wouldn't I? Do you think I like relying on you?"

Whitney breathed heavily, her chest rising and falling. "You keep changing your mind about what you want. It isn't fair."

Her mom rolled her eyes. "Life isn't fair, Whitney. You know that."

Resentment filled Whitney's body. Her mom was never going to let her win. It was all just a game to her.

"Oh, my goodness! Whitney Remick, is that you, darlin'? I think you've grown more gorgeous since I last saw you!"

Fuck. Just what I need—a visit from the D.C. welcoming committee.

Before Whitney could open her mouth, her mother shifted into schmoozing mode in one fluid movement.

"Hi, I'm Tracey Mills, Whitney's mother."

Libby Ballou and the tall, old guy with her took turns shaking her mom's hand. "Libby Ballou. I had the pleasure of meeting Whitney and your handsome husband at a little welcoming tea party at my home this summer. I'm so pleased that my daughter, Laura Beth, has become such fast friends with your Whitney." Libby patted the arm of the guy with her. "Where are my manners? This is my dear friend Senator Jeffrey Ives."

Whitney's mom flashed them a dazzling smile. "It's so lovely to meet you at last, Mrs. Ballou. William told me about the wonderful welcome you gave him and Whitney. And the senator and I, of course, go way back. He's from my home state, after all."

Senator Ives grinned. "Tracey even convinced me, in a weak moment, to appear on her TV show in Los Angeles."

"And of course, he was one of the first people I contacted after I moved here," Whitney's mom said. She squeezed his hand, and Whitney could have sworn Laura Beth's mother looked jealous.

Mrs. Ballou interrupted. "I do hope you're enjoying Washington. How is your husband? Such a nice man and such interesting work, too."

Whitney couldn't decide who had the biggest fake smile—her mom, Laura Beth's mother, or the tight-ass senator.

"William loves his job. He's a policy animal," her mother joked.

LB's mother and the senator laughed politely.

"I've been following your column with great interest," she said, all sugary nice.

If you call airing people's dirty laundry a column.

Her mother laughed. "It's nice to know someone out there is reading it."

"So you'll be here for the holidays?" Her mom nodded. "How wonderful! We have the best season here—the parties at the embassies are just amazing. Of course, nothin' compares to the White House parties, do they, Jeffrey?"

God. Does she ever shut up?

The senator chuckled. "A real taste of Christmas in America. I go whenever I'm invited."

Oh, puke.

Her mom shifted in her seat. "So the parties aren't partisan?"

"Not really. With fifty thousand guests pouring through the doors over Christmas, they have to include some of us Republicans." He chuckled again.

"Oh, Jeffrey's just bein' modest," Libby Ballou gushed. "Anyone who's anyone in this town gets an invitation to at least one of the parties, especially political superstars like him." She gazed up at him adoringly.

Whitney thought she might throw up her Diet Coke right there on the table.

"I'm sure you'll get your invitation, Tracey. There's always a party just for the media. But if I were you, I'd try to finagle my way into the Prices' *private* Christmas party. It's something to behold. My dear friend Deborah Price is a marvelous hostess—only the crème de la crème of Washington society and politics. Fascinating people, exquisite food, and wonderful gossip!"

Whitney rolled her eyes and shoveled half her salad into her mouth to stifle a guffaw.

"Oh, my Lord. Jeffrey, look at the time! You're going to be late for the afternoon session if we don't scoot.

"Tracey, such a pleasure to meet you." Libby amped up the fake smile. "And Whitney, darlin', don't be a stranger, now. You hear?"

"Hopefully, we'll see each other again soon," her mom said in her slightly higher, kiss-up voice.

The senator dipped his head to them. "Ladies."

Her mother watched them exit the restaurant before slapping her hand on the table. "*That's* the kind of thing I need, Whitney. Invites to the private parties."

Whitney stared at her plate. "Cuz I'm your social planner?"

"Don't be a smart-ass. Get me into the Prices' exclusive Christmas party and not only will I treat you to a trip back home, you won't ever have to come back to D.C. for as long as you live."

Laura Beth laid two dresses on the bed and frowned. Last night's Homecoming was a total bust. Nothing had better go wrong with the New York trip—not the fashion show and definitely not her rendezvous with Sol.

She couldn't believe what Jackie had told them about Andrew sleeping with Taylor. Surely not *her* Andrew? But of course it *was* true, no matter how much she wished it weren't.

And the more Laura Beth thought about it, the more convinced she was that her theory was right: He'd been driving that night.

It made sense, the way he'd been behaving since the accident. It was just grieving. . . . He'd practically changed his whole personality. He'd always been so in control and now it was like something controlled him.

But even if he *had* been driving, surely that didn't mean he was responsible for the accident? Jackie said Taylor was screaming and hitting him. That could be enough to drive anyone off the road.

She sighed and pulled the V-neck Ralph Lauren sweater dress over her head. It fell softly over her hips and she scrunched up the arms a little to give it a more casual look.

Still, Andrew and Taylor had slept together. That was unforgivable.

Poor Jackie, she's been carrying this burden all alone. No wonder she's been so depressed.

Laura Beth rolled a pair of Wolford tights up her legs before fastening the straps of her three-inch heels. A skinny belt around the waist and a thick gold chain finished the look.

She admired herself in the mirror and ran her finger over a nonexistent bulge near her hip bone. "I've got to stop eating so much."

The three girls had stayed up until three in the morning, when Jackie finally went back to the White House. She and Lettie fell asleep on Laura Beth's huge bed. Which of course meant her breakfast plans with Sol had to be changed to late lunch plans.

On her way downstairs, Laura Beth heard her mama's musical laugh coming from the front sitting room.

"Is that you, Laura Beth?"

Crap. The last thing she wanted was to undergo a Libby Ballou interrogation.

"Yes, Mama."

"Then get in here, sugar. I want to hear all about last night."

Laura Beth gritted her teeth and checked her phone.

"Mama," she said entering the room, "I have plans with—" She stopped abruptly. Sol was still persona non grata around here. "Jackie and Lettie in thirty minutes."

Libby Ballou sat snuggled up next to Senator Ives. Each held a glass of something strong in their hands.

"The girls can wait." She waved her hand dismissively. "Tell me all about the dance. What did Whitney Remick wear? You know, I saw her today—with her mama. Poor thing looked downright miserable." She turned her head slightly to look at the senator. "Don't you think so, Jeffrey? Like she wanted to be anywhere but at that table?"

The senator knocked back the rest of his drink. "I defer to you on that one, Libby."

She smiled. "Anyway, you need to invite her over sometime soon. I haven't seen you with her in ages."

Anger erupted inside Laura Beth. *First Whitney blackmails me into being friends, but now Mama is ordering me to hang out with her, too? Ugh.* She kept her smile firm. "Mama, Whitney's very popular. In fact, I don't think she has time for *us* anymore—with her boyfriend and all."

"Well, that explains that awful bruise she had on her neck. Looked like a vampire had his way with her. Who's her boyfriend, anyone I'd know?"

Laura Beth struggled to keep from rolling her eyes. "Franklin Johnson."

Libby Ballou's mouth dropped open before she remembered herself.

Ha! That surprised her. Now maybe she won't make me hang out with Whitney.

"As in Councilman Johnson's son? The"—she held up her hand so the senator couldn't see and mouthed—"drug addict?"

Laura Beth nodded. It was no secret among D.C.'s elite that Frankin had spent a few weeks in rehab during sophomore year and that his father frequently paid off the local police to cover up his son's drug arrests.

"Oh, my Lord. I wonder if her mother knows?" Her mama began rambling about protecting our youth and moral standing. "I should call her. If you were fraternizin' with boys like that, I'd want to know immediately."

Laura Beth shifted her weight and tried to look calm. If her mama ever found out about Sol, she'd be grounded for the rest of the year. But she couldn't turn her back on him. Not after what he'd told her about Andrew, his so-called friend, suddenly avoiding him. And besides, his parents were innocent. No one had produced any evidence of them having terrorist links.

"Mama, I really have to go. Can we discuss this later?"

Libby accepted a freshly poured drink from the senator, who had gotten up while mother and daughter gossiped. "We surely can, darlin'."

As Laura Beth stepped into the foyer, her mama called out, "Don't stay out too late, you have to pack for New York tonight."

Butterflies fluttered in her stomach. Mama was right, she had a lot to get ready for—especially her two days of freedom and alone time with Sol.

Last night hadn't gone well, but Laura Beth had New York planned right down to her Brazilian wax appointment later that afternoon and the hot-pink lingerie (black seemed too trashy) she'd picked up a few days earlier.

New York was going to be epic.

"Knock, knock."

Jackie turned around at the sound of her mom's voice. "Mom!"

Even though Jackie was living at the White House, where her mom spent most of her time, they'd barely run into each other the past couple of days. She and Aunt Deborah had been locked in meetings, hashing out policy positions for the coming year. Plus, they were distracted by the PAPPies, who'd been disrupting every public appearance by the president, accusing the administration of corruption and yelling about impeachment.

Carolyn Shaw wore a crisp, fitted pants suit and her hair was twisted into a simple knot. During the first presidential campaign, critics often dismissed Aunt Deborah and her top aide as nothing more than two "pretty women." Jackie knew the president worked harder than she should just to prove she deserved to be commander in chief.

"Hey, kiddo." Carolyn tugged on Jackie's ponytail. "Packing for New York? Or running away?"

The girls were going for only two days, but it looked as if Jackie's entire wardrobe covered her bed. "I'm not sure what to bring. Laura Beth said to bring 'club clothes,' whatever that is. And Friedrick's hosting a pre- and post-party in my honor. I'm not sure if I'm supposed to wear this." Her fingers jabbed at the blue sequined dress she'd worn to Homecoming. If she had her way, she'd never wear it again.

Her mom stretched out on the pillows, the only empty spot on the bed. "As a master packer, I must advise you to take as little as possible." The famous Carolyn Shaw megawatt smile lit up her face. "Besides, I'm giving you this." She held out a credit card. "So you can have a little fun."

Jackie snatched it from her hand. "A Visa card?"

"Not exactly. It's a prepaid debit card. Your dad and I both pitched in. It has a thousand dollars on it."

It wasn't anywhere close to Laura Beth's credit limit, but it was better than nothing. And it was all for the trip.

"Thank you!" Jackie dove onto her bed and wrapped her arms around her mom.

Her mother kissed her head. "I know things haven't been easy for you lately, and I want you to have fun."

"I will."

Her mom hugged her tight. "Please be careful, Jackie. I worry about you enough as it is. New York is a totally different place, and we're still not confident that kidnapping threat was a one-off."

Jackie furrowed her brow. "What's going on?"

Her mother hesitated. "It's nothing to worry about; you know the White House gets crank calls and letters all the time. There's nothing major enough to make me think you *shouldn't* go to New York."

"But you're sending an agent with me, aren't you?" Even

though her every movement was watched in D.C., Jackie had hoped that leaving town would give her some freedom.

"Sorry, but yes." She sat up. "For my peace of mind. It's that young female agent—you liked her, didn't you?"

"Agent Fellows is great. I had her last night."

Her mom stood up. She studied Jackie's face. "This isn't forever, you know. Just until we think it's safe for you to go home."

"When will that be? When I go to college? Or is Yale out of the picture now?" She didn't mean it to sound as snappy as it did.

"Jackie . . ." Her mom smoothed the hair off Jackie's brow and cupped her face in her hands. "You are the most important thing in the world to me. I'm only doing this because I love you. And so does Aunt Deborah."

"I know. It's just . . . I want to go home. Please? I miss *my* bed and *my* room." Jackie swallowed. "I hate being watched all the time. I can't even pee without someone knowing."

Her mother stood and walked toward the door. "We're trying to protect you. When we think it's safe, you can go home."

A nasty thought shoved its way into Jackie's mind. *What if it's never safe again?*

FOURTEEN

Lettie hated New York. Today, at least.

Cars honked angrily and people raced past. Laura Beth squealed with excitement, and Jackie actually seemed relaxed. Unlike Lettie, they loved the city.

Just like Taylor.

Everywhere she looked, Lettie only saw Taylor. Taylor running out of the train station; Taylor flirting with the hot-dog guy; Taylor throwing her head back and yelling, *"Are you ready for me, New York?"*

Thinking about Taylor hurt too much right now. Like a wound that refused to heal.

"Can you believe we're here—for two days—with no chaperones!" Laura Beth spun around on the sidewalk and nearly knocked into a guy wearing a suit. He scowled at the girls as he passed.

Jackie adjusted her purse and pointed with her thumb over her shoulder. "You forgot someone."

Agent Fellows stood nearby. She was the only reason Lettie's parents had let her go on this trip. That and Laura Beth's mom picking up the entire bill—something Lettie's papá gave up arguing about years ago.

They pulled rolling suitcases behind them. Laura Beth's was twice as large as Jackie's and three times the size of hers, and Lettie wondered what exactly she had brought. Her own bag was nearly empty—just toiletries, shoes, PJs, a dress for tonight and the fashion show, and a pair of jeans and a shirt.

Jackie had convinced Miss Libby it was silly to take a car eight blocks from the train station to the hotel. Which was fine with Lettie. She'd much rather walk than ride anytime. They followed the crowds up Eighth Avenue to Forty-second Street and walked another block until they were surrounded by neon signs in every direction.

"Oh. My. Lord," Laura Beth gasped. "No matter how many times I see Times Square, I still love all the lights and the people!" She posed. "Jackie, take my picture."

Jackie fiddled with her phone and snapped a shot of Laura Beth.

"Now get your agent to take one of the three of us!"

Agent Fellows was at Jackie's side before she even lifted her hand.

Poor Jackie. I couldn't live like that.

Laura Beth stood between Jackie and Lettie, her arms draped over their shoulders. "Smile, girls!" she shouted over the din of the city.

"C'mon, let's get to our hotel. I need to freshen up after the train ride." Laura Beth set off toward the W Hotel with Jackie, Lettie, and Agent Fellows trailing behind.

Such a change from the quiet train ride up. For the most part, Laura Beth had flipped through a stack of fashion magazines while Jackie had listened to her iPod with her eyes closed. Lettie had sunk into her corner seat and worked her way through her assigned English reading. It was as though Jackie's revelation two days earlier had sucked all the joy out of their time together.

But now, here they were. Laura Beth raced ahead, Jackie laughed, and even Lettie felt the anger of the past two days slowly melt away.

She'd spent most of yesterday with Daniel, going over the fight with Andrew and trying to understand what he'd meant. Then she had lain awake the entire night, trying to decide if she should tell him about Andrew and Taylor.

Finally she realized she had no choice. As much as she wanted to, she couldn't break her promise to Jackie to tell no one, especially Daniel. Because if Daniel knew that his sister and Andrew had had sex, he wouldn't be able to stop himself from confronting Andrew and demanding to know everything else that happened that night—what led up to it and what occurred afterward.

She felt horrible lying to Daniel. Not exactly lying, but withholding the whole truth. In the end, she pleaded with him to let it go, so he could move on with his own life. Daniel had just shaken his head, his jaw set.

"I can't, Lettie. She was my twin. No one was closer than Taylor and me. I owe it to her to get to the bottom of this." He looked so sad and vulnerable all I

wanted to do was kiss away the hurt. His lips were warm and soft. Our kisses, gentle at first, got deeper. I could hear his heart hammering wildly in his chest, matching mine, beat for beat.

When he dropped me off at the corner near my apartment—Papá would have died if he'd seen me alone in a car with a boy—we kissed softly and quickly.

Lettie watched as her two best friends ran through the enormous suite Mrs. Ballou had booked. It was seriously larger than the home she shared with five other people.

What other secrets are there—that I'll have to keep from Daniel?

"You can't wear that!" Laura Beth stared at Jackie in disbelief. "Jackie, this is the pre-party. You *have* to wear something stunning. We *all* do."

Jackie ran her hands over her Marc Jacobs maxidress. "It's a rooftop party in October, Laura Beth. The invite said city casual and it's going to be cold. I'm not wearing sequins and feathers."

"I'm not, either," Lettie said.

Of course Lettie wouldn't. She probably thinks it's too pretentious or something. But her yellow sundress just wasn't cutting it. Wrong season. Wrong time of day.

"Good Lord. They'll have heaters, you know." Laura Beth dug through the closet where she'd hung all her outfits. "Here, Lettie, you wear this." She held up a slinky black cocktail dress with strategically placed cutouts and a bare back.

"I . . . I . . . ," Lettie stammered.

"Lettie looks fine, Laura Beth. And so do I. Friedrick said he wants me to seem natural, untrained. A breath of fresh air."

This is going nowhere. Why do I even bother with these two?

"Fine, but I'm wearing this." Laura Beth held up a cobalt-blue Marchesa with an Empire waist and a scooped neckline. "It's beyond cute on."

Jackie's eyebrows shot up. "It's a little like a cross between a milkmaid and Napoleon's Josephine."

"It's fashion!" Laura Beth scooped up the dress and stormed into the bedroom to change. *I try to be helpful and they tell me I look like a milkmaid. Well, Jackie looks like she's about thirty in that dress, and Lettie looks all kinds of wrong.*

She tugged on her favorite dark blue Chantelle bra and panties. Laura Beth hadn't come to New York just to be part of Jackie's entourage. She planned on seeing Sol as much as possible. In fact, they were supposed to meet tonight, after the pre-party. *Thank the Lord tomorrow is the big night, or I'd be pulling my hair out right about now.*

Laura Beth hadn't told her friends about her plans. She was waiting for just the right moment—like tonight, when they were back from the party and sitting around watching movies on the sitting room's plasma TV. *Lettie's going to be scandalized, I'm sure, but Jackie will understand. Before her fallout with Andrew, all she wanted was to jump him. Taylor kept telling her to go for it.*

She paused. *And then she slept with him herself. Nice one, Taylor.*

The car ride—thankfully Agent Fellows put a stop to Lettie and Jackie's silly notion about taking the subway—took about twenty minutes. The whole time, Jackie kept her iPhone in hand, scrolling and typing.

She can't possibly be texting Andrew—not after what she told us.

But if it wasn't Andrew, who was it?

The car stopped in front of a run-down-looking set of metal garage doors.

"Is this it?" Lettie asked, wrinkling her forehead. "It looks like we're at a skate park or something."

Jackie checked her phone and leaned closer to the driver. "Is this right?" She showed him the address.

"That's this place right here," he said in an accent Laura Beth couldn't place.

Agent Fellows got out of the car first. To the left of the garage doors was a smaller door with a sign taped to it.

"FVD Party Here," it read.

Laura Beth patted her hair and adjusted her dress. Time for a real New York party. "Okay, ladies. We're on!"

For a moment, Jackie thought they'd crashed someone else's party. Or non-party. There were no canapés or even a bar. Just a few people sitting on floor cushions, drinking and passing joints around, while everyone else huddled in tight groups.

There were no heat lamps.

And it was cold.

Unlike the girls, everyone wore dark skinny jeans—even the guys!—heavy coats, fabulous scarves, and hats.

Laura Beth stood in stunned silence next to her. *Bet she wishes she was wearing something else now.*

"Jaaaa-ckieeee!" A stocky, muscular guy wearing dark-rimmed glasses and a pale purple scarf bounded across the roof toward her. "You look fabulous! Absolutely exactly as I thought you'd be!"

He had a heavy Midwestern accent. She'd expected someone tiny, effeminate. Someone European. But this guy . . .

"It's nice to meet you, too, Friedrick."

She held out her hand, but he wrapped his beefy arms around her and pulled her close. "We're huggers around here."

Jackie smiled politely. *We're so not in the District anymore,* she thought as he released her. "These are my friends, Laura Beth Ballou and Lettie Velasquez."

Laura Beth giggled when Friedrick extended the same full-body hug to her. "Call me LB," she said.

Since when did she *like* that name?

"I just love what you've done up here. Are those the models for tomorrow?" Laura Beth asked in a breathy voice.

Next to Laura Beth, Lettie stood stiffly with a forced smile on her face, bracing for her hug.

"Did you forget someone?" Friedrick asked, moving his eyes in the direction of Agent Fellows, who stood near the door but still within easy reach.

"That's Jackie's Secret Service agent," Laura Beth babbled. Jackie groaned inwardly. She didn't want everyone knowing she had to travel with an escort. "She doesn't care what we do, as long as you don't hurt Jackie."

"Fancy," Friedrick said, leading the girls over to the circle of people sitting on the ground.

"LB, I do approve of your choice of dress this evening," Friedrick said to a beaming Laura Beth. He reached over and grabbed Jackie's arm and pulled her in front of him.

"Hey, everyone, this is Jackie Whitman and her two friends, LB and Lettie. And that darling creature back there is a Secret Service agent." He play-whispered the last words loudly: "So don't mess with Jackie, or you might get laid out."

The group on the floor laughed.

Great. Now everyone knows. Way to go, LB.

A few people moved around so that the three girls could sit down. Friedrick took a spot directly across from Jackie.

"Are you nervous about walking tomorrow?" asked a girl in a gray peacoat and beanie. Her straight brown hair hung down past her breasts. "I was the first time, you know. It's freaky seeing all those people out there, staring at you. Waiting for you to fall or something so they can tweet it or YouTube it."

Laura Beth leaned across Jackie. "She stands in front of crowds all the time. Jackie's a pro."

The girl snorted. "Standing and walking are two completely different things."

Someone passed Lettie a joint, and she handed it to Jackie without taking a hit.

"Do you girls not smoke?" Friedrick asked, raising an eyebrow.

"Of course!" Laura Beth took the joint from Jackie and inhaled.

"Oh, good! I thought maybe we had some cherries here!" The group laughed again.

Lettie rolled her eyes at Jackie. "Who *are* these people?" she whispered.

This isn't at all what I expected. It's more like what I imagine an art school party to be, not a fashion event. Where's the wine and magazine editors? Where's the glamour?

Once the joint had made its way around the loose circle, Friedrick tilted his head back and inhaled deeply. "Picture time, girls. Let's see what you have."

The girls, or women—Jackie wasn't sure how old most of them were, but the youngest looked about sixteen—shrugged off their jackets and began posing provocatively. A few of the guys snapped pictures on their cell phones.

Uneasiness rolled over Jackie. This was too similar to what had happened at Princeton. The last thing she needed was pictures of her at a stoner party splashed across the *Washington Tattler*.

"Jackie, doll, don't be shy. This is how I warm the girls up before the show." A girl prowled the ground on all fours, like a tiger. "It's fun! Isn't it, girls?"

It looked ridiculous, not fun. Lettie was basically holding Laura Beth down so she wouldn't join in. *Good Lord. That's just what we need, Laura Beth high as a kite flashing her undies at everyone.*

Jackie smiled politely. "I'll pass. I don't want to ruin my dress."

"Then take it off. We're all friends here. Besides, it's not like we haven't seen a little T and A before."

The models around her laughed, and Jackie felt herself blush. The camera flashed in her direction.

"Umm . . . Friedrick, I really wish you wouldn't take pictures of me."

Laura Beth rolled onto her back and stared up at the sky. "Live a little, Jackie. We're having fun. Right, Lets?"

Lettie shook her head and motioned to the door. Jackie bit her thumbnail. She'd love to leave—everything about this situation seemed wrong—but she didn't want to seem rude.

The camera flashed in her face again. Before she could register what was happening, Agent Fellows was in Friedrick's face.

"Miss Whitman asked that you not take any pictures, sir." Agent Fellows took his camera, deleted the pictures, then handed it back. "Please do not do that again."

"C'mon, Jackie, let's go," Lettie said, pulling her jacket up closer to her neck.

A very stoned Laura Beth leaned against Jackie's leg. "Do we have to leave?" She giggled. "I'm havin' a great time."

Jackie bit her lip. This looked like a setup. What if all Friedrick wanted were some candid shots to sell to the tabloids? The only thing the girls knew about him, after all, was that he was a rising designer. They'd come to the party expecting a highbrow fashion event, not some pathetic pot party on a warehouse roof. What if his show was more of the same thing? Jackie couldn't afford to associate with people like this. It could ruin her mother's career.

Friedrick touched Jackie on the arm. "Jackie, darling, I didn't mean to upset you. Forgive me a thousand times?" His pupils were dilated, but he looked genuinely repentant. Like a naughty kid caught doing something bad. "I swear, it was all in good fun. Wasn't it, friends?"

A chorus of voices filled the air:

"Yeah!"

"Sure!"

"It's totally cool!"

Jackie scanned the group. Maybe she *was* overreacting.

"I'm tired, Friedrick. If you want me to look my best tomorrow, I need to get some sleep."

Friedrick clapped his hands in excitement. "So we're still friends! Excellent!"

Lettie had pulled Laura Beth to her feet and was ushering her toward the door, where Agent Fellows waited.

Friedrick embraced Jackie. "Remember. Fresh face tomorrow. No makeup, no hair product. Just you and your natural beauty. Okay?"

"Okay."

The designer kissed her cheek. "Fantastic. See you tomorrow."

FIFTEEN

The little party from the night before had mushroomed into a thousand-person mob arguing at the doors for a seat at the fashion show. Jackie peeked between the curtains separating the side stage from the audience. Fashionistas and reporters filled every seat plus all the available standing space. Through the double doors at the back, she could see frantic event workers trying to hold back the crowd.

Behind her, Friedrick paced nervously and yelled orders to the dressers: "Not the green hat, you ninny. Lola wears the blue. Lola *always* wears the blue."

As Jackie watched him work, she let go of her worries from the night before. Friedrick was a businessman. That's all. He hadn't wanted to embarrass her or sell photos to the tabloids. She was being crazy.

"Tell me." He paused next to Jackie. "Is it empty? Did no one come?"

She dropped the curtain and smiled at the designer. "A packed house. Not even standing room."

Friedrick grabbed her face with both hands and kissed Jackie firmly on the lips. "Ah-may-zing!"

So they're huggers and *kissers around here,* she thought as Friedrick rushed off, barking orders at the models and dressers.

Jackie still wore a robe and curlers in her hair. Since she walked last—in the signature piece of the collection—she had a few extra minutes the other girls didn't have.

"Laura Beth would love it back here," she whispered as she watched the finely tuned chaos backstage. Half-dressed models, dressers with pins in their mouths, hairstylists making last minute fixes to the ridiculously high hair Friedrick demanded.

She hadn't seen her dress yet. Friedrick insisted it be a surprise. Which, to be honest, worried Jackie a little. So far, all the other girls wore sheer dresses and no bras.

I can see the headlines now: "First Girlfriend Shows All." Right above a picture of my nipples. Mom and Aunt Deborah will love that.

"Miss Whitman? I need to finish your hair."

Jackie followed the hairstylist through the throng of models to a chair. A team of two yanked the Velcro curlers from her hair and began jabbing in bobby pins.

"What are you doing?" she asked, and wished that they had let her face the mirror.

"Your hair," replied the younger guy stylist in a snooty voice.

A woman walked toward them carrying what looked to be a giant set of crystal antlers. It took Jackie a second to realize they were for her. To wear.

Oh, God, no.

"Hold still now, sugar pie, we have to make sure these don't slip. Otherwise my ass is grass."

"I'm wearing *antlers*?" Jackie sputtered.

"One-hundred-and-fifty-thousand-dollar crystal-and-diamond antlers. This is haute couture, don't you know."

Suddenly, Jackie regretted the milkmaid costume jokes she and Lettie had lobbed at Laura Beth the night before.

The antlers weighed a ton and made her neck hurt. "So, I guess I'm stepping into my dress?"

"You're about to find out." Another woman—a dresser— took her hand and led Jackie to a rolling rack with only one black garment bag on it.

As the dresser unzipped the bag, Jackie held her breath.

The multitone dress was stunning. Friedrick had draped feathers on the shoulders to resemble moss. And the sheer skirt flounced midthigh, over crinoline. But there was something earthy and natural about the whole look.

Jackie stepped into the dress and waited for her team to lace and hook her in. She rolled her shoulders and hoped the elaborate headdress didn't make her walk funny.

One last check from the makeup artist and it was go time.

Don't fall. Whatever you do, don't fall.

Camera flashes blinded Jackie when she turned the corner onto the catwalk.

"Walk from your hips. Shoulders back, head up," Laura Beth had told her before leaving the hotel room. *"And whatever you do, don't look down. You'll trip if you stare at your feet."*

Jackie's stomach churned when she took the first step forward, but she kept her head up. It was impossible not to with the antlers perched precariously on her head. The model from the night before was right, walking in front of people was a lot harder than standing.

Music pulsed around her. Jackie reached the end of the runway. Moved right, pivoted left, and strutted back up the catwalk.

"You were brilliant! Brilliant!" Friedrick crushed Jackie to him, completely disregarding her headgear. "I couldn't ask for a better woodswoman to close the show. My little deer in the headlights. So fucking brilliant."

Jackie froze. "Your what?"

Friedrick grinned. "The theme of my collection was invasion of privacy. Who better to illustrate that than you? The girl who has a Secret Service agent with her at all times."

Jackie glared at him. Oh, hell, no.

"I thought it was about milkmaids and woodland creatures."

Friedrick shrugged. "This is my art, and art is always political. We live in a culture where anyone can be famous, and where those who are often don't want what goes with it."

She knew exactly what that meant, but she didn't care. Friedrick had used her, and it pissed her off.

"Come, it's time for me to take my victory lap." He wrapped his arm around Jackie's shoulder and guided her toward the stage.

Asshole.

He laced his fingers through hers and dragged Jackie out onstage. Laura Beth and Lettie waved wildly from the front row right.

"Oh, my gosh! Thank you. Thank all of you. I'm so happy

you've blessed me with a chance to share my designs." The crowd clapped loudly.

And Jackie saw her opportunity.

She smiled sweetly at Friedrick. "I know this is unorthodox, but I have to let you all know how wonderful Friedrick Von-Drak is—he's donating one hundred percent of the proceeds from the auction of this dress—and the antlers—to a charity that's dear to my heart—the Veterans Rights Activist Group. Isn't he wonderful?"

She felt the designer tense up next to her, but he kept smiling.

"The auction will happen at the after-party. I hope to see you all there!"

Jackie spun around, leaving the stunned designer alone on the stage.

"I nearly peed myself. Seriously. What made you do that?" Lettie giggled as the three girls piled into a town car for the ride back to the hotel. After her announcement, Jackie decided to skip the after-party, saying she'd already done enough for that asshole. After all, most of those people probably came to see her, not his weird clothes.

Jackie slumped into the backseat and kicked off her shoes. "I don't know. It just seemed like the right thing to do. VRAG needs money, so why not?"

Lettie nodded in agreement. As depressed as Jackie had been lately, it was nice to see her laugh.

"Can y'all drop me off somewhere? I have plans with Sol."

Laura Beth dug through her bag like she wasn't excited, but a huge smile stretched across her face.

Jackie noticed, too. "Plans? As in dinner or something else?"

Laura Beth dropped her bag and Lettie caught a glimpse of something pink and lacy inside. "Well"—Laura Beth blushed—"I've decided tonight's *the* night. I'm going to sleep with Sol." She winked. "After we go to dinner."

Lettie twisted her hands together. She'd replayed Aamina's party over in her mind a hundred times, and every time she swore it *was* Sol who went off with Whitney. "Laura Beth, do you think you should? I mean, your mom doesn't even want you dating him."

Jackie shook her head. "What better place? She's far away from Miss Libby and her prying eyes. I swear, Laura Beth, your mom should get a job working for the Secret Service."

Laura Beth bounced nervously on the seat. "Should I tell him? Would that be weird? Or should I just let things unfold?"

"Don't tell him! It would be too weird sitting across from each other at dinner thinking about what you're going to do next," Jackie said.

Jackie pulled open the partition between the girls and the front seat back. "Can you drop Laura Beth off at this address?" She held out her hand to Laura Beth, who handed Jackie her phone.

"Yes, Miss Whitman. Should take about twenty minutes."

Once she'd closed the partition, Jackie grinned and said, "Our little Laura Beth is growing up, Lettie!"

Laura Beth ducked her head. "You guys! Stop teasing me! This is serious."

Jackie's iPhone buzzed and she flipped it open. As she read, her face moved from amusement to excitement.

"Lettie!" she yelled. "You get to stay! Mom and Aunt Deborah did it! You don't have to go to Paraguay!"

The world went fuzzy and warm and quiet before sound rushed back into Lettie's ears. "What? I'm staying? It's okay?"

Jackie practically bounced in her seat. "Yes! Listen:

"Excelsior has agreed to keep Lettie on as an 'exchange student,' which will be good until the end of the school year."

Lettie's elation evaporated. What about after graduation? What about college?

But Jackie was still reading.

In order to stay on in the U.S., however, she needs to petition the Justice Department to change her legal status under the new immigration law. We can hire an immigration lawyer to help her do that. I'll give her parents a call tomorrow to explain everything to them, through a translator. Hope you're having fun in New York. Love you! Mom.

Jackie studied Lettie's face. "What's wrong?"

Lettie felt awkward, not wanting to sound ungrateful.

"What if my application gets rejected, Jackie?"

Jackie leaned forward and looked right into her eyes. "We'll cross that bridge when and if we get to it. But I doubt that will happen. You'd be a wonderful candidate for legal residency. They'd be lucky to have you."

Laura Beth hugged her friend. "Of course they would!

Anyway, by the time Mama, Jackie's mom, and the president weigh in, they won't dare say no."

Lettie tried to squelch the nagging doubts—or at least tuck them away into a far corner of her brain. "Thanks, guys."

"Looks like this is a big night for two of us!" Laura Beth said. "You get to stay and I get my man."

Lettie gazed out of the window. Maybe it would all come true. She could stay. With her friends. Finish her senior year and go on to college.

But Mamá and Papá and Maribel and Christa wouldn't be here.

The candlelight cast a warm glow across Sol's face. So far, everything was perfect: the food, the atmosphere, the conversation.

Before leaving for the show, Laura Beth had nervously folded her lingerie into her handbag just in case, along with a bottle of perfume and a few scented candles. She wasn't chancing anything. And when Jackie decided to skip the after-party, Laura Beth immediately called Sol and moved up their date. He'd asked her to meet him at a place near his apartment.

"I'm happy you're here," Sol said, reaching across the table and rubbing the back of her hand with his fingertips. "It's fun getting to show you *my* city."

Sol often joked that everywhere they went in D.C. had a Capital Girls story connected to it. Maybe that was true, but what did he expect? She'd lived there her whole life, and it was a small town after all.

The waiter left the check on the table, and Sol placed his credit card inside without even looking at the total.

"So, do I get to see your apartment tonight? I've been wondering about it all day." Laura Beth hoped it didn't sound too forward. The whole time they were eating, she couldn't help thinking that everything she said sounded like "I want to have sex with you."

I like your shirt . . . translation: Take it off. You have crumbs on your lips . . . I want to kiss you. It was like there was a whole new way of speaking now that she'd made up her mind to sleep with Sol.

Her boyfriend laughed. "I'm warning you, it's nothing like my parents' place in D.C. I don't have a maid—my dad thought I should learn to take care of myself."

I hope it's not too messy. That will destroy my mood.

They linked arms as they strolled along the Upper West Side near the Columbia campus. Laura Beth inhaled deeply, wanting to remember every minute of this night.

"This is it." They'd stopped before an old but attractive brownstone building.

"Welcome home, Mr. Molla," the doorman said as they entered. They stepped inside the elevator.

Laura Beth's heart raced faster with each floor they passed. This was happening. Tonight. To her.

Sol squeezed her hand and smiled. "I don't bring many girls here." He gave a nervous laugh. "I mean, I don't, you know—"

"It's okay. I know what you mean." The elevator doors parted and they stepped out, not into a hallway, as she'd expected, but into the entryway of a penthouse.

Laura Beth spun around, admiring the massive pristine space. It wasn't exactly the simple bachelor pad she'd imagined. "This is some dorm room!" she joked.

Sol watched her carefully. "Do you like it? I know it's a bit much for college, but . . ."

"It's gorgeous." She shimmied away from Sol and batted her eyes. "Kind of like you."

He closed the small distance between them and pressed his soft lips against Laura Beth's neck. She sighed as heat radiated from every spot he touched. When she threw her arms around his neck, Sol scooped her up and carried her to the dark gray couch. Just like Rhett Butler and Scarlett O'Hara.

He set her down gently, so that her head rested against the low arm of the couch, and stared at her. His eyes looked ebony in the half-light.

Her breath hitched slightly when he kissed each of her fingers, one at a time.

I need to change and get everything set up. I need . . .

Sol rested on his side, his body pressed into hers. *Should I unbutton his shirt? Or wait for him?* This was when she needed Taylor. Jackie and Lettie had no idea how any of this worked, either, and if she messed this up because she didn't know what to do . . .

"Laura Beth?" Sol said, tracing her lips with his finger.

"Hmm . . ."

"I meant it when I said you're unlike any girl I've ever met." He nibbled on her neck. "I've totally fallen for you."

Laura Beth's heart skipped and she reached over to pull Sol closer to her. *Maybe I don't need the candles and lingerie after all.*

Her fingers shook as she unbuttoned Sol's shirt. His skin was so smooth. "You look better like that," she said. And then she wondered if that was too slutty.

Sol ran his hand up her back and gently pulled down the zipper on her dress. Laura Beth gasped.

"Is this okay?" Sol asked.

You can stop if you want to. If you're not ready, you can stop, Laura Beth reminded herself. She lifted her head and found herself gazing into Sol's eyes. "Yes."

Her dress slipped lower and Laura Beth instinctively folded an arm across her chest, before dropping it to her side. *You're being silly,* she thought. *He's seen you in a bikini.*

But this was different. Everything was coming off. And when it did, there was no going back.

She reached out to Sol and pulled him to her. When they kissed, she tasted the wine they'd had at dinner and the mint candy afterward. Laura Beth opened her eyes and admired the way the soft light in the room backlit him. He looked better than gorgeous.

Suddenly Sol sat up, breaking the spell surrounding them.

"I need to tell you something first. The truth."

Time stopped and fear crept into Laura Beth. She forced a smile, the way her mama taught her to do when faced with unpleasant news. "You mean about the rumors about your parents?"

Sol pinched the bridge of his nose and then ran his hand through his dark wavy hair. "No. Things are better. They convinced their donors to come back, even if they haven't convinced the press to change their story. We're moving past it."

"Then what?" Laura Beth ran through a list of possibilities, but nothing seemed serious enough to stop what they'd started. At least not that abruptly.

"I'm telling you this because I don't want any secrets between us. Do you understand?"

Laura Beth nodded.

"At Aamina's party this summer, right after I got there, Andrew introduced me to Whitney, and . . ."

Laura Beth felt sick.

Sol paused, his eyes locked on hers. "I don't how it happened, and you've no idea how sorry I am, but we hooked up."

It was as if he'd punched her in the stomach, but she kept herself calm, the way a real lady would. "A few kisses the night we met? We barely knew each other, Sol. It's okay."

"No. We went further than that." He paused, staring at her like he didn't want to say anything more. But he went on. "We had sex."

"You *slept* with Whitney Remick?" Laura Beth's hands shook. "With that awful girl? What were you thinking?"

Sol moved to take her hand in his, but she pushed him aside and leapt off the couch.

"Laura Beth, wait. We need to talk about this. Don't go," he pleaded. "I can't explain why it happened with Whitney. I don't usually sleep with girls I've just met. You know me well enough to know that." He came up beside her. "I made a huge mistake and I'm trying to set it right because I'm falling in love with you."

He'd just said the words she'd been dying to hear. *He's falling in love with me.* She hesitated. *Maybe I should hear him out.* Then she thought of Sol with Whitney, and the warmth his words had brought fled. *Or maybe I should get out of here before I do something I'll regret for the rest of my life.*

With a flip of her hair, Laura Beth zipped up her dress and snatched her handbag off the sofa. "I have enough problems in my life. I don't need one more."

She stormed over to the elevator and left.

SIXTEEN

"Thanks for ditching me," Whitney said to Angie Meehan as she leaned heavily against the wall of lockers. They ignored the crush of students pushing past them, all sharing their college tour stories from fall break.

Angie rolled her eyes as she fumbled around in her locker. "I can't help it that my parents made me tour colleges. Trust me, spending time with my mom is worse than listening to Jackie talk about how fabulous she is."

"Whatever." Whitney spun the combo lock on some kid's locker. For the past four days, she'd been bored out of her mind, trapped in D.C. Bored. Bored. Bored.

"You and Franklin had fun, didn't you? Carter said the three of you hung out, like, every day."

Whitney bashed her head against the locker and huffed. "If

you call sitting in a dark basement smoking pot and watching Three Stooges movies fun. . . ."

Angie leaned closer to Whitney and patted her hand. "What's wrong? Is D.C. not as exciting as L.A.?"

"Is that even a question?" She'd been in a bad mood since her mom dissed her dirt on Ankie. She didn't need Angie mocking her, too.

Angie recoiled. "Don't you think it's time you stopped moping and tried to like it here? We're not all boring, you know."

Whitney clenched her jaw and bit her lip. When she wasn't with Carter and Franklin, she'd spent the entire break trying to figure out how to get her mom invited to the White House parties. Angie's dad had connections, but he was a Republican. And Jackie hated Angie, so she wasn't likely to get an invite without . . .

LB.

Whitney spied her first. Unlike most other times of the day, this morning she was alone.

"Hey, LB, what's with the sour, grinchy frown?" Whitney called, her voice suddenly upbeat.

Angie chuckled and slammed her locker shut.

Laura Beth kept walking, as if she hadn't heard her.

What the fuck?

"Laura Beth! Are you deaf? I'm talking to you," Whitney said louder.

When Laura Beth turned, her hazel eyes flashed with anger.

"Slut." Even though the hallway was packed with girls, the word hung in the air and sucked up all the space around it.

Okay. I've been called worse. Whitney kept her face impassive. But her mind was spinning. Something had riled Laura Beth and she needed to know what. "Looks like someone woke up on the wrong side of the bed. Walk with me to class, LB. We can talk."

Laura Beth tossed her hair and kept walking, completely ignoring Whitney's demand.

Angie's eyes grew wide. Whitney had never told her what she had on LB, but Angie had more or less guessed there was something. And now she knew Laura Beth didn't care anymore.

Whitney, Angie on her heels, pushed past the few girls between her and LB. She noticed that despite her best efforts to hide it, LB was nervous. Or scared. Or both.

"Wait up, bestie. I have a secret to tell you," Whitney said when she caught up with her.

Laura Beth stopped abruptly and pivoted. "I'm not your bestie. I'm not even your friend. So fuck off."

She spun around and continued down the hallway.

"Damn. Looks like little LB grew some lady balls." Angie giggled.

"Shut. Up." Whitney's eyes searched the hallway, but LB had vanished. A few younger girls tried to hide their smiles as she brushed past them and headed for the bathroom.

Whitney gave them her best "What are you looking at?" glare, and the girls scattered.

It didn't make sense. LB couldn't turn on her like that—not when Whitney held all the power. Something had changed, but damned if she knew what.

She locked herself in a stall and slouched against the door. "Damn it," she whispered. Clearly, LB was pissed . . . and it must be bad enough that she'd take a chance on Whitney spilling her secret.

Bad enough that she'd risk losing Jackie as her BFF.

"Shit. Shit. Shit." Whitney banged her head against the metal door. *If LB's not vouching for me, there's no way I'm getting invited to any more* Crapital *Girl parties. And my mom will be totally blackballed.*

A long sniff from the stall next to hers.

Fan-fucking-tastic. Somebody else is having a pity party.

Papá had been clear: Lettie had to return to Paraguay. It didn't matter that the president and the chief of staff had pulled a few strings to allow her to stay in the States. It didn't matter that secret angels had offered to pay her tuition. No. All that mattered was that she was a girl, and girls needed to be at home, with their parents, until they married.

Were they planning on moving to Princeton with me? Or were they just indulging my fantasy?

Paz offered to let her stay with him. Insisted, actually. Promising Papá that he'd watch out for Lettie and she'd make sure he ate well. He swore he'd keep her safe and out of trouble.

But in the end, it came down to Mamá. She didn't like the idea of Lettie living with Paz, not knowing what sorts of friends would be hanging around. "No, Lettie. It isn't right. You can't live like that."

So everything was for nothing. She'd told Jackie before first period and watched as her face crumpled.

"Lettie, oh, Lets. No. We'll figure something out. You can't leave now. We need you—Laura Beth and me. And Daniel. You have to stay," she pleaded.

As usual, Lettie found herself being the strong one, hugging Jackie when in fact Jackie should have been comforting her.

That's how it always was. When things went bad, Lettie propped everyone up. That was her role.

Like after the fashion show. Jackie was pissed about Friedrick using her; Laura Beth sat crying on the couch, going on and on about how her night was ruined but wouldn't say why; and the whole time, Lettie sat there, soothing both of them—being their rock.

But who's my rock now that Taylor's gone?

Her heart sank. All these years, she'd thought Taylor was her best friend. The person she was closest to. But she didn't really know anything about her—or her secrets. It made her worry that she didn't really know Jackie or Laura Beth, either.

With one last sniff, she opened the bathroom door and walked to the sink. The cool water felt good on her tired eyes and hot cheeks.

"Need some of these?" Whitney stood a little off to Lettie's left, holding a small bottle of eyedrops. Their eyes met in the mirror. She looked almost as bad as Lettie.

"Thanks." Lettie took the bottle from Whitney and squeezed the drops in her eyes.

I know Jackie and Laura Beth hate her, but Whitney's not that bad. Ever since Whitney's pregnancy scare, when Lettie saw her vulnerable side—she just couldn't hate Whitney. Maybe if her friends tried being nice to her, Whitney would relax and stop being a pain in the ass.

Besides, the night they'd slept over at the White House was fun. Sure, the mood changed when Whitney showed up, but she was good for a laugh and she could drink them all under the table. And her impersonation of Mrs. Ballou was even better than Jackie's.

Whitney definitely had a good side. If only she'd show it more.

Lettie tore off a paper towel and blotted her damp face and neck. "Everything okay?" Whitney asked.

"Not really." Lettie swallowed a huge gulp of air and steadied herself against the sink. "I'm moving back to Paraguay, the day after Thanksgiving."

"Oh, Lettie. I'm sorry." Whitney stretched out her arms.

When Lettie hesitated, Whitney laughed. "What? I won't bite."

The dam holding Lettie's tears opened.

"You know the worst part?" Lettie said between sobs. "Excelsior agreed to change my status to exchange student and Carolyn Shaw found patrons to pay my tuition. But my parents won't let me stay—they don't think my brother is mature enough to look out for me."

Whitney held Lettie at arm's length. "Wait. The only reason you can't stay is because your parents want you to be with real adults?"

Lettie sniffed. "Uh-huh."

A smile stretched across Whitney's face. "Why didn't you say something? We have a big apartment and two empty guest rooms. I bet my parents would totally let you stay with us."

Hope filled Lettie's heart. Maybe this was the solution. Maybe she could stay after all. But this was *Whitney*—the girl Jackie and Laura Beth hated.

But did it matter what her friends thought, if it meant she could stay?

Lettie dropped her used paper towel in the garbage. "Do you think your parents would say yes?"

Whitney winked. "We'll be picking out furniture by this afternoon."

Laura Beth picked a carrot out of the organic salad from Excelsior's catered lunch offerings. For the first time in days, she didn't look as if she'd been crying. In fact, she looked almost . . . relieved.

She still hadn't told Jackie or Lettie about what had happened that night with Sol in New York. But it was obvious things had gone horribly wrong. When Laura Beth had returned to their hotel room, no amount of chocolate from the minibar or room service ice-cream sundaes had calmed her down. But she wouldn't talk about it.

"What are we gonna do?" Laura Beth said, spearing a slice of roasted artichoke with her fork. "We can't let Lettie move in with Whitney."

"Do you have a better idea?" Jackie asked. "She can't stay with me—not while I'm at the White House. Plus, her parents know Mom is hardly ever home."

Laura Beth swallowed. "I'm calling Mama. She'll take care of this. I won't have Lettie living in that viper pit. Lord knows Tracey Mills will probably start pumping *her,* too, for info about all of us." She tapped the keyboard of her phone. When Jackie frowned, Laura Beth added, "Have you forgotten the whole 'pretend engagement' leak?"

Jackie sighed. Of course she hadn't forgotten. But what choice did Lettie have?

"Mama?" Laura Beth was saying into her cell. "You need to do something about this. Lettie is movin' in with Whitney Remick."

Laura Beth rolled her eyes. "I know they're both my friends, Mama. But have you forgotten who Whitney's mama is?"

Poor Lettie. She's totally going to be a ping-pong between Libby Ballou and Tracey Mills.

Laura Beth scrunched up her face and huffed. "Mama, Whitney's parents are Democrats. And Whitney runs around with Franklin Johnson! You can't let her live there."

Jackie could hear Libby's Southern twang through the phone but couldn't really make out her words. She kept her eyes on Laura Beth, watching her lips go from tight and pinched to smiling.

"You're the best, Mama! Mwah. Love you too!" Laura Beth hung up the phone and beamed at Jackie. "Lettie can stay with us! Isn't that wonderful!"

"What did your mom say, exactly?"

Laura Beth waved her hand around. "Oh, just some nonsense about Tracey Mills and the elections and gossip or something. I don't know. I wasn't listening to that part." She gathered all her lunch and shoved it back into her bag. "Let's go find Lettie and tell her the good news!"

Jackie shook her head. "She's with her counselor, remember? Going over her transfer plans."

"To *Paraguay*? They're practically having a civil war, Jackie!" Laura Beth put her hands on her hips. "Besides, this is so excitin', and she doesn't need those plans now. C'mon. We've got work to do."

Libby Ballou or Tracey Mills. Not a choice I'd want to make.

Jackie followed Laura Beth to the counselor's office. Laura Beth knocked once and entered without waiting. Lettie sat in a chair with her back to them.

"Excuse me, Mrs. Preston, but Lettie doesn't need to be here."
She turned to Lettie. "I've fixed it! You can stay with us!
Isn't that wonderful? It'll be like havin' a sister—except I know
you already have two, but you know I don't and I've always
wanted one. It'll be so much fun."

She's in Mama mode, Jackie thought as she watched Laura Beth
completely ignore Lettie's stunned look and the counselor's stern
glare.

"But I'm staying with Whitney—that is, if Papá and Mamá
agree."

Laura Beth pulled Lettie out of the chair and toward the
door. "You don't mind if I take her, do you?" she said to the
counselor.

"I'll be right back, Mrs. Preston," Lettie said over her shoulder.

"No, she won't," Laura Beth sang from the hallway.

When Laura Beth got going, it was better just to stand back
and watch. Unless you enjoyed being steamrolled.

"Lettie, you don't want to stay with Whitney. Not after . . ."
Laura Beth's face clouded for a second. "Well, you know who
her mama is. That says it all right there."

Jackie's eyes darted between her two friends. Lettie clearly
wasn't comfortable, and Laura Beth was totally oblivious to it.
"Laura Beth, why don't you give Lettie some time to talk it over
with her parents. They still have to say yes."

Lettie played with her ponytail, her eyes trained on the
floor. "It's okay, Jackie." She smiled at Laura Beth. "I appreciate
your offer, but if my parents say it's okay, I'm going to stay with
Whitney."

Laura Beth's pale complexion flushed red. "You're what?
You're pickin' Whitney over me? Is that what you're doin'? Cuz I

fail to see the logic in this." Her Southern accent came out thick as syrup.

This isn't going to end well.

"It's not between you and Whitney, Laura Beth. It's just that . . ." She paused and looked at Jackie. Her eyes said everything, and Jackie nodded. "I'm not sure if I could live with your mother."

And here it comes.

Laura Beth recoiled. "What's wrong with Mama? She's offerin' you a place to live so you don't have to go back to that horrible country."

Silence.

Jackie stood waiting, with her mouth slightly open. But instead of crying or getting mad, Lettie simply raised her chin, looked Laura Beth in the eyes, and said, "And that is why I can't stay with you. Allowing your mother to treat me like some sort of abandoned puppy who needs rescuing."

Shock registered on Laura Beth's face. But before she could say anything, Lettie continued: "And by the way, Paraguay is *not* a horrible country." Her voice rose an octave. "It is beautiful and has *chipa guasu* and *guarania* and it's the reason I'm here today."

The group fell silent again. The tension was so thick, Jackie felt as if she couldn't breathe. Lettie had never let Laura Beth have it like that before, even if she deserved it.

For a few moments, something unspoken passed between them. Then Laura Beth nodded and blinked back tears. "You're right. You're probably better off at Whitney's." She flashed a meager smile. "I'll see you girls later, I have to call Mama."

When she was gone, Jackie said, "Are you sure you want to live with Tracey Mills?"

Lettie sighed. "Not at all, but between Mrs. Ballou and Tracey Mills, I'll take my chances with Tracey. Besides, I'm too boring to gossip about. But you'd better stay far away while I live there."

Jackie nodded. "Don't worry, I will."

SEVENTEEN

Logs crackled in the fireplace and the whole house smelled like Thanksgiving turkey and sweet potatoes. Laura Beth's stomach growled like a starving dog. She placed her hand over it and blushed.

"I've been savin' up all day. Our cooks make the most amazin' feast," she said to the petite girl sitting on the love seat across from her. "There's no way I can eat anything during the day without blowin' up like a balloon."

Dina Ives, the senator's daughter, rolled her eyes. "Laura Beth, there's not an ounce of fat on you anywhere. I can't imagine, with all the dancing Daddy says you do, that you could gain weight if you tried."

There was something condescending about the way Dina said it. But ever the good host, Laura Beth said, "Well, just you wait till you see what Mama dreamed up this year. You won't be eatin' until Christmas either."

"I'm looking forward to it."

Laura Beth stood and walked over to the large picture window overlooking the street. In the fall and winter, this was one of her favorite scenes—the streets of Georgetown filled with partygoers moving from one house to another. When she was little, she used to sit there for hours and watch the ladies in furs and men in tuxedos step out of their town cars before being swallowed up by the mansions lining her street. She couldn't wait to grow up and be just like them.

"How are you liking Excelsior?" Laura Beth turned around and asked. When Dina had first transferred, of course, her mama had volunteered Laura Beth to show her around. She hadn't minded—*at first*. It was always good to get in with another senator's daughter. But Dina gave Whitney a run in the "most irritating" category. *So now I have two Cali misfits I gotta put up with.* And then she starting hanging out, not just with Whitney, but with Angie, too.

Dina fidgeted with her skirt. "It's so nice to be at an all girls' school, but I miss competing with boys. I mean, we *are* going to have to learn to work with them in the real world, right?"

Laura Beth's lips pressed into a tight smile. She loved Excelsior and her all girls' education. *Real ladies don't compete with boys, we charm and manipulate them into givin' us what we want.*

"If you say so," she said.

"How come your friends are Democrats?" Dina tossed her glossy black hair over her shoulder. "That did surprise me—the way you all hang out together. Doesn't it ever get weird? Like when your parents are on opposite sides of issues?"

"No." Laura Beth clenched her jaw. Her eyes darted to the large clock sitting on the mantel. *How much longer do I have to entertain her? Thank God her sister came down with a cold and had to cancel.*

Dina lifted her eyebrows. "Really? You mean to tell me, when Jackie's mom pushed immigration reform, neither of you discussed it? How about your other friend, Lettie? Doesn't she get to stay here because of that law? I know we *true* Republicans were against it."

"We leave politics out of our friendship."

Dina tilted her head and smiled. "Interesting."

There is nothing, not one thing, I like about this girl other than her fabulous hair. Dina's hair was everything Laura Beth longed for: perfectly straight and raven black. She also had skin that looked as if it would turn golden brown after five minutes in the sun, and the fullest lips.

"Miss Ballou, Miss Ives, dinner is ready," Maria, the maid, wearing a crisp white apron called from the doorway.

Thank the Lord.

Dina walked ahead of Laura Beth, not waiting. As if she were in charge or something. *At least Whitney was fun, before all the blackmail and Sol stuff. Dina Ives just has a huge stick up her backside.*

Standing in the dining room doorway, Laura Beth heard Dina take a sharp breath. *So even Little Miss Senator's Daughter is impressed,* Laura Beth thought with a satisfied smile.

The staff, under her mama's direction, had laid out the best silver and the Ballou family china (which dated to the 1860s and had miraculously escaped the Yankee occupation unscathed). The table was covered in a creamy lace cloth, and the low arrangements of roses and poppies picked up the shades of red in the china. The Dale Chihuly chandelier that hung over the table sparkled in the light of a dozen silver candlebra.

"Mama!" Laura Beth said. "It's gorgeous! You've outdone yourself!"

Her mother beamed. "I thought you'd like the new table-cloth, darlin'. I had it specially made at the Royal School of Needlework in Hampton Court Palace."

Across the room, Libby Ballou stood arm in arm with Senator Ives as her thirty guests mingled and sipped champagne. "Elite leftovers," was what she called her annual collection of those who couldn't get home for the holidays, all of them D.C. power players, of course. Her mama blew Laura Beth a kiss.

"Are you and Dina havin' a nice time?"

No.

"Laura Beth is a great hostess, Mrs. Ballou. She's taken me under her wing and I feel right at home at Excelsior."

"Now, you know you're supposed to call me Miss Libby," she said to Dina before beaming at Laura Beth. "If anyone knows anything about navigatin' that school, it's my Laura Beth."

"Sweetheart, should we sit?" the senator asked. *Sweetheart? That's new.*

"Of course." Libby moved toward the head of the table. "Won't y'all have a seat? We have a feast that's just waitin' to be tasted."

A few people in the crowd laughed as they searched for their place cards. Her mother had spent hours agonizing over the seating arrangements. Every year, she tried to play matchmaker, hoping to kindle at least one romance at the table. Though no one had made it to the altar yet, she'd come close, with a few steady daters. She and Laura Beth liked to wager on who would end up getting married. It was their time-honored Thanksgiving tradition.

I should have picked Mama and the senator. I've never seen her happier.

The two of them seemed so comfortable together, as if they were two halves of a whole. So in sync. Just like she had thought she'd been with Sol.

It had been weeks since she'd rushed out of his apartment. Sol, of course, had tried calling her immediately and all the following day, but Laura Beth just let his calls go to voice mail before deleting them. She thought maybe he'd gotten the point, but last night he'd texted her and tossed her feelings upside down.

She wanted to be upset with him. And she had been. But the fact was, what happened with Whitney happened before she and Sol got together. And he had told her himself. That was honorable.

Ironically, knowing about Sol had freed Laura Beth from Whitney. She no longer cared what that Cali slut did or didn't tell Jackie. Because she believed their friendship would survive any challenge or shocking revelation. That Jackie, ultimately, would understand that Laura Beth had been trying to protect her.

Forgiveness is the best virtue. And Jackie's full of virtue, Laura Beth thought as she scanned the place cards, looking for her seat. To her complete dismay, she and Dina were seated directly across from each other, on either side of her mother. Which meant Laura Beth would have to engage in more small talk. She didn't know how much more of Dina Ives and her snotty act she could take.

"Dina," her mama said, before taking a sip of her champagne, "your daddy tells me you're gonna start an internship with that congressional education panel your sister works on. How inter-estin'."

A waiter placed a chilled endive-and-walnut salad before Laura Beth.

"Y'all, I hope you don't mind. We eat our salad first, unlike some people," the hostess said to her guests. Laughter circled the table. It was a dig at President Price, who last week had hosted the French president and served salad at the end of the meal. *And* a cheese course after dessert. Like the French. You would have thought she had proposed making French the national language, the uproar it caused in Republican circles.

Dina chewed a small mouthful of salad and patted her lips with the starched white napkin. "It's just once a week. It starts after Thanksgiving break."

"How wonderful!" Mama exclaimed.

Laura Beth had another word for it: nepotism.

Who am I kidding? All D.C. is is a bunch of connections.

"I'm looking forward to it—and learning more about Bob Price's educational initiative, although we disagree over vouchers."

Laura Beth had to blink to keep her eyes from glazing over. At school, all Dina talked about were boys and parties and the best places to shop. Even Jackie, the biggest teenage political junkie Laura Beth knew, didn't talk about education reform at Thanskgiving dinner. Dina was obviously putting on an act for the adults.

"Well, I wouldn't give Bob too much credit," her mother said, picking at her salad. "Every idea he comes out with is usu-ally fed to him by either the president or Carolyn Shaw."

"Oh?"

"Don't sound so surprised, sugar. Do you really think the president would let him run around spouting off his own ideas? Oh no. Deborah Price watches everything that man does. Poor thing." She smiled warmly down the long table to where Senator Ives sat at the other end. "Unlike Laura Beth's daddy, Preston—God rest his soul—Bob Price is a sorry excuse for a man. The way he lets those women boss him around."

Laura Beth jabbed at her food. Sitting here listening to her mother and Dina talk about the First Husband was hardly stimulating dinner conversation. She wished she had her phone so she could at least text Jackie, but her mama was a stickler about phones at the table. She'd even reprimand guests if she caught them sneaking a glance.

Dina set down her fork. "I didn't realize the president and Bob Price were close. Frances says they barely speak."

Laura Beth stared across the table. *What in the world? Why would she say that?*

"I'm good friends with Andrew Price," she said, "and I can tell you, his parents not only speak, but see each other *all the time*." Okay. So it was a lie. But still.

Her mother waited while the waiter refilled her wineglass. "I wouldn't say all the time, not with the way Deborah's always flying off all over the place." She clucked her tongue. "Really, is that any way to run a family?"

This time, Laura Beth's mouth dropped open. "She's the president, Mama. That's her job."

Dina shook her head slightly. "From what I hear, maybe she should be spending more time at home."

"What does that mean?" Laura Beth's blood boiled. It was one thing to attack the president's policies, but going after her home life was unfair. And who was Dina Ives but some know-nothing high school junior? She'd never even met the Prices.

Mama signaled the maids. "Bring out the next course, please." She turned her attention back to the girls. "Oh, hush, Laura Beth. It's nothing but a little Washington gossip. Dina's not hurtin' anyone."

Laura Beth narrowed her eyes and studied the perfectly polished girl across from her. *I don't like her and I don't trust her.*

Dina Ives, I'm watching you.

"I'm going to miss Thanksgiving," Papá said, kissing Lettie's forehead as she stood at the kitchen counter smearing peanut butter on a piece of celery. "All this wonderful food. Maybe it's a tradition we should continue in Paraguay."

Mama swatted him with a dishtowel. "And where, exactly, would we find canned cranberry sauce? Or the ingredients to make the culinary masterpiece known as green bean casserole?"

Lettie giggled. The entire time the Velasquez family lived in the United States, her parents insisted on preparing a traditional American Thanksgiving feast. Sweet potatoes with marshmallows, a stuffed turkey, deviled eggs . . . all the things Papá learned about from watching the Food Network when he couldn't sleep. Thankfully, Mama put her foot down the year he wanted to make a turducken. Not that they could have afforded such an extravagance.

"Maribel, the table looks gorgeous," Paz said, snatching a piece of celery.

Lettie turned around to look at her sister' s handiwork. With everything packed for the move, she'd used cheap paper plates and cups, but she'd added bright green napkins and arranged orange plastic flowers on the table to make it look nice.

"Does the president really eat the turkey, Lettie?" Maribel asked.

Lettie scrunched up her eyebrows for a second before she realized what she was talking about. "No," she said cheerfully. "Even though President Price only pardoned one of the birds, both of them are sent to a farm to live out their lives."

"Then what turkey do they eat?" Maribel asked.

Paz laughed. "Yeah, Lettie, which turkey do they eat?"

She tossed one of Mama's homemade rolls at her brother. He caught it and took a bite. "They get a turkey from the store, just like everyone else."

Maribel seemed satisfied with the answer.

Lettie's heart lurched. All day she'd tried to stay positive, to focus on the time she had left with her parents and sisters, but as the hours ticked away, the minutes grew more precious.

One time, though, the tears had spilled down her cheeks and Paz had guided her into her bedroom, where he'd hugged her tightly and stroked her hair.

I'm scared, too, Lettie, he'd admitted. *But Papá and Mamá and the girls will be okay. They'll be under the protection of the ambassador and the government. And when this is all over, we'll apply for new visas and convince them to come back here to live.*

Now, Lettie bit her lip to keep from crying again.

No more tears till tomorrow.

"After dinner, Mamá, I'll wash the dishes and help you finish packing up the kitchen," she said to distract herself.

Cardboard moving boxes were stacked in the living room, waiting for the embassy movers. Papá, Mamá, and the two girls would be leaving for Paraguay first thing in the morning, while Lettie and Paz stayed behind. All of Lettie's possessions filled two duffel bags and a cardboard box.

Tomorrow, her life would change. Lettie had known this day would come, but she'd always thought she'd be the one leaving— for college. Instead, most of her family was going to board an airplane for South America and she'd load her things into William Remick's car. Paz was moving in with an old friend, someone Lettie knew still ran with his old gang. But Paz swore it was temporary and that he'd move out as soon as he got a paying job.

She believed him. Even though he was officially a college student now, Paz's immigration status still depended on him getting a paid internship or a job. But in the meantime, he was going to be around his old crew, and that worried her.

Christa, Lettie's youngest sister, wandered into the kitchen, her eyes red from crying. Paz noticed and lifted her high into the air. He looked so handsome, his black hair falling over his eyes and his strong arms holding up Christa, who was wearing her white Sunday church dress. It was a hand-me-down from Lettie and Maribel, but it was starched and pressed and had a brand-new blue ribbon tied in a bow around her waist.

"No tears, Christa." Paz stared at Lettie as he said it, obviously realizing how hard she was struggling to keep it together. "Thanksgiving is for celebrating." He tossed the little girl higher until she giggled.

My heart is going to break into a million pieces when they go.

With a heavy sigh, Lettie said, "I think dinner's ready. Mamá?"

Her mother smiled. "Sit down everyone. Lettie and I will serve."

They started with Papá, piling his plate high with food. There was no need for leftovers this year. Everything had to be eaten.

When Lettie and her mother finished serving everyone and took their seats, Papá bowed his head to pray.

"We give thanks for our health and our family. We give thanks for the food and gifts You provide. We ask that no matter where our family is, or what paths we may take, that You continue to watch over us."

"Amen," they all said.

"Let's eat!" Paz lifted his fork and shoveled a heap of mashed potatoes into his mouth.

No one mentioned the civil unrest in Paraguay or the danger that awaited them. Despite her badgering, Paz refused to tell Lettie anything about the situation other than it was "tense."

As she listened to her parents tell the girls, who were too young to remember their homeland, about all the fun they would have in Paraguay, she knew no matter how far away her family was, they'd always be with her in her heart.

Lettie touched the silver charm bracelet dangling from her wrist.

At least she wouldn't be alone.

EIGHTEEN

"This is the crappiest Thanksgiving ever," Jackie said out loud to the empty room. She checked her iPhone for the hundredth time, doubled-checked to make sure she hadn't turned off the ringer or vibrate mode, and slumped into a chair.

Her mom and the president had taken an early morning flight to western Florida to console victims of a late season hurricane that had ripped through the previous night. They also wanted to make sure federal emergency workers were doing their job. Last thing they needed was another Hurricane Katrina.

But it left Jackie alone on Thanksgiving. Her dad, as usual, had canceled at the last minute. He said it was a work crisis, but Jackie bet his newest way-too-young girlfriend wanted to ski Aspen for a few days. It wouldn't be the first time he'd ditched Jackie for a girlfriend.

I could call Lettie at home, but it's her last day with her family. Jackie tossed her phone on the couch. *And why isn't Laura Beth answering my texts?*

She picked up a fashion magazine lying on the coffee table. That was one of Aunt Deborah's dirty little secrets—she loved to read *Vogue* and *Harper's*. And she wasn't above glancing at an *In Touch* every once in a while. She said sometimes her brain just needed to be off, and frivolous magazines helped.

As much as Jackie liked to look at the gossip rags, she hated actually being in them. Since the whole Friedrick debacle, her name hadn't graced the pages—no Ankie, no "First Girlfriend Speaks Out!" She'd asked Dr. Rosen to give her behind-the-scene tasks, and while he'd protested, saying how much good she—*Jackie Whitman*—could do for the group, he'd reluctantly agreed. She'd be working instead alongside Dr. Rosen's protégé, Vic Hazelton, whose shyness was slowly evaporating. He'd even started confiding in her, describing the war flashbacks that could be triggered by a car backfiring or the sight of a Hummer rumbling down a D.C. street. He'd described how, once he was stateside, Pentagon red tape had held up his paychecks for months and how military psychiatrists had dismissed his hallucinations and doctors had shrugged off the pain that sometimes sliced through his brain. He'd even shown her some of the poetry he liked to write.

Jackie threw down the magazine with its cover of Taylor Swift and her latest boyfriend.

I'm seriously considering calling Whitney. That's how effing bored I am.

"Miss Whitman?" a maid said from the doorway. "Dinner will be served at four. Mr. Price has asked that you join him and Andrew in the dining room."

Awesome. Nothing says holiday like an awkward dinner with people who aren't even your family.

"Thanks." She hadn't spoken to Andrew since the Homecoming debacle.

Her phone buzzed next to her. "Finally," she muttered, picking up the iPhone. She grinned as she looked at the text. It was from Scott.

Hey Jackie— Sorry I didn't make it home. I bet you're bored out of your mind. But I'll see you soon—hopefully alone.

Her heart gave a little flutter, which was completely ridiculous because it was *Scott*. As in Andrew's younger brother, Scott. As in the boy who used to steal her Barbies and hold them for ransom.

And right now, she wanted to see him more than anything.

Her fingers moved quickly over the keypad.

Ugh. So boring. No one is around. I could use some company. When do you finish up at school?

Jackie picked up *Vogue* and flipped through the pages. When she came to a picture of Friedrick at a charity event, she flicked his face and grinned. The dress she wore at his fashion show brought in over two hundred thousand dollars for the veterans. If he was pissed, he certainly didn't say anything in public. Besides, that little bit of revenge by Jackie grabbed him a ton of press.

Her phone buzzed.

On the 12th. Leave the day open, I plan on touring DC's finest burger joints and need a partner in crime.

Jackie smiled. During the presidential campaign, she and Scott had been in ninth grade. Neither of them had as many command performances as Andrew, and they often snuck off to find burger joints in the cities they visited. They'd kissed a few times, but it never got serious. Then, after the cops caught Scott with a small amount of marijuana, the Prices promptly shipped him off to reform school.

Overnight, Scott went from being her carefree friend to a brooding, grumpy guy who glared at Andrew whenever he was allowed home on break.

But this Scott—the one who'd started texting her now—sounded like her old friend.

Maybe reform school's been good for him after all.

"Miss Whitman? Dinner is ready."

Jackie tossed the magazine on the table and followed the maid to the dining room, where a waiter was filling the water goblets and wineglasses. Bob Price sat at the head of the table, scowling, his lips pressed tightly together.

"Jackie, we're just waiting for Andrew before we start," he said, staring intently at the empty seat across from Jackie. "Where is he?" he asked gruffly.

Looks like he wants to be here as much as I do.

Jackie swallowed a bitchy remark. "I haven't seen Andrew at all today." Which was true. He'd moved back to his dorm after their moms had returned from the South Africa trip and was even sleeping there over Thanksgiving break. Which was fine with Jackie.

Just as Bob Price was about to answer, Andrew teetered into the room, obviously drunk, and collapsed into his chair.

"Hey, guys. Happy Thanksgiving," he said, slurring his words.

A waiter set a plate of stuffing and turkey and cranberries

before Jackie, but she barely noticed it. Her eyes were fixed on Andrew. Nothing about him said sober or even sane. His sandy brown hair looked as if it hadn't been brushed in days, dark circles ringed his bloodshot eyes, and at least three days' worth of stubble dotted his chin.

"Are you drunk?" Bob asked his son in disgust.

Andrew cut off a piece of turkey and shoved it in his mouth. "So what?" he said. "I'm celebrating Thanksgiving. I've got so much to be thankful for." He gave a bitter laugh.

Jackie nearly choked on a piece of turkey. Andrew rarely mouthed off to his parents. "Andrew," she said sharply, hoping to take some of the tension out of the room.

Bob slammed his hand on the table and the glasses rattled. "I've had enough of this, Andrew. Your behavior has been outrageous for weeks. Your mother and I cut you some slack, especially in light of the car accident, but I've got news for you—it ends. Tonight."

Andrew went to grab the full wineglass sitting in front of him and knocked it off the table. It shattered and sent red wine spraying all over the wall and floor. From where she sat, it looked like blood.

Jackie's breath lodged in her throat, and suddenly it was too hot.

"Do you think it's so easy? To just forget?" Andrew shouted. "Taylor died. *Died.* I saw her lying there. I held her dead body in my fucking arms. How do I forget that?"

Jackie blinked back tears while she listened to the two Price men scream at each other.

She pushed her chair away from the table. "I'm done. Thank you both for such a wonderful Thanksgiving."

As she ran from the room, she heard Bob Price say, "See— you've upset Jackie. Don't you even care anymore, Andrew? Don't you see what you're doing to her?"

Jackie didn't wait to hear Andrew's answer. She didn't care. Not anymore. Andrew was losing it and there was nothing she could do without making the truth known. And that would just make everything worse.

The walls of her bedroom—prison—pressed in around her. *Why am I even here? It's been months since the kidnapping threat. I should be home. Not here.* She paced back and forth, iPhone in hand. *Damn it, Laura Beth, where are you?*

When she reached the window, Jackie stared across the lawn at the throngs of people standing outside the White House fence, hoping to get a glimpse of the First Family.

I'd give anything to be out there right now.

Then leave, Taylor whispered in her mind. *Get the hell out of here.*

Jackie sighed. "Great, now *I'm* hearing voices. And talking to myself." But the idea stuck in her head. Leave. Just go.

Before she lost her nerve, Jackie raced to the study, grabbed a backpack, and shoved a change of clothes and toiletries inside. She changed out of her dress and heels and put on a pair of jeans, a sweater, coat, and boots.

She cracked open her bedroom door and stuck her head out. The hallway was empty.

If anyone stops me, I'll say I'm going to Laura Beth's.

Her heart beat furiously as she slipped down the staircase, giving the agent at the top of the stairs a casual hello as she walked past him. At the far end of the Center Hall, a maid vacuumed the floors with her back to Jackie.

Outside, the cool night air stung Jackie's face and she paused for a moment, breathing it in. Even though the White House felt like an island, it was the heart of the city. She could hear traffic and voices through the trees separating her from freedom.

"Going out tonight, Miss Whitman?"

Jackie turned slowly, her fingers clenched around the strap of her backpack. "Agent Davenport! Why aren't you home with your family?" She forced herself to sound upbeat, as though standing on the lawn, near the trees, was exactly where she should be.

"My family's in Colorado," he answered, and pointed at her backpack. "You haven't answered my question. Are you going somewhere?"

Jackie shifted her weight. *Smile, it will make you seem less nervous.* "Just to my friend's—Laura Beth Ballou. She called and asked me to stop by."

Mark Davenport closed the short distance between them and took Jackie's backpack from her shoulder. "The car is in the other direction."

Jackie stuck out her chin stubbornly. "I was going to get a cab—I didn't want to interrupt anyone's meal." *Okay, that's lame. They're at work, so obviously I wouldn't be interrupting them.*

Agent Davenport spoke into his microphone. "Agent Fellows, I have Jackie Whitman on the lawn. Did Ms. Shaw clear this with you?"

Heat burned across Jackie's face. She was an adult—eighteen—legally allowed to make her own decisions, and yet she couldn't leave without permission.

She pretended to look confident as the agent listened to his earpiece, but the whole time her heart raced. She had to get out of here before she went crazy.

"Miss Whitman, I'm sorry, but you need to go back upstairs. Your mother gave orders for you to stay on the grounds today. And we have no record of the Ballous inviting you to their home."

Anger pulsed through Jackie's body and her hands shook as he escorted her upstairs. The whole way, she fought back tears. Thank God no one saw.

Agent Davenport lingered, his eyes studying Jackie. A chill ran up her spine. Something about him bothered her—and it wasn't just the way he'd covered up the truth about Andrew and Taylor's accident. There was something not right about how he looked at her. With her foot, she walked to her room and kicked the door shut on him.

"Creep!" Jackie screamed, not caring if he or anyone else heard her. Besides, what did it matter? Andrew walking around drunk was way more outrageous than her screaming.

She dumped the contents of her backpack on the floor and sat down hard. *I can't believe I'm back in prison.*

With tears in her eyes, she stripped down to just her lace bra and undies and climbed into bed. *Fuck my life,* she thought as she sobbed into her pillow.

The door creaked. Jackie opened her blurry eyes but didn't move. She was facing the opposite direction—toward the window—but a sliver of light from the hallway appeared on the wall.

The door squeaked again.

Her breath hitched and every muscle in her body tensed. *Mom won't be back until tomorrow at the earliest. So who's sneaking into my room?*

Two names popped into her head: the stalker and Mark Davenport.

"Come one step closer and I'll scream. Secret Service agents will be all over this room before you can touch me." She kept her voice even and strong. Of course, if it was Agent Davenport, there was a good chance no one would come. Better to not think about that.

The bed dipped and two strong, warm arms turned her around and scooped her up. She gasped.

Andrew.

"Andrew," she whispered sternly. "You scared me. I thought maybe you were the stalker."

His lips found hers. Jackie bristled.

"What are you doing..."

She moved to the other side of the bed. If she wasn't ready to talk to him, she definitely shouldn't be kissing him.

Andrew hesitantly ran his hand up her bare back, and she began to warm to his touch. He kissed her gently on the lips. He tasted like toothpaste, which surprised her. Jackie expected bourbon or vodka, not Colgate.

"Maybe I am the stalker," he murmured. "Maybe that's the only way I can get time with you—to kidnap you."

"Not funny."

He nuzzled her neck, his hot breath chasing the cool touch of his kiss and sending shivers down Jackie's spine.

"I know. Sorry."

It was almost as though the past couple of months hadn't happened and all her anger was no longer real. Not gone. Just irrelevant. Maybe this was what she needed: to just do and not think. Maybe it would fix everything that was wrong between them.

She fell back on the pillows and pulled him down to her. Andrew's hands were everywhere at once, on her thighs, her arms, brushing over her bare stomach. She arched her back, pressing into him, and he groaned appreciatively.

"I've missed you. God, have I missed you." Andrew kissed her again, harder, as if his life depended on it.

Jackie's hands slid down to the elastic waistband of his basketball shorts—the hideous Georgetown ones he insisted on wearing to bed. She pulled on them, and this time Andrew gasped.

"Are you sure?" he asked.

Her mind screamed, *No!* but her heart was acting on its own. She needed more than anything to feel close to Andrew again. To feel they were together, not on opposite sides of a battle neither could win.

"Yes," she said breathlessly.

Andrew kicked off the shorts and leaned over her. He kissed the tops of each of her breasts and then made a trail of kisses down her stomach.

"Forgive me, Jackie. Please. We can't do this anymore . . . be apart from each other."

Jackie closed her eyes, and in an instant she saw Taylor's face. Taylor laughing. Taylor kissing Andrew. Andrew and Taylor . . .

All the feeling drained from her body. She shook her head as tears rolled down her cheeks. "I . . ."

"Can't." Andrew finished the sentence for her as he sat up. Away from her.

The space between them felt cold on Jackie's skin, and she

wanted to wrap herself around him again, but her body wouldn't obey.

Andrew looked down at her. "Do you still love me?"

"I . . . ," she stuttered. "I'm not ready. Not yet. I need more time."

Andrew stood up and scooped his shorts up off the ground. "If I could, I'd undo it, Jackie. But I can't. It was wrong. But I still love you. Always you."

Jackie wiped her tears with the sheet. "I know you do. But I think you should go."

"Give me another chance," Andrew pleaded. "Please."

She squeezed her eyes together to stop the tears. If Taylor hadn't died, what would have happened? Would Taylor and Andrew have pretended everything was normal and kept lying to her? Or would one of them have confessed and ruined all their friendships? Or would Andrew have dumped her for Taylor?

"Maybe someday, but not now."

NINETEEN

Lettie shut the door to her new bedroom and threw herself down on the pale gray cotton duvet cover. Nicer than anything she'd ever had. So far, life with the Remicks hadn't been bad—Tracey and William (that's what they'd said to call them) were hardly ever home. And Whitney seemed excited to have Lettie around—making bowls of popcorn, watching movies, insisting they order take-out whenever they were left on their own for dinner (which was almost every night). Lettie couldn't complain.

Having Whitney constantly around meant not having to think about her family and how far away they were. But Mamá had just called to let Lettie know they'd made it to Paraguay okay. It had been six days since they left. Apparently telephone service was spotty. Hearing her mother's voice so close, as if they were back in their old apartment, made Lettie's lips tremble and her heart ache.

She needed to be alone.

From the bedside table, she picked up *Freakonomics,* found her place, and began reading.

A knock on the door. Lettie sighed and set the book next to her. *I'm beginning to think I have less privacy here than when I shared a room with Maribel and Christa.*

"Lettie? Can I come in?" Tracey Mills called from the hallway.

Lettie's eyes widened. Tracey hadn't been home when her mom called. Maybe Whitney had told her how upset Lettie was.

"Of course."

Tracey held something behind her back and wore a large smile. "I wanted to give you this." She held out a small white box with both hands.

"Is that—"

"An iPhone. Whitney told me your old phone was broken. And since you're living with us, I really would feel better if I had a way of contacting you."

Lettie blushed. It was so expensive, and she no longer had a job at the embassy. "That's very kind, and I don't want to sound ungrateful, but I can't afford an iPhone. I don't have a job anymore."

Tracey dropped the package on the bed. "It's a gift, Lettie. William and I will pay the bill, don't worry about it." She slid the box apart and held out the phone. "It's all set up. All you have to do is add in your contacts." She handed a piece of paper to Lettie. "This is your phone number. Ours are already in there."

The tiny phone weighed a million pounds in Lettie's hand. She turned it over and admired its sleek design. Unlike Jackie's and Laura Beth's, Lettie's last phone had been a rehab.

"It's for safety. And our peace of mind," Tracey repeated with a smile.

A sinister thought popped into Lettie's head. If Jackie was right and Tracey Mills was responsible for all those Ankie leaks over the summer, now she'd know every single person Lettie called or texted.

She looked up at Tracey and was greeted with another warm smile.

Or maybe Tracey Mills is just a really good person.

"Are you serious?" Jackie tossed aside the newspaper. "Has Lettie seen this?"

Laura Beth licked chocolate icing from her fingers. "I don't know. I mean, I could call Whitney's house, I guess. But I really don't want to. And besides, if she did see it, she's probably dying, don't you think?"

Dying or not, Lettie deserved to know. "We're going over there."

Color drained from Laura Beth's face. "I really don't—"

"Laura Beth," Jackie snapped, "we're going to Whitney's and we're going to check on Lettie."

Jackie basically dragged a reluctant Laura Beth to her BMW. They'd taken a break from Christmas shopping at Georgetown Cupcake when Jackie had spied the *Washington Tattler* headline: "How Opening Our Home Opened Our Hearts," by Tracey Mills. The article was worse than anything they'd imagined. It was all about Lettie, her dreams, her achievements, and how the Remicks were acting as her "guardian angels," providing her with a home so she could live the American Dream.

The whole thing made Jackie want to scream.

When Laura Beth pulled up in front of the Watergate, Jackie jumped out of the car and stormed into the foyer, paper in hand. Laura Beth sat huddled in the car, as if she were afraid to get out.

Jackie turned around and motioned to her friend. "Laura Beth, get over here. What are you doing?"

She'd heard through the grapevine that Laura Beth and Whitney had had a blowup at school. But when she'd asked her about it, all Laura Beth had said was, "It wasn't a big deal. I just got sick of her, you know?"

Jackie didn't really care about what had happened, to be honest. She was just happy that Laura Beth was no longer dragging Whitney around with her everywhere.

Laura Beth fed quarters into the meter and slinked to Jackie's side, fidgeting with her jacket as Jackie buzzed Whitney's apartment. Much to their relief, it was Lettie who answered and Lettie who opened the apartment door.

"Oh, my God, Lettie! Are you holding up okay? How could she do this to you?" Laura Beth launched herself at poor Lettie and pulled her to her chest.

So much for "What if she doesn't know?"

Lettie tried to pull away from Laura Beth. She looked as if she'd been surrounded by a human tornado and didn't know where to run. "What's going on?" she squeaked.

Jackie held up the paper. "I take it you didn't see Tracey's article today?"

Lettie shook her head and grabbed the paper from Jackie. As she read, her face grew more crimson.

"No. No. No," she muttered. When she'd finished the first page, Lettie dropped her hands and looked first at Jackie, then at Laura Beth. "Why would Tracey do this?"

"Because she's a lyin', connivin' bitch like her daughter." Laura Beth put her arm around Lettie. "You can still move in with Mama and me. No one would blame you. I could have the movers here in an hour."

Jackie resisted reminding Laura Beth that Lettie didn't need movers—she barely owned anything. Instead, she put her arm around Lettie's other shoulder and said, "Is anyone else here?"

"No. Whit's out with Angie, Dina, and Aamina. William and Tracey don't get home till late."

"Then there's plenty of time to figure out what you're going to do."

Lettie led the girls into the living room. Like the rest of the apartment, everything in it looked brand new, shiny, and hardly used.

"We should pack your things," Laura Beth said, pulling her phone from her bag. "And I have to call Mama and let her—"

"I appreciate the offer, Laura Beth, but I think I'm going to stay here."

Silence.

The clock on the mantel ticked. One second. Two seconds. Three—

"What?" Laura Beth asked huffily.

Lettie studied her nails. Her long dark hair fell across her face. Jackie could tell she was uncomfortable—anyone would

be with Laura Beth breathing down her neck—but she didn't
know what to say.

"I hate the article. And maybe Tracey is using me. But don't
you think it's better to have someone on the inside? Now that I
know what she's up to, I won't trust her. But if I'm here, I can
keep an eye on what she does."

Jackie's mouth fell open. "You're offering to *spy* on Tracey
Mills?"

"And Whitney?" Laura Beth prompted her.

Lettie hesitated. "Maybe."

"You're like a mini Jennifer Cane!" Laura Beth giggled, until
Jackie gave her a stern look.

Lettie shrugged off the comparison to The Fixer, Washington's biggest secret keeper. "One good deed deserves another, no?"

Whitney looked up as Lettie's new phone rang.

*Bitch. Mom buys her the newest iPhone and I'm stuck with a year-old
piece of crap.*

The phone rang again.

"Do you need help answering it, Lets?" Whitney asked.

Lettie threw her a dirty look. "No."

"Then answer your phone."

So far, Lettie wasn't awful to have around. The trouble was,
she was *always* around. Especially since the *Tattler* article. It was
like she was too embarrassed to leave the apartment other than
going to school. Which was weird. The article was great, in
Whitney's opinion. All it did was talk about how amazing

Lettie was. If she didn't use it for her college applications, she wasn't as smart as everyone said she was.

Across the room, Lettie spoke quietly in Spanish into the phone. Whitney pretended to be busy searching through the fridge. Seventeen years of living in L.A. and ten years of school Spanish had made her conversational—but she kept that under wraps. No need for Lettie to know Whitney understood what she was saying.

Whitney closed the fridge empty-handed and turned around when she heard Lettie say good-bye.

"Was that Paz?" she asked. Seemed safe enough—who else would Lettie speak to in Spanish?

Lettie nodded. "He wants to meet up for dinner."

Hmm. Paz. He's hot. Let's hope he's chill. Not stressed like his sister.

"Cool! Let's go! I'm so bored anyway, and Mexican food sounds awesome."

Lettie hesitated. Whitney knew, from listening to her end of the conversation, that Lettie wanted to get away from her, but she didn't know how to do it politely.

"We're just going over to a place in my old neighborhood. You wouldn't like it."

Whitney raised her eyebrows. "Anyplace with guys, I'll like."

Lettie shook her head and laughed. "You're hopeless."

"Then let's go. Don't want to keep Paz waiting."

The drive over to Mount Pleasant wasn't too long, only about twenty minutes, but the whole time Lettie fidgeted with her phone, her purse, her seat belt. Basically anything she could touch, and it drove Whitney crazy.

Seriously, you'd think she's on the way to meet Daniel or something.

"Turn right at the stop sign and park anywhere. The restaurant's on this block," Lettie said.

The neighborhood wasn't exactly gangbanger land, but it definitely wasn't Georgetown. A few run-down cars parked outside shuttered shops lined the street.

Shit. I'm totally getting carjacked.

"Is it safe to leave my car here?" she asked.

Lettie shrugged. "Jackie does." She opened her door. "You don't have to stay. You could just drop me off."

Yeah, fat chance. "It's cool. In L.A. we have way worse neighborhoods. Ever hear of the Eighteenth Street Gang? They're like the worst of the worst in L.A."

All color drained from Lettie's face and she swung her head left and right. "Just because I'm Latina doesn't mean I'm up on my gangs, Whitney," she snapped.

"Touchy." Whitney slammed her door shut. "Just making conversation."

"Well, stop."

Whitney smirked. She'd never seen Lettie irritated before, and it was kind of funny.

"So where's this hot brother of yours?" Whitney had seen Paz Velasquez—the brother who had returned from the dead—only once, on the morning Lettie moved in. But what she'd seen, she'd liked. Lean and muscular, thick dark hair, eyes like onyx, and a complexion the color of warm honey. Yummy.

Lettie held open the restaurant door. "Probably inside."

Sure enough, Paz sat in the back corner, reading a book.

Bad sign.

The dimly lit restaurant had a seedy, wrong-side-of-the-tracks feel. Worn red vinyl booths and a few tables and chairs in the middle of the room. Other than them, the place was empty. Whitney loved it.

She watched Paz and Lettie exchange kisses and waited to be introduced. Paz looked over at her, but Lettie didn't introduce them. Instead, she started babbling about the lame book he'd been reading.

"Isn't it great? I loved the part where—"

Whitney cut her off.

"Hi, Paz, I'm Whitney. We met the other day. At my place." She slid into the booth and touched his arm on the table.

She turned on her megawatt smile and leaned forward a little to give him a better look at her breasts.

On the other side of a grinning Paz, Lettie scowled.

"So you're my sister's angel. Thanks for helping her."

Whitney raised her eyebrow. "I can be yours, too, if you want."

"Whitney!" Lettie kicked her under the table.

Paz just laughed. "I'm not into high school girls."

Whitney sensed a challenge. No way was Paz Velasquez going to forget her. Plus, he smelled delicious. "We'll see about that."

Lettie clenched her fists under the table. Through the whole meal, Whitney basically forgot she was there. Even mentioning Franklin didn't stop Whitney from draping herself all over the table and laughing at Paz's bad jokes. And Paz, despite saying repeatedly he wasn't interested, seemed to be eating up the attention. Although admittedly he had mouthed, "Help!" to Lettie a few times.

"We should go, Whitney. Your parents will be home soon."

Whitney pulled her attention away from Paz. "They don't care, Lets. They probably don't even realize we're gone."

"I have to finish my homework." It was a lie. She'd finished it as soon as she got home.

Paz signaled the waiter for the bill. She watched her brother flip over the check, glance at it, and insist on paying for all of them. As if it were no big deal.

Lettie raised her eyebrows. Paz had just started an on-campus job in the dining hall. He hated it and it paid hardly anything, but it was temporary. In the new year, he'd begin a part-time job assisting Carolyn Shaw's body man. An honor that still shocked Lettie. Paz would help keep track of her personal and professional details—like making sure she always had a cell phone or briefing papers and knowing where she was at all times. And with the campaign gearing up next summer, he'd go on the road whenever the campaign needed him. As far as Lettie was concerned, Paz had walked into a dream job.

Late afternoon light filtered through the buildings, and a crisp breeze blew leaves down the sidewalk. Lettie turned to her brother and wrapped her arms around him. "Don't be a stranger."

He hugged her back tightly. "I'll call you. We'll do something next weekend."

"Paz? Paz Velasquez?" a guy called from the other side of the street.

Lettie stiffened, recognizing the short, stocky guy from the crowd Paz used to hang with.

"Paz?" she said, her voice shaking.

He squeezed her arm and whispered, "It's okay, *mi hermana*. I'll handle this."

The guy crossed the street, his hands shoved deep in his pockets. The hair on Lettie's neck stood up. This guy was dangerous—even Whitney seemed to know it. She'd suddenly gone quiet.

Paz turned and greeted the guy in Spanish. "Ramon, hey. Long time no see."

Ramon leered at Lettie and Whitney. His eyes lingered a little too long on Whitney, and for the first time ever, Lettie watched her shrink from a guy's gaze.

"I heard you were back," he said in a menacing voice. His hands were still in his pockets, which made Lettie nervous. What did he have in there?

Paz scratched the back of his head. "Yeah, I'm back."

Ramon moved closer to Lettie. "Does Miguel know?"

Lettie felt Paz's arm encircle her waist. He pulled her and Whitney closer to him. "Can't say I've had a chance to get over there. Been helping my little sister move."

"This Lettie? Damn, girl. You grew up." Ramon let out an appreciative whistle.

Whitney cleared her throat, as if she were offended Ramon hadn't complimented her. Which was totally ridiculous—first, there was no doubt he was a gang member and dangerous, and second, they were speaking Spanish.

"Who's the gringa?" He pointed his thumb at Whitney and gave a one-sided smile.

"This is my friend Whitney," Lettie said quietly.

Holy shit.

Whitney's eyes latched on to the tattoos across Ramon's knuckles. XVIII.

No wonder Lettie froze up when I mentioned the 18th Street Gang—Paz must run with them.

Ramon turned back to Paz.

"If you're back in the 'hood, you need to let Miguel know. He doesn't like surprises, especially from old friends," Ramon said, laughing in a mean way. Even Whitney picked up on the threat.

"You know and Miguel knows I'm not up in his business. We used to hang, but I was never part of his chain."

"That's not what I heard from Miguel. He was real pleased with that favor you just did him."

"That's all it was. One favor. Period."

Whitney saw Lettie recoil as if the guy had hit her. *Whoa. So that's how Paz sneaked back over the border. Doing a job that could land him in prison for the rest of his life. That's too freaky. Even for me.*

She tugged on Lettie's arm and said in Spanish, "We have to go. My parents are waiting."

Lettie, Paz, and Ramon gaped at her.

"What?"

Ramon laughed louder. "For a *gringa,* you don't speak half-bad Spanish."

Oh shit.

TWENTY

Carolyn Shaw rolled her shoulders to try to ease the crick in her neck. Three hours of meetings and still no progress. And now the Republican leadership had the nerve to demand the president cut her beloved jobs creation program because they said it favored new immigrants instead of lifelong citizens. If she didn't, Senate Budget Committee chairman Raymond Milton had just warned her, they'd refuse to pass the budget.

There's a reason the American public thinks we don't accomplish anything. We're in the middle of a budget crisis and they don't want a jobs program that puts thousands of people to work. I don't get it.

The president had joined them moments earlier and sat at the head of the table, to Carolyn's right.

"With all due respect, Senator Milton, what you're proposing is unacceptable and you know it," Deborah said. "You're simply trying to score points with your Republican base by scapegoating new citizens. But the numbers don't support it." Carolyn slid a piece of paper toward her. "We've had three quarters of job growth—minimal, yes, but still growth. Interest rates are low, consumer confidence is up." She let the paper drop to the table. "So tell me again, how exactly have I destroyed the economy?"

Before the senator could respond, an aide handed Carolyn a note. She held it under the table and read quickly.

"Ladies, gentlemen. I'm afraid we've run overtime and the president has another appointment. I'll have our staff arrange our next meeting for tomorrow." Carolyn pushed back her chair and stood. The president sat still at the head of the table, her eyes asking what she dared not say in front of the group: *What's happening?*

The room emptied quickly and both women walked briskly to the Oval Office. Carolyn turned on the TV and perched on the edge of the president's desk.

"Carolyn, what's going on?" Deborah asked with concern in her voice.

"It's the PAPPies." She didn't tell her what the note said. She wanted to see it on TV first, to see if it was as bad as it sounded.

Every channel showed the same thing: Republican Senator Hampton Griffin and his top aide, Eric Moran, surrounded by a group of PAPPies.

"When is an accident not an accident?" the senator asked. "When it is a *cover-up*." He held a stack of papers in his hand and waved it at the camera. "Nearly a year ago, Andrew Price—the son of our president—was involved in a fatal car accident that killed a sweet, young woman. At the time, no one asked questions. But we're asking them now. Why did the First Family wait more than a week to release a statement? What are the president and her staff hiding?"

Carolyn watched the color drain from Deborah's face. "Is he implying . . ."

"Yes."

"Oh, my God." She covered her eyes with her hands and leaned on the desk. "Where's Andrew?"

She reached across her desk and buzzed her private secretary. "Lindsay, find Andrew and send him directly to the family quarters—"

Carolyn interrupted. "Better make it my house. There are no reporters there. Not yet, anyway."

Deborah nodded. "On second thought, have him go to Carolyn Shaw's town house and tell him to wait there for Jackie. And Lindsay, please clear my schedule for the rest of the day."

The lines between Deborah's brows deepened. "I don't need this, Carolyn. Not now. Not in the middle of budget talks."

"It's been a rough few months, and it's only going to get worse when the campaign season starts."

"Hasn't it already? Look at the PAPPies, circling like a pack of wild dogs, whipped up by Griffin. They're taking shots at my son. *My son.*"

Carolyn had seen Deborah upset many times over the course of their long friendship—usually about Bob—but this was different. She radiated fury.

"I wouldn't be surprised if they were behind the threats against Jackie, too," Deborah added.

It had been almost three months since the first kidnapping threat and still no leads. Whoever was leaving the phone messages was a master of evasion. Carolyn tried not to worry about it, but it frightened the hell out of her. Especially lately—the number of threats about Jackie had increased, and Carolyn worried that every time she let her daughter out of her sight, she might never see her again.

Carolyn drummed her fingers on the desk. Something Jackie had mentioned nagged at her. Something about Andrew and Daniel fighting at the Homecoming dance. At the time, it seemed insignificant—a disagreement among teenagers. Jackie hadn't elaborated, and Carolyn hadn't pressed for more info.

Everything slid into place. "Do you think Jennifer Cane's behind this?"

Taylor's parents had been friends of the Prices—before Deborah decided to run for president. But once the campaign started, Jennifer Cane became a major liability—so they'd distanced themselves from her, and Jennifer had seemed to understand. She'd faded into the background and stopped calling.

Deborah pressed her hands together tightly, as if to keep them from trembling. "I hope not. Jennifer Cane can destroy us. All of us."

"Jackie, hand me the garland. Not that one—the one with the holly berries." Laura Beth balanced at the top of the ladder, one hand stretched toward Jackie and the other clutching the top step.

"At some point, you're going to have to stop messing with it." Jackie tilted her head back to get a good look at her friend. Laura Beth's zeal for decorating and shopping had kicked into high gear since the New York trip. She seemed to buy a new designer dress every other day, although it was obvious she wasn't seeing Sol anymore. When Jackie and Lettie asked her about it, Laura Beth grew quiet before saying, "Some things are meant to be private." She never talked about Sol, and she barely spoke about Juilliard.

Something wasn't right, but what?

Laura Beth positioned the garland and shoved a pushpin into the wall. "Christmas decoratin' is a talent. And I plan to use my talent to put a little cheer into this place."

So far, her cheer consisted of donating not one or two trees but *six* to the veterans hospital, tacking white lights around every door, and swagging garlands over every window. At least fifty poinsettias sat in the corner waiting for Laura Beth's attention.

Across the communal lounge, Whitney tied herself in a large red velvet ribbon and posed seductively. "What do you think, Angie? Aamina? Do I make a pretty present?"

"The vets would like it better if you stripped down a little," Angie said.

Aamina laughed. "Don't you think she should save that gift for Franklin?"

Whitney ripped off the bow and let it drop on the floor. "He'd probably be too high to even notice."

Jackie rolled her eyes. *Oh no! Someone not paying attention to Whitney. The world might just end.*

"This. Is. So. Boring," Whitney complained, and stretched out on the floor. She arced her hands over her head and moved her feet. "Snow angels."

"Whitney, get up," Jackie snapped. "We have to finish decorating."

She stood up and shook her wild hair. "Whatever. I need to buy a dress for the Prices' Christmas party." She smiled at Jackie. "Lets, Angie, feel like shopping? Aamina?"

Lettie blushed and kept her eyes focused on her work. "I'm just going to wear something I already have."

"Translation: Borrow something from LB. C'mon," Whitney pleaded. "Mom said we could use her credit card and buy what we wanted."

Of course she did. Tracey Mills is on cloud nine after getting her invite to the White House Christmas party. Amazing what a fluff piece about being Lettie's guardian angel and the importance of immigration reform will get you.

From the way Lettie kept her face hidden with her hair, Jackie could tell she was embarrassed. When would Whitney learn that offers like that mortified Lettie?

Angie and Aamina grabbed their coats off the chair, but Lettie shook her head. "I don't want to get in trouble for skipping out."

Whitney rolled her eyes. "Whatever. I'll see you at home. With a fabulous new dress."

After the three girls left, Laura Beth climbed off the ladder. "I can't believe she and her mama are goin' to the party. What happened to the 'no journalists' rule?"

Jackie checked Lettie's reaction before saying anything. "Well, she *is* Lettie's guardian. I guess it's no different than letting your *Republican* mama in," she teased.

"Oh, please. Everyone knows Libby Ballou is a Washington power player. Tracey Mills is just a gossip columnist with no class. Couldn't her daddy just go alone? At least he's *someone*."

"I think he has political aspirations. At least that's what it seems like. I heard him tell Tracey to keep her ears open about any White House jobs," Lettie said as she untangled another row of lights. "I think his dream job would be to write economic policy for the president."

"I thought he was just an economist who came to work for a liberal think tank? Ugh. How can you live with those people?" Laura Beth climbed off the ladder and admired her work.

"William's not bad. He's nice, actually. And Whitney's okay. She's different when you guys aren't around."

"Whitney!" Laura Beth slammed a poinsettia on each of the three coffee tables. "That girl gets on my last nerve."

Lettie drew her eyebrows together and pressed her lips tight. As though she wanted to say something but couldn't.

Interesting how Lettie never fully defends Whitney, Jackie thought.

A blast of Christmas music blared through the overhead speakers, and the girls jumped.

"Let's take a break," Jackie said.

Laura Beth nodded and sat in one of the rec room's overstuffed chairs. "I need to tell you somethin'."

Jackie's heart flopped and she felt a little queasy. It had been weeks since the fashion show—and Laura Beth's big night with Sol. *Please, please, please don't let Laura Beth be pregnant.*

"I didn't sleep with Sol."

"What? Why would you lie about it?"

Laura Beth kept her eyes on the far window. "I didn't lie. I just didn't talk about it. I was embarrassed."

"Because you didn't go through with it?" Lettie asked.

"No. I'm happy I didn't." Laura Beth gave a weak smile. "He told me he slept with Whitney. Over the summer."

Next to Jackie, Lettie let out a huge sigh. As if she were relieved.

"Before you guys were going out?" Jackie asked. She could understand being upset. After all, who wants to think of her boyfriend with another girl? Especially Whitney. And when did he even have time to hook up with Whitney? Sol and Laura Beth were practically joined at the hip from day one.

Laura Beth, twisting a piece of her auburn hair around her index finger, filled them in on Sol's hookup at Aamina's party.

Sleazy, Jackie thought. But it wasn't as if Sol had cheated on Laura Beth. Not like Andrew and Taylor.

"I know. I know. But he kept it from me. And here I was ready to give him *everything.*"

Lettie reached over and rubbed Laura Beth's hand. "I think it's honorable that he told you. He could have kept it a secret, but he did the right thing."

A slow smile spread across Laura Beth's lips. "He did, didn't he?"

"Yeah. Maybe you should give him another chance, Laura Beth," Jackie said.

Just then a soldier on crutches hobbled through the door. "You girls don't mind if I turn on the TV, do ya?"

"Of course not," Laura Beth said perkily, the air of sadness that had been hanging over her for weeks all but gone.

Jackie went back to the box of lights she and Lettie had been untangling. "Hold this end, Lettie, and I'll work on finding the other end inside the box."

"Jackie," Laura Beth said softly.

"What?" Jackie kept working her hands through the box.

"You need to see this," Laura Beth said.

Jackie looked up, expecting to see her friends holding up some ridiculous Christmas decoration, like the cigar-smoking Santa they'd found earlier. Instead, everyone's eyes were focused on the TV.

———

Mark Davenport walked briskly beside Andrew to the front door of Jackie's Foggy Bottom town house.

"Chin up, Andrew. It's not the end of the world."

Andrew scowled. "You know your ass is on the line, too, right?"

"Not if we stick to the same story," Mark said with a hint of a threat.

Taylor's death was an accident. No one can blame me. I wasn't drunk. But now . . .

The squeal of tires on pavement caught his attention, and Andrew turned his head toward the street as a navy Prius jerked to a halt at the curb.

Jackie. Fucking wonderful.

The way her long blond hair fanned out behind her as she ran toward him reminded him of the way she'd looked as a little kid when he'd push her on the swings. *She always wanted to go higher, and I'd push her until she felt like she was flying. Look where that's got me.*

"What are *you* doing here?" he asked with a bitter edge to his voice.

She recoiled, her bright blue eyes full of concern. "My mom called me. And this is my house, remember?"

"Haven't you done enough already?"

Mark had moved to the curb, far enough away to give them privacy but close enough in case he was needed, and Agent Fellows was already unlocking the front door. Andrew instinctively darted his eyes up and down the quiet street for any sign of reporters. He and Jackie had been out of the news for a few weeks, so there was a good chance no one was watching them.

"You think I did this? Tipped off Senator Griffin?" Jackie crossed her arms.

Anger burned inside him. "Who else, Jackie? Who else knew besides you and me?"

It was hard to believe the last time they saw each other, she was wrapped in his arms. Back where she belonged. Sure, it ended badly. But . . . How could it go from that to this? Screaming at each other in the street?

Jackie cast her eyes toward the sidewalk and then back to Andrew.

She's got to be kidding. My Secret Service agent? God, she's desperate.

"Did you tell anyone else? Laura Beth? Or Lettie, maybe?"

She stared at him defiantly. "They're my best friends, Andrew. You told me you cheated on me with Taylor. What did you expect?"

"How much did you tell them?" He grabbed her by the shoulders. "How much?"

Jackie stiffened under his touch. "Just about you and Taylor. Not the other stuff," she said.

He dropped his hands to his sides. "Lettie is Daniel's girlfriend. Did that occur to you? That she might tell him?"

Before Jackie could answer, he shoved past Jackie's agent, pushed open the heavy front door, and stormed inside.

Screw Jackie. And screw all her friends, too.

"Andrew, sit down, please." Deborah paced in front of the fireplace. Across the room, images flickered silently from the TV. On the drive over, Deborah had fallen apart. It was in these private moments that Carolyn remembered that no matter how powerful her friend was, she was, more than anything else, a mother.

A mother who'd known from the start that her son had been driving that night.

After dialing 911 from the accident scene, Deborah was the next person Mark Davenport had called.

I was in the Oval Office with Deborah when the call came through on her speakerphone.

"Madam President, your son is fine. But he's been in a car accident with Taylor Cane, and unfortunately, ma'am, the girl is dead."

I'm not sure if either of us or both of us screamed. But I'll never forget what Agent Davenport said next: "It was Miss Cane's car. I think it's safe to assume she was driving."

"What do you mean, you assume?" Deborah said sharply.

"Andrew hasn't corrected me and I've already told the police that's what happened."

I watched Deborah's face age ten years as the truth of who'd really been behind the wheel sank in. "Was the driver at fault?" she asked.

"No ma'am. The car turned a bend on a slippery road and skidded into a tree. No one was to blame."

"Thank you, Agent Davenport."

She hung up and we stared at each other wordlessly. The tears were streaming down both our faces. We each took a step forward and held each other tight. We'd been through so much together over the years, but nothing like this.

"No one, not even Jackie and especially not Jennifer Cane, must ever know that my son was driving. We must do whatever it takes," Deborah said finally, pulling away. "And let's make sure Agent Davenport stays happy in his

job. When it comes to protecting Andrew, it's obvious he's willing to go above and beyond his official duties."

I didn't voice out loud what Deborah was surely thinking: That by telling the president the truth from the get-go, Mark Davenport was also protecting his own butt if it ever came out.

In the following weeks, I tried to do everything to help Jackie deal with the loss of her best friend while hiding the facts from her. I was grieving, too. I'd known Taylor since she was a toddler and thought of her as the sister Jackie never had.

I also knew Deborah was devastated. She had to watch helplessly as the guilt ate away at her son. While she desperately wanted to share Andrew's burden with him—and help him heal—the risks of a leak were too great.

"I assume this is about Griffin's bullshit press conference?" Andrew asked sourly, grasping the top of a wingback chair. "What's the big deal? Everybody knows there was an accident and Taylor died. End of story."

"He was driving." Jackie spoke up suddenly, her voice shaking. "He told me this summer. They were fighting, and he lost control of the car."

Andrew moaned. His body sagged against the chair and Carolyn could read the shock and despair in his eyes.

"Jackie, how could you do this to me?" Andrew said dully. He turned to Deborah. "Mom, I'm sorry. I'm so sorry I lied to you. It's true, what she said . . ."

Deborah rushed over to her son and hugged him fiercely. Carolyn took Jackie in her arms.

"Andrew. Jackie. Both Carolyn and I know what happened that night," Deborah said, her voice strained. "We've known all along. We didn't tell you because we wanted to protect both of you."

Andrew stiffened and pulled away, staring his mother in the eye.

"What! You knew all along? Oh, my God." He sank into the armchair, his head in his hands.

Carolyn led her daughter to the sofa, sat down, and pulled her close, inhaling the scent of Jackie's shampoo, the way she used to when Jackie was a baby and fresh from her bath.

"How did you find out?" Andrew asked, raising his head.

"Mark Davenport told me. He wanted to protect you. And me, in case the truth ever got out," his mother answered.

Jackie began to sob, her face buried in her mother's neck, her shoulders heaving. Carolyn couldn't understand why Andrew wasn't rushing to Jackie's side. Instead it was as if they weren't even in the same room.

"Carolyn and I are sorry, too, more sorry than you'll ever know. We love you two so much and we thought we were doing the right thing," Deborah said sorrowfully.

How could we have screwed this up so badly? If we'd come clean from the start, our children would not still be suffering. They'd be coping and healing and helping each other. Instead, they're both shattered and they're barely even speaking to each other.

But she knew the answer. *We two mothers made a political decision. And our children are the casualties.*

Jackie untangled herself and sat up straight. "What happens next?" she asked. She blew her nose and wiped away the tears. "What do you want Andrew and me to do?"

Carolyn marveled at her daughter's strength. She looked over at Andrew, who was still slumped in his chair.

"Senator Griffin didn't produce any evidence to back up his allegations. It's obvious he has none. He's just on a fishing expedition," she said.

Deborah interrupted, a small smile playing on her face, obviously hoping to dispel some of the tension. "Brian Gillespie suggested we create a diversion . . . like an Ankie engagement."

Jackie gasped and her body visibly stiffened. Andrew's head shot up, his face in a scowl. Carolyn expected him to object, for Jackie's sake. But instead, he demanded: "What does Gillespie know?"

"Nothing, he knows nothing," Deborah said soothingly. "He was just reacting to Hampton Griffin's press conference. Don't worry, the engagement idea was a joke."

"We're going to issue a simple statement dismissing his groundless innuendos and accusing him, once again, of playing politics with teenagers' lives. It'll all blow over in a day or two," Carolyn said, trying to sound more confident than she felt.

Deborah walked over to Jackie and took her hand. "Jackie, I think you deserve some good news after this."

What's she talking about?

"I think you should move back home with your mom in a couple of days. You two need to be together. Carolyn, don't worry, I'll see to it that she has plenty of security."

I will worry, though, Carolyn thought. She looked at her daughter. The tiniest of smiles was creeping across her face. *At least someone's leaving this room happy.*

TWENTY-ONE

Snowflakes drifted softly from the sky and Jackie stuck out her tongue, trying to catch one.

"Do you remember—when you were maybe five—how you believed snowflakes were little bits of powder sugar? You said Mrs. Claus put too much on her Christmas cookies and it drifted all the way down here."

Jackie smiled at her mom. "I remember that. And how sad I was because it didn't taste anything like powdered sugar."

They'd been holiday shopping most of the afternoon, and it was the first time in ages Jackie had more than a few minutes alone with her mom. After the horrible scene with Andrew a few days earlier, her mom suddenly cleared her schedule to spend time with Jackie. That included helping her move back to their town house. Even with the two extra agents assigned to her, Jackie was happy to be home. In her own bed. And away from Andrew and politics.

"Feel like hot chocolate? Or are you too grown-up for that?" her mother teased.

"I'll never be too old for hot chocolate," Jackie said.

"Me neither." Her mom laughed.

They found a cute café nestled among the shops and not too busy with late season shoppers. As usual, they sat in the most secluded spot at the back so no politicians or lobbyists inter-rupted their mother-daughter time.

"Who else do you have on your list?" her mom asked once they had arranged themselves and all their packages around the table.

"Just Laura Beth. She's tough this year. I thought maybe tickets to a Broadway show or something, but I kind of want to give her something more meaningful."

Her mother blew into her cup, and steam swirled around her face. "I think tickets would be lovely. You know she'd love it."

"I guess."

"Have you gotten Andrew's present yet?" There was a hint of hesitancy to her mom's question. Almost as if she weren't sure she should ask.

Jackie sighed. After the way he'd treated her at her house the other day, Jackie had all but written off their relationship—and friendship. Yet he'd seemed so loving that night at the White House.

"Hey, are you still worried about Senator Griffin?" her mom asked. "It's already died down. The press is fickle and the Amer-ican people have short memories. Most of them won't remember his empty allegations after New Year's."

Yeah, but what about Jennifer Cane? Jackie thought. *She won't be so easily persuaded.*

It was weird. The day everything blew up, Jackie wanted to grill her mom. She wanted to know what else they'd kept from her. But she knew she did the right thing by holding her tongue. Aunt Deborah and her mom did what they did to protect Andrew. Just like they'd do anything to protect her.

"I know." Jackie tore a piece off her chocolate cookie. "Andrew was a mess, wasn't he?"

Her mother placed her hand on top of Jackie's. "Jackie, honey, what's really going on? Andrew's been walking around like a zombie, and he's been spotted drunk more than a few times. I barely see the two of you together anymore. And at the house the other day . . . well, it was like the two of you were enemies, not dating."

A tiny crack formed in Jackie's façade and she struggled to keep it together. With a deep breath, she said, "Things aren't good between us. He told me some things—about another girl— and . . ."

"Oh, baby, I'm sorry." She moved her chair closer and wrapped an arm around Jackie. Tears slipped down Jackie's cheeks, but she felt safe. Like her mom could fix all her problems.

"I know Aunt Deborah and I always talk about how we love seeing the two of you together. And I know the press loves it, too. But don't ever feel like you have to stay with someone. Not for me. Not for anyone."

Jackie sniffed and wiped her hand across her face. "Sometimes, it feels like I'm living my life for everyone else. For what they expect of me."

She lifted Jackie's chin so that the two of them were eye

to eye. "You're your own person, Jackie Whitman. You can be whoever you want to be and date whomever you want to date. I'm proud of you no matter what."

She released Jackie and settled back into her chair. "You know what? Scott gets in today. Why don't you go pick him up at the airport?"

A smile danced across Jackie's face. How was it December twelfth already? She'd lost track of the days.

"I have a surprise for you," her mom added with a grin. "He's coming home for good. He'll finish his senior year at St. Thomas."

"That's the best news I've had in weeks!" Jackie exclaimed. Her heart fluttered at the thought of having him back in her life. Someone she could depend on. Or something more . . .

"But I don't understand." Jackie frowned. "How come Aunt Deborah's changed her mind?"

"Two years away from the media and the drug scene seems to have done him a world of good. Deborah and Bob say he's a changed kid. If he stays clean—"

"Oh, so he's just on probation?"

"You could say that."

Jackie stood up and handed her mom her coat. "What time does his flight get in?"

"I'm not sure. Call Lindsay and find out." She kissed Jackie's forehead. "Now, if you don't mind, I have one last person to shop for." She tapped Jackie's nose with her finger. "And she needs to get over to the White House to catch a limo, or something."

Jackie giggled. "Okay, okay. I'm going."

"Give Scott a hug for me."

"Mom?"

"What, sweetie?"

"Thanks."

As his plane made its final approach into Reagan National Airport, Scott Price frowned. The city lay stretched out before him, glowing in the dark, but all he saw was another prison.

It had been two years since he'd been caught with a small amount of marijuana after getting pulled over for rolling through a stop sign. It hadn't mattered to his parents that it was Taylor's and he was just dropping it off. Hell, no, that made him a dealer in their eyes. Tay had left it at Jackie's and he was just being a good friend. Okay, he was going to smoke it with her . . . but hey . . .

God, it's going to be weird without Taylor around.

His other prison—school—had refused to let him go to her funeral, and he'd decided to do another summer of wilderness survival camp just so he could avoid D.C. He hadn't been ready to face everyone. Or the fact that Taylor was gone.

The plane bumped over the tarmac as it taxied to the gate. Once the doors opened, Scott grabbed his backpack from the overhead compartment and hurried off the plane and through the airport. He traveled light—the way his school taught him—and had no checked luggage, but he made a beeline for the luggage claim, looking for his driver. All of his gear from school was being shipped later.

A stocky guy held up a placard with the name "Scott" printed neatly on it. He doubted anyone would recognize him, unlike his media-darling brother. Still, his mom insisted he never use the name "Price."

"Hey," he said, walking up to the Secret Service agent. "I don't have any luggage."

The agent held out his hand. "Let me take that for you, Scott."

Scott shook his head. "I think I can manage."

The limo was parked in the red zone, with another agent positioned near the hood.

One more thing to hate about being the president's kid, constant babysitting. Jackie had told him about her agent and how she felt suffocated and how every move she made was monitored. After so much time away, he'd almost forgotten what that felt like. But seeing the agents brought it all back.

"Hi, Scott. I'm Agent Bowen," the nondescript woman said.

Couldn't they at least have given me someone good to look at?

"Hey, nice to meet you."

Agent Bowen nodded in return. The driver swung open the back door of the limo and Scott slipped out of the cold air and into the warmth of the vehicle.

It took him a second to realize someone else sat across from him. He noticed the long legs first, crossed neatly at the ankles. Scott let go of his bag and raised his head until his eyes met two deep blue ones.

"Jackie?"

Her smile stretched from ear to ear. "Surprise!"

She looked gorgeous, and Scott ran his eyes over his one-time playmate. His pulse raced.

"Are you going to say something or just stare at me all night?" she asked with a giggle.

Scott leaned back into the seat and tried to look nonchalant. Who was he kidding? He wasn't over Jackie Whitman, and he probably never would be.

———

It took all of her self-control to not gasp out loud when Scott got in the car and raked his eyes over her. He looked nothing like the boy who left after ninth grade.

He still had the same Price-family sandy brown hair, but the once floppy mess had been buzzed off. Somehow his eyes seemed darker and richer—more like liquid chocolate—now that she could actually see them. And even though he wore a parka, Jackie could tell he had more muscle than lankiness.

Basically, Scott Price had turned drop-dead delicious during his time away. Not that he hadn't been cute—they'd flirted and kissed a little freshman year, but not enough for it to ever turn into a real romance.

"Bring me up to date on everything," Scott said, flashing her a lopsided grin. "What's Laura Beth up to? And how's Lettie?"

Before she and Andrew started dating, Scott had been like the fifth Capital Girl—only a guy. He'd also been Daniel Cane's best friend until Daniel moved to L.A. for boarding school and Scott got shipped out of state.

"They're good. Laura Beth dated a guy for a while, but I'm not sure what's going on with them right now. And Lettie's dating Daniel. Didn't he tell you?"

Scott unscrewed a bottle of water and took a swig. "We haven't really talked since . . ."

"Taylor?" Jackie whispered.

He slipped off his parka and laid it neatly next to him on the seat. *Oh, dear God,* Jackie thought as she tried, but failed, to not look at him. It was as if the tight white T-shirt stretched across his chest and arms had a laser hold on her eyes.

"Daniel blames Andrew, you know. And I guess I'm guilty by relation." Scott's expression turned serious then. "I'm sorry about the stalker. The guy sending threats?"

Jackie blinked and swallowed the sudden lump in her throat. She didn't want to think about that right now. Everything was fine. She was okay. Her family was fine. Fine. Fine. *Fine.* "Let's talk about something else. Something happier." She fished around for something—anything—to change topics. "I can't believe you're home for good."

Scott shook his head and moved across the aisle so he sat right next to her. His leg grazed hers. "I want to hear about you."

Jackie's heart pounded. What was she doing? This was Scott. Andrew's younger brother.

"Well, I just found out I got into Yale. Early action," she managed to say.

"I'm not surprised." He grinned and ran his hand over the back of his shaved head. Jackie found herself wondering what it felt like. Her cheeks grew hot and she turned her head away from him.

Scott touched the back of Jackie's hand and a shiver ran through her. She turned back toward him. His chest rose and fell in quick succession as his deep brown eyes locked on hers. "Are things good with Andrew?"

He's asking me if we're still together. He's asking me because he doesn't want us to be. The realization frightened and thrilled her.

"Not really." She threw the words out before she lost her nerve.

Scott exhaled and a slow grin danced across his full lips. "I'm sorry to hear that."

Jackie tried to look upset, to send Scott the message that

Andrew was her boyfriend (although not one she wanted at the moment), but she couldn't. Instead she burst out laughing.

"What?" he asked.

Jackie bit her lower lip and shook her head. "You haven't changed."

The limo pulled up in front of her house. The lights were on, but her mom was probably still at the White House and would be until Scott's welcome-home party later that night.

Jackie looked at the house again. She could ask him in. What harm was there in that? After all, they *were* friends.

Before she could decide, Scott's arms were around her, pulling Jackie to him.

"Yeah, but the old Scott would never have had the balls to do this."

His lips floated softly over hers, like a whisper. A million butterflies fluttered in her stomach.

Oh, my God. I'm kissing Scott. Scott!

He tasted like spearmint and autumn freshness, as if he had spent a lot of time outdoors. Before she could stop herself, Jackie ran her fingers down his muscled arms. He was definitely working out *somewhere*. Scott groaned at her touch, and Jackie's breathing quickened. She pulled her head back slowly, not really wanting to end the kiss but knowing she should.

His eyes twinkled and he grinned. "I've wanted to do that for two years."

The driver pulled the door open before she could respond. Jackie scooped up her coat and stepped out of the car. She lowered her head so she could see inside the limo. Scott sat propped against the corner.

Lie, Jackie. Lie. "Not a good idea."

He shrugged. "We'll see."

She shook her head, but her mind screamed, *Yes, yes, yes!*

"Later tonight?" he suggested playfully.

Heat scorched her cheeks. "I don't think so."

Still, as she hurried up the front steps of her house, Jackie felt as if she were floating.

Scott Price kissed her.

And even though she shouldn't, Jackie hoped he did it again. Soon.

TWENTY-TWO

The thing about Christmas parties is that they can be either absolutely magical or a total train wreck. As Jackie scanned the room, she didn't hold high hopes for the Prices' annual celebration.

First, there were way too many Secret Service agents. Tonight, this was the safest place to be in Washington—probably the world. With all the dignitaries and senior U.S. officials, security was at its highest. No one was getting in who didn't belong. However, who could relax when they were constantly being watched? Just once, Jackie would have loved to see someone get trashed at a White House party and start a conga line or something.

Second, her mom and Aunt Deborah were jumpy. Her mother had confessed earlier that they had considered canceling

the party but ultimately figured that if you're not safe at the
White House, where are you safe?

And third, Jackie studied the room and wondered who had
made the guest list. *It's like they purposely invited all the Democrats who
hate each other and all the Republicans who are out to get them.*

She watched William Remick, Whitney's dad, chat up Vice
President Ike Sawyer. Of course, Tracey Mills was glued to his
side, soaking up every word and probably planning to spin the
conversation into some sort of "gotcha" article.

"Can I have you for Christmas?" Scott whispered in her
ear. Jackie hadn't heard him sneak up behind her and she
jumped.

"Scott." She punched him softly on the arm. "Stop joking."

His eyes grew serious. "I'm not."

For the past week, this was how it had been. Scott would
make a comment about wanting to kiss her/ask her out/run
away with her, and Jackie would pretend it was all a joke—
even though every time he said it, her heart leapt out of her
chest.

Tonight, he looked unbelievable in his tuxedo. All grown
up. She ran her hand over the front of her strapless Rachel Zoe.
"Aren't you going to tell me I look amazing?" she teased.

"Only if you tell me first."

Jackie rolled her eyes. "Fine. I look freakin' amazing."

Scott snorted. "Smart-ass."

From across the room, Jackie's mom signaled to her. "I'm
being summoned."

"Who are Carolyn and Ike talking to?"

Jackie groaned. "Whitney Remick's parents—Tracey Mills
and William Remick."

"Ah, right. The dreaded Whitney." He darted his eyes around the room. "Is she here?"

"I hope not. But she was invited. Through some bizarre joke."

Scott rubbed his hands together and wiggled his eyebrows. "Fantastic. I've always wanted to meet a conniving bitch."

As they walked up to her mom, Jackie heard William Remick say, "I hear the PAPPies are looking for an attractive centrist like you, Ike, to run for president."

Jackie's ears pricked up. So this was what the Remicks were discussing. Trying to see if the veep would run with the PAPPies? Jackie drew her eyebrows together, watching the vice president and her mom, who just laughed politely. Ike Sawyer was supposed to be on the ticket with Aunt Deborah next election. It was all set. Plus, he was a Democrat. Everyone knew that. Jackie's mom and Ike Sawyer exchanged glances.

"You mean they want an African American war veteran who's strong on fiscal responsibility. So does my own party—*the Democrats,*" he said smoothly. He took two glasses of champagne from a passing waiter's tray, handed one to Jackie's mother with a smile, and shifted his right leg as if uncomfortable. Jackie remembered that he'd lost his lower leg fighting in Operation Desert Storm and he couldn't stand for too long on his prosthesis. "I'm happy where I am."

"You could give Ham Griffin a real run for his money. He'd have no chance of the nomination against you," William Remick persisted.

"Jackie! Have you said hello to the vice president and the Remicks yet?" her mother interrupted, asking a little too enthusiastically.

She wants to change the subject. Fine. I'll sacrifice myself.

"Happy holidays," Jackie said with a smile. "Mr. Remick, Mrs. Mills, this is Scott Price, the president's younger son."

Tracey Mills raised an eyebrow. "Haven't you been away at school?"

Her mom answered, "He has. And we're so happy to have him home!"

Jackie could tell the conversation was veering into dangerous territory. Officially, Scott chose to go away to school—to get out of the Washington spotlight. The Price family had managed to keep his arrest quiet, but that didn't mean Tracey Mills hadn't heard rumors.

Jackie tried another diversion.

"Mrs. Mills, have you met the wounded vets who are here tonight?" She pointed to two uniformed soldiers, one in a wheelchair, who were talking to Bob Price. "Aunt Deborah invited a couple I work with at the veterans rehab hospital—Private Vic Hazelton and Private Tanya Wilson. They'd make a great human-interest piece."

"Honey, that's just wonderful. But I'm not sure the *Tattler* would let me run a story so sad." She smiled.

More like they won't run a story without any dirt.

Jackie quickly changed the subject again.

"Is Whitney here?" she asked. Like she cared.

Tracey Mills waved her hand dismissively. "Somewhere. She went looking for Laura Beth and Lettie."

"Oh. I don't think they're here yet." Laura Beth had insisted Lettie get ready at her house today—without Whitney.

Scott placed his hand on Jackie's bare arm, sending her temperature soaring a hundred degrees. "Why don't we go look for

Whitney?" He smiled politely at the Remicks. "Nice meeting you. Aunt Carolyn, Ike, see you guys later."

He led Jackie through the throng of partygoers already crowding the entrance hall and spilling into the East Room, which was lined with enormous, glittering Christmas trees, each with a different theme. "When did your mom and Ike start dating?"

Jackie froze. "What?"

"Aunt Carolyn and Ike." He stopped next to the bar and lifted two Cokes from the counter. "C'mon. You couldn't see how into each other they were?"

"No."

What the hell is he talking about?

Scott stepped behind the bar, against the protests of the bartender, and poured a little whiskey into each glass. "Shhh," he said to the man before handing one to Jackie.

"The whole time we were standing there, they kept brushing against each other." His hand grazed Jackie's as he lifted his drink to his mouth. "That's a sign of attraction."

"That's silly." She shrugged. "They like each other, they work closely together, that's all."

Jackie realized how close she and Scott were standing to each other. The way their bodies were turned toward each other. She could feel her face light up when he smiled at her.

But all the giddiness disappeared when she caught a glimpse of Andrew over his younger brother's shoulder. His green eyes sliced through the room and drilled into her.

"Scott," she said, touching his hand, "Andrew's watching us."

He shrugged. "So. We're just talking. Or are we not allowed to do that?"

"No. It's just that he looks upset." For the first time in ages, Andrew appeared sober. His eyes weren't bloodshot. He didn't look unbalanced. Just hurt.

But what does he have to be hurt about? He did this to himself. He made bad decisions. Not me.

"Do you need to talk to him?" Scott asked, his voice strained, as if he were trying to hide his irritation.

Jackie shook her head. "We're past talking." She batted her blue eyes playfully at Scott. "Besides, I'm enjoying my current company too much."

"Then let's pretend my brother isn't there, okay?"

"Deal," she said.

Lettie gasped and craned her head to see the top of the tree. The entire East Room smelled like pine. Just this one Christmas tree was easily twenty-five feet tall. She'd never seen anything so beautiful.

The tree was covered in twinkling white lights, red bows, and silver bells, and the design team had wrapped the wall behind it in gold foil, with giant red bows running from ceiling to floor. Standing here made her feel like Clara in *The Nutcracker*.

"Isn't it somethin'?" Libby Ballou asked, pushing Lettie and Laura Beth through the foyer and into the room. "They do it up like this every year."

Sol and Jeffrey Ives trailed behind them. Laura Beth had taken Jackie and Lettie's advice and decided to forgive him. Lettie still wasn't a hundred percent sure about him, but she liked that he'd been honest.

And since no evidence had turned up against Sol's parents, Mrs. Ballou had agreed—to the girls' surprise—to let Laura Beth date him again. Though the whole way over, she barely spoke to him beyond a polite "hello" and a "thank you" when he offered his hand to help her out of the car. Still, Laura Beth didn't seem to mind. She'd been floating around all afternoon, talking about how much better things were between her and Sol. How their relationship had matured.

Mrs. Ballou had insisted they make a fashionably late appearance—which meant an hour after the start of the party. And it paid off for her. As she and the girls walked through the room, guests stopped to either kiss her cheek or shake her hand. Laura Beth seemed thrilled by the parade, but Lettie just wanted to find Jackie and Daniel. And Paz.

Her eyes roamed the crowded room, but there was no sign of her brother. Carolyn Shaw had personally invited Paz, saying she wanted him to get used to the crowd without the pressure of being on the job.

So where is he?

"Lettie! Laura Beth!" Jackie waved at them from behind another massive Christmas tree. The two girls exchanged knowing glances. Scott Price was glued to Jackie's side, and Andrew was nowhere to be found. It had been that way all week.

"What is she doin'?" Laura Beth whispered. "I know Andrew made a horrible mistake, but does Jackie need to run around with Scott? It looks bad."

Lettie pursed her lips and shook her head slightly. "They've been friends forever, Laura Beth. And Scott is one of our friends, if you haven't forgotten."

"Of course not! I'm just sayin'." Laura Beth laced her arm

through Sol's as though he might run away if she didn't keep him tethered to her.

"Hi, girls! Sol!" Jackie spoke a little too fast. Too bubbly.

Lettie's eyes fell on the near empty glass in Jackie's hand. *Looks like someone's been in the liquor cabinet.*

Laura Beth quickly introduced Sol to Scott. "Isn't this great? We're all together again. And with new friends, too! This is just what the holidays are for!"

"Speaking of old and new friends, have any of you seen Daniel or Whitney?" Lettie asked.

Scott grinned and wiggled his eyebrows in the mischievous way Lettie remembered. Taylor always said Scott had the face of an angel and the mind of a devil. She would have known, since she was created from the same cast.

"I can't wait to meet Whitney. Jackie's told me lots of . . . interesting things about her," Scott said.

"Don't listen to them. Whitney's not bad at all. She does dumb things, but who doesn't?" Lettie said.

Jackie and Laura Beth both rolled their eyes. "That's our Lettie, always seeing the good in everyone."

Sometimes they treat me like a naïve fool. But I'm the only one who has to deal with real life. With real stuff.

Lettie turned away from her group of friends to hide the redness creeping into her cheeks. She pretended to admire the Christmas tree, while her friends continued to make fun of Whitney.

A piece of white stood out on the tree. An envelope. *That's strange. Why would there be an envelope on the tree?*

She moved closer to it until she made out the word JACKIE printed in neat block letters across the front.

"Hey, Jackie? There's a card here for you." Lettie plucked it from the tree and handed it to her friend.

"On the tree?" Scott asked.

Lettie nodded. "Yeah. I thought it was weird."

Laughing, Jackie slid her finger under the tab and pulled out a piece of crisp white card stock. Her smile disappeared.

She let out a scream of horror.

Fear pounded through Jackie's body. Hot, shivery, and fast, it started in her gut and spread to every part of her body until she stood trembling and unable to move.

Scott tore the letter from her hand, read it, and immediately signaled for the Secret Service agents mingling among the guests.

This isn't happening. Someone is playing a sick joke. But why? Why would someone want to scare me?

The words on the note card flashed through her mind.

You look so sexy in blood red.

That's all it said. And yet it terrified her. Someone had walked through layers of security—supposedly the best in the world—and left this card for her.

She fought the bile rising in her throat as she realized what it meant: Someone at the party did this.

"Jackie?" Scott asked gently. "Are you okay? You're shaking like a leaf."

"Leave her alone." Andrew shoved his brother out of the way. "I've got this."

Scott crossed his arms. "Right, like you've 'handled' every-thing else?"

Andrew grabbed the card from Scott, read it, and handed it to a Secret Service agent, and slipped his arm around Jackie's waist, guiding her toward the foyer. Being in his arms felt safe and Jackie relaxed into him.

"Thank you," she muttered. "I . . . I needed to get out of there."

Andrew leaned his head down and kissed the top of her head. Her heart didn't speed up the way it did with Scott, but it felt nice. As though a missing piece had slotted back into place.

"I'll always take care of you, Jackie. Always."

The Cane family appeared in the doorway, blocking their way out of the room. "Jackie! Andrew!" Jennifer Cane said cheerfully. "You can't be running off already?"

Jackie felt Andrew stiffen next to her as Daniel shot him a dirty look.

"Not now," she said to both guys. "I'm not in the mood." She forced herself to smile at Jennifer Cane. "We have to go. But my mom and Aunt Deborah are in the reception room."

Jennifer Cane gave a conspiratorial smile and winked. "Well, have fun, you two."

A Secret Service agent calmly strode up to Jackie and guided her and Andrew the rest of the way out of the party and upstairs to the family quarters. Jackie sat on a plush couch, her heart hammering in her chest, trying to make sense of what happened. Before her, Andrew paced.

"Can I get you something? A drink?" he asked.

Jackie studied him. She had been right earlier. His eyes were clear and he was fully composed. There was no sign of the screwed-up drunken mess he'd been for the past couple of months.

"Something strong," she said.

Andrew hurried to the bar and poured out a whiskey. "Drink this. Fast. I have a feeling we won't be alone for long."

Sure enough, within minutes the rest of the Price family and her mom joined them in the living room.

"What's happening?" Jackie asked as soon as everyone made sure she was fine.

"The Secret Service is sweeping the party. But for now, we've been asked to stay up here until they determine the source of the note and the threat level," Aunt Deborah said.

Jackie held her head in her hands. She had ruined the party. Now everyone was going to think she was a weak little girl.

"I'm sorry," she said as fat tears welled in her eyes.

"No, Jackie. Don't cry." Her mom draped an arm around Jackie's shoulder. "This isn't your fault. And it will be easy to get to the bottom of it. We have a record of every person who walks into the White House. Our list of suspects is narrow."

Scott sat down across from her. "What do you say? After this, we blow off the party and do that hamburger tour we talked about?"

Jackie tried to smile and sniffed. "I doubt I'll be allowed to leave. And all our friends are still down there. They're probably freaked out."

Andrew knelt next to Jackie. "Don't worry about them."

She moved her gaze between the two brothers. The one

who had done nothing but make her feel miserable for the past few months, and the one who always made her laugh.

Suddenly, she didn't want to be around either one of them. She didn't want to feel like a prize the Price brothers were fighting over.

"I think I want to be alone with my mom," she said. In the corner, Aunt Deborah and her mother were engaged in a heated discussion.

"Mom?" Jackie asked. "Is everything okay?"

She didn't answer, but Aunt Deborah did. "There's no need to panic, Jackie. But just as a precaution, I'm increasing your security detail."

Jackie pressed her eyes shut and counted to three. "Because of the note?"

"Because this sicko penetrated security tonight. And we're supposedly fully prepared." As Aunt Deborah spoke, she turned her hard eyes on Agents Davenport and Fellows. "This should not have been possible."

Air caught in Jackie's lungs, and she had to force herself to breathe. Air in. Air out. One. Two. Three.

"That's why there was so much security?" Jackie asked. "Because there was another threat against me?"

She wondered what she'd done to draw this kind of attention. Why would someone want to harm *her*? She was just a kid, not a politician.

Her mom rubbed her eyes. In the past half hour, she had gone from elegant party guest to ragged-looking mother. While her hair and dress still looked impeccable, dark shadows ringed her eyes and lines creased her brow.

"Can we be alone?" her mother asked her boss.

Aunt Deborah turned to Agent Davenport. "Mark? Are we clear yet?"

He held his finger to his ear, listening. "Madam President, you and your family may return to the party. However, we'd like to keep Jackie and her mother up here for a while longer."

Aunt Deborah nodded. "Take all the time you need. I'll make an excuse."

She walked over to where Jackie sat and squeezed her hand. "This ends here, Jackie. I won't have you terrorized."

Jackie smiled weakly at the most powerful woman in the world and felt . . . nothing. She wasn't sure if Aunt Deborah could protect her anymore. Because Jackie was beginning to believe whoever was threatening her might be someone close. Someone the family trusted.

She shivered.

Andrew lingered in the doorway as the others left, staring at her.

She couldn't read his expression, and for a second, she wondered if he was her stalker. She shoved the thought out of her mind. *That's absurd.*

Her mother nudged her slightly. "I think he wants to speak to you."

Jackie walked across the room on shaky legs. Andrew turned his back so that he blocked her mom's view.

Something cold and hard pressed into Jackie's hand. She looked down at the phone Andrew had given her.

"I wanted to give this to you ever since I told you the truth, but I just . . . couldn't."

Before Jackie could ask him questions, he slipped out the door.

In her hand was Taylor's cell phone—the one that had gone missing the night of the accident.

The one Andrew had had all this time.

"Daniel, why don't you take Lettie somewhere nice and quiet? Away from all these people?" Laura Beth squeezed her trembling friend's hand and tried her best to remain calm. After all, that's what Ballou woman did—they kept things moving.

Around them, people laughed and hugged and greeted each other with air-kisses. Fortunately, no one seemed to have noticed the incident, apart from a couple of people nearby, and Laura Beth had done her best to cover it up. Make it seem like some silly teens getting a little too rowdy.

"Where?" Daniel asked. "The White House is packed."

Laura Beth clucked her tongue at him and his lack of imagination. "Maybe the family quarters? Go check on Jackie?"

Daniel pried Lettie's fingers from Laura Beth's and put his arm around her. He leaned close to Lettie's ear and whispered, which made Lettie smile.

They make such a cute couple: the skateboarder and the scholar.

"So now what, Miss Ballou?" Sol's deep brown eyes twinkled. No matter how many times Laura Beth looked at him, she felt like she found a new, more beautiful part. Like his eyelashes. Or the way he rubbed his finger and thumb together when he was nervous. Or how the hair at his neck had a slight curl.

Laura Beth moved away from the Christmas tree. The Secret Service had taken the note card and there wasn't any evidence of the threat Jackie received. It was like it didn't happen.

Only it had. Again. And this time, inside a heavily guarded building.

But Laura Beth didn't want to think about that. After all, there was nothing *she* could do. Besides, Jackie was fine, tucked safely away upstairs.

"We could join the others upstairs," she suggested coyly.

"I've always wanted to have a tour of the White House family quarters," Sol said. "I've heard there are ghosts up there on the third floor."

She lifted her eyes to his and her heart sped up. "And secret passages."

"Really?" Sol was already pulling her toward the Grand Staircase.

Two Secret Service agents stood guard at the bottom. "I'm Laura Beth Ballou and this is Sol Molla. We're close friends of Jackie Whitman and Andrew Price. I'd like to check on my friend."

The agent on the left studied her for a moment. She couldn't tell if he was being very thorough and assessing them for danger or if he was checking her out. Either way, it made her skin crawl.

He spoke quietly into his mouthpiece, but Laura Beth still heard her name. He nodded as he listened.

"ID?" he asked.

Laura Beth pulled hers from a tiny silver purse and Sol produced his. They handed them to the agent. Satisfied, he let them by.

"That was intense," Sol said.

Laura Beth giggled and led him away from the living room, where she knew Jackie would be, and up the stairs to the third floor. "Not as intense as what I have planned," she said a little ambiguously.

"Really?" From behind her, Sol wrapped his arms around her and lifted her slightly off the floor. Her back pressed against his solid frame, and heat flooded her body.

She reached out in front of her and pushed against a door. It gave way.

"What the hell?" Whitney's voice floated from behind the wall.

Laura Beth huffed. "Oh, good Lord, Whitney. What are you doing in there?" she said as she shoved open the door, revealing Whitney and . . .

Paz!

Oh, Lettie is going to die if she hears about this!

Whitney threw an amused glance at Laura Beth. "Obviously more than you."

Paz looked way beyond embarrassed.

"It's not how it looks—" he started to say.

That's it. I've about had it with this girl. Stay calm. Just like Mama taught you.

Laura Beth cut him off midsentence.

"Did you know someone threatened Jackie tonight and the White House is being searched top to bottom? Hiding away in here seems very suspicious."

"Someone threatened Jackie?" Paz asked with true concern.

Whitney rolled her eyes as she stepped into the hallway. "When isn't Jackie threatened? Every week it's something new."

Laura Beth swallowed every foul word that popped into her head. No way would she stoop to this brass bitch's level. "You should be more careful, Whitney. You never know who's listening."

"Where's Lettie?" Paz asked.

"She's really upset, so I had Daniel bring her up here to the family quarters," Laura Beth replied. Paz nodded curtly before hurrying off. Not a good-bye to Whitney or anything.

Definitely true love.

Whitney shook her full head of curls and chuckled. "Watch your back, LB." She winked at Sol, and flashes of red pulsed behind Laura Beth's eyes. Whitney sashayed down the stairs, making sure she threw a little extra wiggle into her walk.

Sol wrapped his arms around Laura Beth and gently smoothed her hair. She felt the tension melt from her body. "Why don't we find your friends?" he suggested.

Calm, Laura Beth. Calm. You're a Southern lady. Act like one.

"That's a great idea!" she said a little too perkily, and flashed a megawatt smile at her boyfriend. "I'm sure Jackie could use some cheering up, and poor Lettie . . . Don't tell Lettie what we just saw. It would upset her."

Lettie and Daniel sat in the family room. Daniel had a glass of amber liquid, and Lettie played with what looked to be a glass of water but was probably vodka.

"Where's Jackie?" Laura Beth asked, taking the seat across from them.

"Her mom took her to Andrew's bedroom so they could be alone," Daniel replied.

That was for the best. After all, Jackie probably wasn't in the mood to socialize anymore.

Daniel tapped his pocket. "Why don't we go out on the balcony and have these?"

He held up a couple of cigars.

Sol immediately stood up. "Sounds good. Laura Beth?"

She placed her hand in his and walked to the Truman Balcony. When she was younger, she'd fantasized about standing out here with Andrew—after their wedding. Like English royalty at Buckingham Palace. Below them, loving citizens would fill the lawn, admiring the happy couple.

Daniel lit a cigar, took a long drag, and passed it to Lettie, who—to Laura Beth's surprise—placed it in her mouth and puffed.

Oh, what the heck, if she can, so can I.

But before she could take her first drag, voices from the lawn distracted them. Daniel leaned over the edge, his feet dangling off the ground.

"Dudes, you've got to see this," Daniel whispered.

She leaned over the edge, Sol's arm around her waist. In the fresh snow on the lawn, Senator Ives was bent on one knee. In front of her mama!

Laura Beth threw her hand over her mouth. *Oh, my Lord, he's proposing!*

With a racing heart, she strained to hear every word.

"I want you by my side, Libby. For life. And I want you there when I run for president."

"Oh, my Lord," Laura Beth squealed, and grabbed on to Lettie's arm. "Are you hearin' this? My mama is gettin' married! She's gettin' married!"

Below them, they watched Libby Ballou throw herself into

the senator's arms. Daniel let out a catcall and the happy couple looked up, laughing.

"Laura Beth, darlin'! The senator and I are gettin' married!" Libby shouted.

"I know, Mama!" Laura Beth's grin stretched across her face, and she didn't know if it would ever stop.

After her friends shouted down their congratulations, Daniel smirked. "Looks like you and Jackie will both be on the campaign trail next year."

The smile faded from Laura Beth's face as she played with her charm bracelet. They swore nothing could come between them—not boys, not jobs, not politics. Nothing. And so far nothing had.

But what if that was all about to change?

TWENTY-THREE

Jackie stirred whipped cream into her hot chocolate and watched it turn from dark to mocha. She, Lettie, and Laura Beth were sitting in the corner of Seasons in the Four Seasons Hotel in Georgetown, one of their favorite haunts. They were getting ready to exchange presents. Just like every year. Only this was the first time without Taylor.

Next year will be easier, Jackie thought. *There won't be so many firsts.*

But would it really? The hole Taylor left behind could never be filled, and it seemed like it kept growing bigger and bigger, sucking them all into it. Even more since Andrew gave Jackie Taylor's cell phone.

That night, after she and her mother had been safely escorted back to their home, Jackie had tentatively scrolled through Taylor's calls. One number came up again and again, with a couple of phone messages from a frantic woman begging Taylor,

"Don't tell Daniel. Please, please." And another warning Tay of danger.

Try as she might, Jackie couldn't figure out what it all meant except that Taylor had been involved in something. Something that had apparently spun out of control.

"Can I just say how happy I am that Whitney is gone for the rest of break? I swear, I thought she'd never leave." Laura Beth tossed her hair over her shoulder and broke off a piece of cookie.

Lettie sighed. "I know you all hate her, but try to remember I live with Whitney. And she isn't that bad—when she's not hitting on Paz."

"Or my boyfriend," Laura Beth said.

"Or plotting to ruin my relationship-slash-life," Jackie added.

The three girls giggled.

"Here's to Whitney finally getting her trip to California," Laura Beth said, raising her mug. "She must have spilled some really good dirt to her mom. I guess we'll find out sooner or later. . . . May she come back less bitchy and less slutty."

Jackie clinked mugs with her friends. "So, who wants to go first?" she asked.

Laura Beth bounced up and down in her seat. Ever since Miss Libby had gotten engaged, she'd been walking on springs. And why shouldn't she be? The senator seemed like a great guy—even if he was a Republican.

"Me, me, me," Laura Beth said, sounding like a little kid. She pulled two presents wrapped in shiny red paper from her bag and handed one to Lettie before giving Jackie hers. "I hope you like them."

The two girls carefully peeled off the tape and wrapping. Inside each package was a small white box with the words L. M. WINSTON, JEWELER stamped in gold lettering.

Jackie set the lid on the table. A single silver charm lay on the white cotton. She picked it up with a sinking feeling.

"I know you haven't worn your Capital Girls bracelet in a long time, Jackie. But they still mean something to me—to us." She nodded at Lettie, who was holding hers up with a wide smile. "I had this made to show we're indestructible. Nothing can tear us apart—not men, not politics. Nothing.".

The charm was completely different from the clover-shaped charms they'd added every year since seventh grade. This one was a simple infinity loop. With heaviness in her heart, Jackie traced the charm with her finger.

"We'll always be friends. No matter what," Jackie whispered, leaning over to kiss her friends' cheeks.

But even as she uttered the words, she had a feeling that things were about to happen—over Taylor, over the presidential race, over guys—that no charm could protect them from.

Turn the page for

a sneak peek of

TRUTH OR DARE

ella monroe

A CAPITAL GIRLS NOVEL

Available in April 2013

from St. Martin's Griffin

ONE

The past month had been hell.

Scratch that. The past *year* had been hell.

And now this?

Jackie Whitman threw herself onto the sofa and glared first at the TV, then at the gold-embossed card in her hand.

Mrs. Elizabeth "Libby" Ballou, Miss Laura Beth Ballou, and Senator Jeffrey Ives

Kindly Request Your Presence at

A Celebration of the Life of Taylor Cane

Jackie could hardly believe a whole year had passed since Taylor was killed in a car wreck. It still seemed unreal. Yet it was also too real. Too raw.

Unreal to think that Taylor—her best friend, the one who

taught her that life should be fun and *loyalty* a given—had had sex with Jackie's boyfriend the night she died. Andrew's devastating confession, though, was as real and as raw now as the day she heard it.

A whole year later, and she still hadn't discovered the answer to "Why?" What dark secret had forced Taylor to betray her?

Seething, she re-read the surprise invitation to an event she'd known nothing about, then shoved it back in her purse and snapped the clasp. She didn't need this. Not today of all days.

In less than an hour, unless a miracle happened, Senator Jeffrey Ives—Laura Beth's soon-to-be stepfather—would be announcing his candidacy for president of the United States. Running against President Deborah Price, Andrew's mother and the boss and best friend of Jackie's mom.

Throwing Jackie and Laura Beth into enemy camps. Threatening to destroy what was left of the Capital Girls. If Whitney Remick didn't do it first, of course. Jackie shoved away thoughts of the two-faced Cali transplant. She didn't need that worry today, either.

Senator Ives's announcement was why Jackie was sitting in the First Family's private living room in the White House, waiting for President Price and Jackie's mom, Chief of Staff Carolyn Shaw, to arrive. So they could all watch it together. Like one big, happy family.

Jackie stared at the TV, where a blond, Botoxed reporter was standing outside the senator's brand-new Iowa campaign headquarters.

Jackie couldn't believe her ears. The presidential election was almost two years away and Senator Ives hadn't even won the Republican nomination. Yet the reporter was already referring to him as President Price's "worst nightmare" and "her most formidable obstacle to a second term."

"What crap!" she said out loud.

Without warning, Jackie felt a pair of warm hands on her shoulders. She shivered in delight as the strong fingers began to gently yet firmly massage the tense muscles in her neck.

Andrew, she thought, surprised, but also thrilled by his touch.

"Should I stop?" Andrew's brother, Scott, said from behind the sofa. "Or should I see what else needs my magic touch?" he whispered teasingly.

A wave of guilt washed over her. His hands felt so good she didn't *want* him to stop. But what if their mothers walked in on them?

Or Andrew? Though their relationship had hit rock bottom, they were still a couple in the eyes of their parents and the public. After all, the Ankie romance, as the media dubbed it, was fodder for the tabloids and great family-values publicity for the president.

There was no denying the chemistry between her and Scott. But what if it was more than that? As she had with Andrew, she'd grown up with Scott. He was a good listener, someone she'd always been able to talk to. Hang with. Trust. The way she used to with Andrew.

Despite her anger toward her best friend, Jackie tried to imagine how Taylor would handle Scott's flirting.

"Maybe we can continue this later," she purred.

"I'm down with that. Just name the time and the place."

She could hear the smile in his voice. "Be careful what you wish—"

A voice cut her off. "Jackie!"

Lettie Velasquez walked into the room, beaming.

"I'm here to cheer you up," she said. "Your mom arranged it. Sorry it took so long. They've really amped up the security around here."

Jackie sighed. For most of winter break, she had barely moved an inch without a Secret Service tail.

All because some insane person keeps threatening me.

Her skin crawled at the thought of the terrifying note the stalker somehow smuggled into the White House Christmas party. She felt violated all over again.

"Hi, Scott," Lettie said, then her eyes fell to his hands on Jackie's shoulders. "Where's Andrew?"

"He's helping Dad bake brownies," he said.

Scott let go and sat down next to her. Jackie rubbed her arms where the goose bumps were still tickling her skin.

"Too bad Andrew can't slip some weed in those brownies," Scott added. "That'd really cheer us up. But Number One Perfect Son would never do that."

"Behave!" Jackie slapped him lightly on the arm, her hand lingering.

Scott's fondness for pot had landed him in a Midwestern reform school, under orders from his parents. Now he was on family probation—the Prices had just agreed to let him stay in D.C. for the rest of his senior year.

Unfortunately, his crack about Number One Perfect Son was anything but true. Actually, Andrew's "perfect" façade was crumbling. At least behind closed doors. He'd been drinking way too much, his grades were slipping at Georgetown University, and he'd generally been acting like a jerk. So Jackie wasn't about to defend her so-called boyfriend. Besides, she didn't want to get stuck in the middle of another Andrew-Scott rivalry thing, which was about as old as they were. When they were little kids, they'd fought for their mother's attention or argued over who got to bat first in a game of T-ball. It was the same thing today, only worse.

So she bit her lip. And withdrew her hand from Scott's arm when she saw Lettie giving her a puzzled look.

"Scott, move over," she said. "Lettie, come sit next to me."

"I'm good," Lettie said. "You know me, I like to sit on the floor when I watch TV."

Jackie shifted her legs so Lettie could lean against the sofa between them, which forced Scott to move a few inches back. She picked up Lettie's long, black ponytail, pulled out the hairband, and started to make a Katniss braid. Lettie, with her dark hair and eyes and olive skin, could have easily passed for the *Hunger Games* heroine.

As she divided the hair into three thick strands, Jackie thought of the irony of Lettie being here to cheer *her* up. It was really Jackie who should be comforting Lettie, whose entire family, apart from her brother, Paz, was trapped in a near–civil war in their home country of Paraguay.

"Have you heard from your mom and dad?" she asked.

Lettie shook her head slowly. "Not for a while." She was quiet for a moment before continuing. "That's the hardest part, Jackie. It's so difficult getting letters in and out, and the phone lines are down a lot of the time, so it's impossible to call. And of course, the government has shut down the Internet."

"Lettie, you are so unbelievably brave," Jackie said, and meant it. "I don't know how you do it."

"I don't have any choice. I force myself to focus on my

studies, and I convince myself that the ambassador will keep them safe as long as Mamá and Papá continue working for him."

Jackie knew that Lettie followed every single news item about her country and that right now, there seemed to be a lull in the fighting.

"It can't be easy living with Whitney and her mom," Scott added. Jackie had thought the exact same thing since the day Lettie moved in with the Remicks.

"I'm surprised Whitney didn't force you to bring her along today," Jackie said, using both hands to twist the ribbons of hair into a braid.

"Oh, Whitney's not as bad you think. Anyway, she's still in L.A. Fortunately, her mom didn't know I was coming here, otherwise she would have made Whitney fly back early."

"Did you get your invitation yet?" Jackie asked.

"What invitation?"

Jackie rolled her eyes.

"We've been summoned to a memorial celebration for Taylor. Didn't you know? Hosted by Laura Beth and her mom. And Senator Ives. Mrs. Mills probably got to yours first so she could steam it open."

Lettie twisted her head around to look at Jackie; her mouth gaped open. "A Taylor celebration? You're not serious."

"I wish."

Not that an event to mark the one-year anniversary of Taylor's death was a bad idea. It was the sneaky way Laura Beth had done it, not even discussing it first with Jackie or Lettie. And why was Senator Ives's name on the invitation? He never even knew Taylor.

The campaign hadn't even started and yet the two Ballou

women were already plotting behind Jackie's back to make sure Senator Ives scored political points with the media and Washington's powerful elite—starting with Taylor's mom. Jennifer Cane. The Fixer. The keeper of Jackie's secrets, whom Jackie owed big time.

My name should be on that invitation, not theirs.

She wrapped the hairband around the end of the braid and Lettie draped it over her shoulder, her Capital Girls charm bracelet jangling. Taylor had come up with the name of their exclusive clique in seventh grade, and Libby Ballou had ordered four identical bracelets, adding a charm every year to represent each year of the girls' friendship.

After Andrew's confession, Jackie had thrown her bracelet in a bedroom drawer. She hadn't taken it out since.

Jackie suddenly thought of a whole new reason to be terrified of a Price-Ives election fight. What if someone dug up the secret fact that it was Andrew, not Taylor, who was driving the night of the fatal crash? What if that someone was Laura Beth, who Jackie worried already suspected the truth?

If Taylor was willing to betray me, why wouldn't Laura Beth?

Until Sol came along, Laura Beth had had a not-so-secret crush on Andrew, probably fantasizing about one day being his First Lady. But that's all it had been—a deluded dream. Becoming First Daughter in an Ives White House, though, that was a real possibility.

TWO

"Mama, please stop fussin' over my hair. It looks fine," Laura Beth said, ducking out of reach. She'd just spent an hour putting up with the team of stylists that her mama and Senator Ives had kept hidden from the press, in order to prevent any negative stories getting out about the privileged Ballous.

"'Fine' just won't do, Laura Beth," her mama chided. "This is our first step on the road to the White House. If all goes as planned, we'll be refurnishing the presidential mansion and presidin' over state dinners with Kate and Will before you can blink an eye!"

Laura Beth held her tongue. She couldn't blame her mother for being on edge. She knew Mama was so in love with Jeffrey Ives she wanted everything to be just perfect for him. Mama had a big stake in his success, too. She'd regain the status she had when Daddy was alive and she was the queen bee of the

Republican Party. Even so, she'd been extra irritable lately, and Laura Beth wondered if there was something else on her mind.

She forced herself to smile sweetly.

Laura Beth had always envied Jackie's place in the spotlight and never understood why Jackie constantly complained about it. But now she was starting to get it. She was stuck in Iowa for what seemed like forever, rushing from one photo op to the next, practically around the clock, and treated like a prop, shoved into the public eye when needed and ignored when the TV cameras turned off.

Obviously, Jeffrey's handlers were incompetent. They didn't seem to understand what an asset she could be to the campaign.

With her political savvy—thank you, Mama and Daddy— her natural acting talent, and her all-American good looks, she'd be the perfect face of the "youth vote for Ives." She pictured her image blasted across social media, from Facebook fan sites to face-to-face interviews with Jon Stewart. She might even be able to swing him Republican.

Yes. She knew *exactly* what her role should be. She just had to come up with a plan to make it happen.

She wished Jeffrey would hurry up and get here so everyone could take their places inside the cavernous Des Moines conference room where the reporters and Ives supporters were waiting for his announcement.

She eyed her two soon-to-be ugly stepsisters, Dina and Frances Ives. They looked like they were actually *into* it—thrilled to be killing time in the middle of freaking nowhere.

Those two—with their flawless skin, naturally straight black hair, prominent cheekbones, killer bodies, and fake sweetness— truly put her gracious Southern manners to the test.

"Listen! They're chanting his name!" Dina squealed, bouncing up and down on her Mary Janes as the noise filled the hallway. "It's so exciting!"

The only thing the roar did for Laura Beth was give her a headache. Which was fast turning into a migraine when she thought about what she was being forced to wear in front of all those people.

Here she was, about to go on national TV, in a no-brand knit dress that looked like something Lettie would choose if left unsupervised. The beige color totally washed out her delicate complexion and the cut was as shapeless as a sack. When she had a divine, perfectly tailored turquoise suit hanging in her hotel room.

But the campaign manager had decided all three girls, especially Laura Beth, needed a down-home makeover. To her horror, the three of them had been dragged to dreary Corn Capital Mall, where Ann Taylor passed for high fashion and the only thing French were the fries.

She pulled out her iPhone.

Promise me you won't watch the announcement. They're making me wear a hideous dress. I look like a librarian and not the sexy kind in the movies, she texted her boyfriend, Sol Molla.

She wondered how much this campaign was going to ruin her sizzling love life. It was tough enough with Sol as a full-time student at Columbia in New York City.

"You look very cute, Laura Beth." Frances interrupted her thoughts, giving Laura Beth a condescending glance while also trying to read the text message over her shoulder. "Your frizz is just *adorable*."

Laura Beth gritted her teeth.

Kill them with kindness, she reminded herself.

Along with being Senator Ives's daughter, Frances was an arrogant congressional aide who worked with First Husband Bob Price on education issues. She was always blabbering on about how great he was, as if he were a hero instead of a two-timing husband and neglectful father.

But Frances's little sister was even worse. A bratty, conniving junior who'd only just started at Excelsior Prep, Dina had quickly become BFFs with Whitney and Angie Meehan, numero unos on the Capital Girls' shit list.

Before she could make nice the way she was supposed to, Laura Beth saw her mama coming at her with the hairbrush again.

"It is not adorable, Frances. It's unruly and she can't walk around looking like she got tossed about in a windstorm."

Nice Southern girls don't sass their mamas, Laura Beth reminded herself.

"Of course not, Mama, thank you," Laura Beth said, flinching as her auburn curls got painfully tangled in the bristles.

She noticed her mother was wearing an antique sapphire instead of her drop-dead fabulous eight-carat engagement ring.

Surely she couldn't have lost it?

"Mama, where's your ring?" Laura Beth panicked.

"Right here," she said, patting her heart. "Jeffrey says it's so extravagant it sends the wrong message, so I decided to keep it on a chain under my clothes, at least until he wins the nomination."

She held her left hand in front of Laura Beth's face. "This little bitty bauble belonged to his grandmama. Its value is of the sentimental variety."

Okay. But what kind of message does that four-thousand-dollar Bergdorf

Goodman handbag send to the voters? Especially if it also turns out to be made from an endangered species.

Her mother dropped the brush into her crocodile-skin handbag. "Now you look adorable. Mercy, I could use a drink right now," she sighed. "Even if it had to be in a paper cup. Just a teeny bourbon and branch would do the trick."

Me too.

Laura Beth remembered the last time Taylor had made them cocktails. All four girls were sprawled on the deep-pile white rug in front of the Italian marble fireplace in the Ballous' family room.

"I fixed a 'Hollywood' for Laura Beth. Cause that's the next step after Broadway, baby," Taylor said, handing me a glass that looked like it was filled with liquid gold.

"An 'Apple Pie,' natch, for the all-American girl," she joked to Jackie, "who's gonna be the second female president of the United States, unless I can persuade her to run off with a Chippendale dancer!"

Jackie grinned and sniffed the drink. "Yum. Apple schnapps? With cinnamon?"

Taylor nodded.

"And for Lettie, a 'Latin Lover' to remind you there's more to life than just textbooks and law school." Lettie blushed as she took the spiked pineapple juice.

"And a 'Sex on the Beach' for moi! What else?" Taylor hooted, shaking her booty as she drained her glass in one gulp.

Her mama, plucking imaginary lint off her dress, brought Laura Beth back to the present.

"Now, remember to smile just the way I told you," she instructed.

"Don't worry, Mama. I'll be a pretty face for you and the senator."

"Laura Beth Ballou, if I've taught you anything, it's that a woman is never *just* a pretty face." Her mother clucked her tongue disapprovingly.

Laura Beth's face got hot.

"Oh, Miss Libby." Dina giggled. "I think Laura Beth only meant that today is my father's show. We don't want to steal his thunder."

"Of course not, darlin.'" Libby beamed at Dina. "We're a perfect example of the new blended American family. We are all smart, strong women who know how to support their man."

Jeffrey Ives suddenly appeared, flanked by aides, putting an end to the nauseating conversation.

"Ready, ladies?" He smiled, taking his fianceé's hand.

Laura Beth took a deep breath. Despite the excitement of the moment, all she wanted was to be back home in D.C. with her two best friends.

Who'll probably hate me after today.

"Shit! Shit! Shit! Shit! Shit!" Jackie hissed at the TV as Senator Ives plunged into the crowd outside his campaign headquarters.

A chill ran down Lettie's spine.

If Jackie's already this flipped out, how's she going to survive the next two years?

It didn't help that Senator Ives had given a great speech. He'd hit all the right notes to appeal to his base without sounding like a wacky PAPPie, the breakaway Republican group bent on destroying President Price. From everything Lettie had been reading lately, it looked like the PAPPies were going to pick creepy conservative Senator Hampton Griffin as their presidential candidate.

Lettie studied the TV screen. No Hollywood director could have picked a better-looking cast to play the newly created Ives-Ballou family.

She glanced at Andrew, who was slumped in an armchair at the far end of the room. Unlike Jackie, who'd kept up a scathing running commentary of the speech, Andrew and Scott had traded jokes—until the topic turned to Jackie.

"Well, at least Senator Ives will be the best-dressed man running for president," Andrew said, taking in Senator Ives's immaculately cut gray suit.

"Yeah, but wait till Mom unveils her spring line of pantsuits," Scott joked.

"Doesn't *anyone* care about the issues anymore?" Lettie joined in.

"Sure they do," Scott said. "But it's a lot more convincing when it comes from a handsome knight in shining armor. Not to mention a few cute handmaidens."

"Yeah, and I bet Laura Beth pulls out all the stops for her national debut," Andrew added.

"Laura Beth's no competition next to Jackie," Scott said, throwing her a big smile.

Lettie watched Andrew's face turn into a scowl. "I don't need you to tell me that," he said.

Ouch.

Fortunately Senator Ives wrapped up his speech at that point.

Scott started playing a game on his iPhone, looking up only when the camera zoomed in on Laura Beth.

"That's the ugliest dress I've ever seen," he observed.

"Obviously someone forced her to wear it. No way would she have picked that," Jackie said, studying Laura Beth in amazement.

"Yeah, even I wouldn't wear that," Lettie joked.

"Don't *you* wear clothes like that on the campaign trail, Jackie. Sexy best always gets more votes. Especially your sexy best," said Scott, prompting another glare from Andrew.

Jackie laughed.

Lettie had never flirted in her life but she knew it when she saw it.

What is the deal with Scott? And in front of Andrew?

As if on cue, Andrew snapped, "Jackie would look good in anything."

Jackie didn't answer. Her eyes were fixed on Laura Beth, who was holding hands with Dina and Frances and smiling like there was nobody else she'd rather be with.

"You'd never guess by her little act that Laura Beth hates those two," Jackie said.

"Laura Beth's right where she's always wanted to be, on center stage," Lettie said mildly. "Politics is in her genes."

"Dirty politics, you mean," Jackie said. "Her father was the king of dirty tricks. Let's hope she doesn't follow in his footsteps."

"She hasn't done anything dirty," Lettie said. "She's just smiling. It's typical Laura Beth. Give her a stage and she'll put on a performance."

"Yeah, well, Laura Beth deserves a Tony for this act."

Andrew stood up.

"I can't watch any more," he said to no one in particular. "If any of you see Mom or Dad, tell them thanks from me for canceling *another* great family bonding event."

He smiled at Lettie, avoided eye contact with his brother and Jackie, and left the room.

Lettie felt sorry for Andrew. President Price's press secretary, Brian Gillespie, had called to say neither the president nor Jackie's mom could join them after all for Senator Ives's announcement. Bob Price had shown up, but only long enough to pass around a plate of his brownies before disappearing.

Scott got to his feet, yawning. "I'm gonna head out, too. Anyone want to go with?"

"No, thanks. Lettie and I are going to hang for a while," Jackie said.

Scott shrugged and left.

Lettie studied her friend. She was worried about her. First learning about Andrew and Taylor hooking up, then the stalker's threats, and now the possibility of a Price-Ives fight for the White House. At least she was over the panic attacks.

"Do you think you'll be okay going to, uh, this thing Friday?" Lettie asked. Calling it a party didn't feel right.

Jackie was staring at the TV as if she hadn't heard.

"Earth to Jackie . . . Are you going to the memorial thing?"

"What?" Jackie blinked and turned to Lettie.

"Taylor's memorial. Will you be okay going to it?"

"Of course. How can we not go?" Jackie said. She hit the off button on the remote and stood up to stretch.

To celebrate someone we thought we knew inside out but obviously didn't.

One of the things Lettie had most admired about Taylor was her honesty. The way she cut through the crap.

Lettie couldn't believe her luck when she got accepted to Excelsior Prep on a full scholarship. But once there, she felt totally out of place. The girls were way out of her league. They were gorgeous. She felt dull. They were rich. Her family barely got by. They were confident. She was paralyzingly shy. Their parents let them do anything they wanted. Her parents didn't approve of her dating and knew nothing about Daniel, her boyfriend.

Jackie was the first to befriend her at school. Taylor was the first to set her straight.

"Get real, Lets," Taylor lectured her. "You're at Excelsior because of your brains. For what YOU have to offer. The rest of us rode in on our parents' names and the fat checks they write every year." Then she roared laughing. "All I got is my parents' money and my hot body to get me where I wanna go!"

A year later, Lettie still couldn't wrap her mind around Taylor sleeping with Andrew.

Daniel, who was Taylor's twin, insisted from the start that her death wasn't an accident. Lettie's gut told her that nothing about that night made sense. She just didn't know how, what, or why.

"Do you want to come to my place and spend the night?" Jackie asked.

Lettie shook her head. "No, Whitney's flying in from L.A. tonight and I promised I'd be home when she got in."

Jackie raised an eyebrow. "And here I was hoping she'd left and was never coming back."

"Whitney can be . . . difficult sometimes . . . but she's still a person." *And the closest thing I have to a family right now,* she thought.

Whitney had confided in Lettie that her father, an economist, was leaving his job at a Washington think tank to work as a campaign policy adviser for President Price. Since he wouldn't have to be based in D.C. anymore, Whitney had launched a 24/7 campaign to convince her family to move back to L.A.

If the Remicks move back, where will I go?

"How are you getting home?" Jackie asked, tearing Lettie away from her thoughts. "Or are you going to see Daniel for a little fun?"

Lettie knew Jackie was just teasing, but that didn't stop her from turning scarlet.

"Oh, Lets, what am I going to do with you?" Jackie hugged her. "You're too cute."

She hugged back, but she thought Jackie was starting to sound almost as patronizing as Laura Beth.

Jackie walked her to the top of the Grand Staircase.

"When Laura Beth gets back, she'll probably want to get together," Jackie said. "Promise me you'll come, too. I can't face her by myself just yet."

Lettie nodded. It was going to be a long campaign and she wasn't sure she was ready for it.

Her heart plunged at her next thought.

At some point, she was going to have to choose sides.

IN THE NATION'S CAPITAL, EVERYTHING IS A POPULARITY CONTEST.

Available April 2013!

Check out the Capital Girls and Ella Monroe online

St. Martin's Griffin